PRAISE
"THE SIMON

The Ultimate Revenge

"Just finished reading *The Ultimate Revenge*—in a word, Phenomenal! Having thoroughly enjoyed the first two books, *Brotherhood Beyond the Yard* and *Noble's Quest*, I was more than anxious to read the final book of "The Simon trilogy." It is an incredible and fitting finale in the lives of characters created by an author who takes you into a world of intrigue where she expertly weaves a story that has the reader pondering the possibility, or perhaps I should say probability, of fiction being more real than we dare to think. A great read that I would strongly recommend!"

—Donna Post, Banking Consultant (Ret.), Florida

"You do not have to be a political junky to love this book of intrigue. *The Ultimate Revenge* takes you to a place that will make you question—could it happen—and if it did? The recherché and insight that has gone into this book will certainly keep you wondering for a long time."

—Ann E. Howells, Wine Consultant, Florida

Noble's Quest

"In a word—WOW!!! Sally Fernandez has done it again. *Noble's Quest* is a great read. I thoroughly enjoyed her first book, *Brotherhood Beyond the Yard*, and it was such fun to meet up with old characters again in this sequel. Sally has given us a great story telling experience, riveting in ways that walk the line between art and life. While *Noble's Quest* is a great standalone story, it was wonderful to follow up on the lives of characters I had come to love (and hate) in Brotherhood. Even with the complexity of the story line and the volumes of research that went into the preparation, the result is an amazingly reader friendly story that grabs you from page one! I would highly recommend the book with just one warning—give yourself plenty of reading time because once you start, you won't be able to put it down!!"

—Donna Post, Banking Consultant (Ret.), Florida

"A captivating second addition to the Simon Trilogy. Intense rhythmic development woven brilliantly—at times haunting and foreboding—at others a palpable sensation of an unerring power, leaving you to confront your own views of contemporary events. The modern political thriller has a strong advocate in Fernandez."

—**Maestro Debra Cheverino, Internationally Recognized Conductor, Fulbright Scholar, Florence, Italy**

"I was anxiously awaiting the publication of *Noble's Quest* as I had read the prequel, *Brotherhood Beyond the Yard*. I was not disappointed! *Noble's Quest* is everything I was hoping for and more. Along with solid characters development (Noble Bishop really comes alive), Ms. Fernandez has a tight grip on the pulse of the high stakes world we live in today. Her ability to merge political intrigue, international terrorism, and state of the art technology into a swirl of tension-filled events brings to mind the writing of John La Carre. I can't wait for the last installment of the Trilogy."

—**William Kelley, Artist, Florence, Italy and Sarasota, Florida**

"Loved the newest installment of Sally Fernandez' trilogy. *Noble's Quest*: Sequel to *Brotherhood Beyond the Yard* was a real page turner...I could not put it down. In the Brotherhood, Fernandez set us a scary...and plausible...scenario. *Noble's Quest* builds on that story and takes you down a path to worldwide terror. In addition to being totally engrossed in this story, I found Fernandez' ability to weave the back-story of the first book into the 2nd book very well done...Also, Fernandez is a master with her research! Which makes the story that much more convincing..."

—**Beth Littman Quinn, Vice President at Marketburst, Massachusetts**

"Put it down, NO WAY! Simon at his tricks with a sparkling cast! There were new unexpected developments that truly enhanced the Brotherhood. So real, it's easy to visualize in real life. Or was it. Making us wait for number three is crazy! Bring it on Sally. I thought it merited 6 stars."

—**Garrett B. Vonk, President-Keiser Career College & Southeastern Institute Florida**

"*Noble's Quest* starts out with an explosion of fireworks and intrigue. The hope and good wishes that always begin with the New Year is quickly put into question. As the sparks settle and the dots are connected, Noble once again finds himself in the high stakes game of intellect and will. His one friend from a past life, now his nemesis, has come back to taunt him into the ultimate game of man vs. power. Simon has surfaced and Noble is ready to confront the friendly face of evil."

—Ann E. Howells, Wine Consultant, Florida

"…As the sequel it met my expectations for another exciting work of intrigue and adventure. Sally does a fantastic job of keeping 3 balls in the air while moving each plot along in a well thought out methodical track. Characters are fully developed so you really know them, as this is critical for the story to move along. Max is just what Noble needs to compliment who he is as an investigator and person. Simon is more sinister than ever and his control is more evident as the reader follows his devious mind. I do not want to divulge the ending, but wait! It's not over! Well written and paced…a great read for any season!"

—Richard Cobello, Director, Information Technology, Schenectady County Government, New York

"I've never been a spy nor an intelligence agent nor a villain, but I would love to be one so I could inhabit the world of *Noble's Quest,* Sally Fernandez' sequel to *Brotherhood Beyond the Yard,* her excellent first novel that took readers through the intricacies of maneuvering a fraud into the office of the President of the United States. Now the intrigue continues as Fernandez brings us into a world where nothing is as it seems at first—places, people, and events morph from one apparent reality to another...Fernandez' writing style is a delightful blend of fast-moving, crisp language presented in a paradoxically unhurried pace that allows the plot to develop slowly and deliberately. We are constantly challenged to think about where she might be going; almost sparring with her to see if we can guess correctly…Finally, the ending caught me by complete surprise. Fernandez won the sparring contest…the clues were there—no obfuscations, just cleverly woven into a very entertaining and thoughtful narrative…"

—Alfredo Vedro, Media Production Consultant, Florida

Brotherhood Beyond the Yard

"Simon Hall, one of the characters in Sally Fernandez' addictive novel, *Brotherhood Beyond the Yard*, is an ace puppeteer, manipulating the people he encounters, taking them and you on a thrilling political rollercoaster. Timely—Could it be paralleled to the current administration?—and masterly crafted, Sally's action prose will have you riveted right up to the last page. I impatiently anticipate a sequel to see Simon's next strategic move."

—Dann Dulin, Senior Editor, *A&U Magazine*

"Unquestionably, this is a book for the thinking reader. The book's combination of intellect, authenticity and believability, led me on several occasions, almost to forget that I was reading fiction. The author's use of language is quite exceptional...I'm still pondering the book's serious dose of reality and am impatient to get my hands on a copy of the sequel!"

**— Edwin Chadbourne, PhD,
Human Resources Professional, Australia**

"A parable for the times in which we live. Fernandez has written a classic fable for our Age of Doubt, just as Kerouac defined the Age of Hippies. Worth reading no matter what side of the political spectrum you inhabit."

—Aladar Gabriel, Florence, Italy

"Ingenious harmonic conception—Dazzling plot with infectious power, nuance, and sparkling wit—in a true potential enigma. Only a select few can ignite the palette of curiosity and blend together fantastical overtones with such power, nuance, and transformative persuasiveness. Sally Fernandez' debut *Brotherhood Beyond the Yard* invites you to ponder the contemporary enigmas of our age and leaves you longing for the sequel. A resounding ovation!"

**—Maestro Debra Cheverino, Fulbright Recipient,
Maggio Musicale Fiorentino, Florence, Italy**

"Two Thumbs Up! *Brotherhood Beyond the Yard* is a gripping story of intrigue from beginning to end. The reader is captured by the ingenuity and daring of the Brotherhood and their unprecedented impact (one hopes) on the political and economic future of our country and the world. In its daring exploitation of the national political process with worldwide implications, the reader is left to ponder the possibility of reality and its consequences. Truly a mystery one is left pondering could it really happen. Can't wait for the sequel."

—Philip Ames, Marketing Director,
General Electric (Ret.), Florida

"Excellent read in these interesting times...well-crafted and contemporary with intelligent twists and turns! Had me missing a few nights of sleep..."

—Roland Marcz, Owner,
Shanghai Malong Construction, Shanghai, China

"I have finished reading *Brotherhood Beyond the Yard*. I commend the author for her imagination and for her use of her expertise and knowledge of politics, finance, academe, and electronics. The plot is a natural for a Hollywood film: I can see George Clooney in several of the roles. *Complimenti!!* I eagerly await the sequel."

—Horace W. Gibson,
Co-Founder of the International School of Florence, Italy

"Amazed and Amused. *Brotherhood Beyond the Yard* far exceeded my expectations from a new writer on the scene. I was pleasantly drawn into the plot, and as it developed, I was often amazed and amused at how well the author manipulated my curiosity and intrigue regarding the characters as they intertwined their lives in order to devise and undertake a 'master' plan. Now I am left wanting to read more of what I hope will the first part of an epic story to come. Did someone say the future is now...?"

—Philip Claypool,
Acclaimed Country Western Singer/Songwriter, San Francisco

"The *Brotherhood Beyond the Yard* is a wonderful story—compelling and all too believable. It is masterfully plotted, with every episode revealing an increasingly tangled but utterly plausible scheme in which fundamentally decent people perpetrate a despicable fraud, manipulated by a master puppeteer. The fast-paced denouement satisfies all the expectations of a political thriller and yet leaves just enough unfinished business to leave readers anxiously awaiting the next installment...This is a story that unfolds both psychologically and visually, almost begging for a cinematic rendering, and I found myself visualizing many of the individual chapters as scenes in a movie..."

—Linda Cabe Halpern,
Dean of University Studies, James Madison University, Virginia

"...I strongly recommend *Brotherhood Beyond the Yard* for those looking for an exciting, pithy read. As you near the conclusion of, I hope, this first book, the pages will jump out of your hands. A great read for either the beach or the fire."

—John Pearl, Partner, Pearl Associates, Greenwich, Connecticut

"I highly recommend this book. Mystery thrillers, detective thrillers, even vampire thrillers are really enjoyable read. *Brotherhood Beyond the Yard* is just that...an international political thriller that's timely and provocative, and contains extremely believable characters placed in well researched locations and situations."

—Baroness Suzanne Pitcher Flaccomio,
Founder and Director of Pitcher & Flaccomio, Florence, Italy

"You'll want to fasten your seat belt to navigate the twists and turns of this global political thriller. Fernandez combines knowledge of banking, technology, and politics to offer a *'Back to the Future'* reading adventure. And, the author's intimate familiarity of Florentine life makes one want to buy a one-way ticket."

—Donna Davidson, Davidson Associates,
San Francisco, California

"Great read! Unfortunately, all the clichés in English are true and have become so firmly entrenched in our vocabulary that few or no fresh phrases have entered the language. So, when we want to give praise we are stuck with the all-too-familiar 'compelling,' 'page-turner,' 'riveting,' and the like—all appropriate for Brotherhood, but I lack the talent to come up with anything more complimentary. So, I hope readers will accept my very simple WOW! I thoroughly enjoyed Brotherhood—plot, characters, setting, and the many subtle little clevernesses and clues the author drops in as the plot progresses—that I can't quote here for fear of giving it away."

—Alfredo Vedro, Media Production Consultant, Florida

"Fascinating story, intriguing title. It certainly is thought-provoking and intellectually stimulating. It easily brings to mind the power of the Pericles quote at the beginning of the book. Kudos to a new and exciting author!"

—Dr. Patricia Ames, Fulbright Scholar, Maine

The Ultimate Revenge

The Ultimate Revenge

A Novel

Conclusion to
The Simon Trilogy

Sally Fernandez

DUNHAM
books

3 1969 02237 0844

The Ultimate Revenge

For information on sales, licensing, or permissions contact the publisher:

Dunham Books
63 Music Square East
Nashville, TN 37203
admin@dunhamgroupinc.com
www.dunhamgroupinc.com

Trade Paperback ISBN: 978-1-939447-83-8
Ebook ISBN: 978-1-939447-84-5

Printed in the United States of America

*Dedicated to Dr. Patricia Ames,
loving aunt, mentor, and teacher
who planted the seed that spurred
my intellectual curiosity.*

"Truth is so hard to tell,
it sometimes needs fiction to make it plausible."
– Francis Bacon

AUTHOR'S NOTE

This story is pure fiction. The Godfather, the Financier, and Stronghold Management have been fictionalized, but the events are real. This does not detract from their veracity. The mention of other real people, organizations, or groups are factual, but weaved into a fictional setting. All facts are in the public domain. The statements voiced by other fictional characters may add realism to the plot, but should not be misconstrued as giving credence to any of the issues raised. The narrative gestated solely in my vivid imagination.

It is a story that brings "The Simon Trilogy" to a conclusion, having been preceded by *Brotherhood Beyond the Yard* and *Noble's Quest*. When facts are blended with fiction, the reader ultimately must draw one's own conclusions. A nagging question that may arise is a simple, "What if?" as one ponders the possibilities raised.

Once again, I must acknowledge from the start the outstanding contributions of my Editor-in-Residence, Joe Fernandez, and his amazing ability to help me shape and define my storyline continued with *The Ultimate Revenge*. The plot is complex and the research was intense. There were times I became tangled in the weeds of facts and Joe was there to pull me out and help me to refocus. Much love and gratitude goes to my husband, best friend, business manager, editor, and occasional research associate.

1
DAY ONE

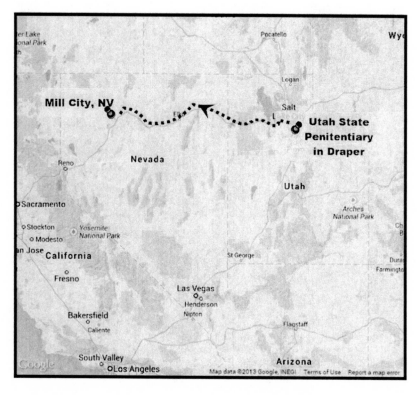

A pale hue blanketed the sky as the sunrise bled into the morning mist. The clock on the dashboard displayed 6:10; he had been driving for over two hours. By chance, he spotted a dirt road approximately five hundred feet ahead. A glance in the rear view mirror reflected nothing other than another dark, empty stretch of highway. *Perfect*, he thought. He gripped the wheel, veered right, and killed the headlights. The first signs of daylight offered enough of a glow for him to inch along through the thick grove of sagebrush. Then he brought the car to a halt.

"Recalculating, recalculating," repeated the GPS's nagging voice.

"Damn thing." He hit the button to silence the stranger who shadowed his every move. The directions were uncomplicated. Straight across I-80 did not require the mile-by-mile instructions. Nevertheless, the GPS did offer a degree of companionship as he drove through the desolate state.

When he stepped out of the car, he hit a wall of frigid air. On instinct, he crossed his arms and hugged his body attempting to allay the cold temperature. Then he removed the duffle bag from the trunk and placed the bag in the back seat. In haste, he changed clothes while bravely ignoring the icy morning dew. Both the fresh clothes and the invigorating air prepared him for the next leg of his trip.

After resetting the GPS, he turned the car around and headed toward the highway. "Recalculating, recalculating," repeated the no longer pesky but welcome voice. He drove for another two hours until the sun finally brightened the rear window.

Up ahead, he observed a sign that read, "Welcome to Mill City, Nevada," and realized he had crossed the state border. Within minutes, another sign appeared. He was elated to see "Travel Centers of America" flashing on an inviting neon light. The fresh clothes partially helped, but as he took a whiff of his malodorous body he mused, *I'm desperate for a shower.* Without hesitation, he turned right into the parking lot and parked next to the "Fork in the Road Restaurant." As if on cue, his stomach growled in relief.

Tucked away in the back booth in the corner he ordered the trucker's special.

"Black or with cream and sugar, hon," the first kind face of the day asked.

"Black, please."

The coffee was satisfying as he waited for the sunny-side up eggs, sausage patties, hash browns, and dark toast; the only hot meal he had had in days. Moreover, the sensation of feeling free again—was overwhelming. Finally, with his hunger sated, he went straight to the Wi-Fi hotspot and began to tap away on his tablet to look for his next destination.

After a hot meal, a lukewarm shower, a full tank of gas, and a firm destination, he once again ventured out onto the long stretch of highway and headed west.

2
THE HUNT GOES ON

Monday was a gloomy day in Washington D.C. It appeared to affect all those within the beltway. Inside the Dirksen Senate Building, the mood was more melancholy.

Already on edge, the knock at the door startled her. "Come in!" the senator barked as she looked up from her computer screen.

"Director Noble Bishop is on the line. He respectfully requests an appointment to discuss some urgent business."

The senator grimaced. *Respectfully requests, I doubt it is a simple request from the director of the States Intelligence Agency,* she thought, knowing exactly the subject of the urgent business. She stared again at the monitor and asked, "Do I have any time this week?"

"Friday morning is open."

"Tell the director I'll see him at nine o'clock—in my office. Thank you," she stated without looking up, a clear sign for her secretary to leave.

⁓

The gloom extended beyond the Washington weather. For the local, state, and federal authorities who had been conducting a massive manhunt, the trail had gone cold.

Two weeks prior, on January 31, SIA Director Noble Bishop had conducted Operation NOMIS from the command center at the Dugway Proving Ground in Utah. Noble and the base commander led a team comprised of Max, his deputy director, FBI Agent Burke, and Major Stanton, along with his Special Forces B Team. Their mission was to enter an underground encampment and capture Mohammed al-Fadl, also known as Simon Hall. The mission was a success. They captured the notorious terrorist, along with men and women trained for an unidentified cause.

On February 2, the ever-slippery Simon escaped from a maximum-security cell at the Utah State Penitentiary in Draper. He simply walked out of the prison—then he vanished from sight.

The authorities pulled out all stops. The prison warden had sent out an all-points bulletin to train stations, airports, hotels, and motels. The state police had established roadblocks throughout the state and at its borders. They required that all passersby submit to visual identification and retina scans—all to no avail. The over-confident warden insisted they would nab him, but Noble suspected Simon had crossed the Utah border—in which direction was only conjecture.

Neither Noble nor Max could add value to the physical capture. Running around the country in lockstep with other authorities on the search for Simon made no sense. They decided it was more important to return to Washington to focus on Simon's game plan, find where he was heading, and stop him in his tracks. The day after the escape, Noble and Max packed up the evidence from the encampment and the Draper prison, and escorted it back to Washington on a military jet. Since then, they had been wading through boxes of documents, manuals, and forensic evidence looking for minute clues.

Noble assigned Agent Burke to remain at the prison to lead the manhunt, much to the warden's chagrin. Major Stanton and his B Team stayed at Dugway to conduct the interrogations of the 109 detainees they had captured in the underground encampment. Unhappily, the number one detainee had slipped through their supposedly flawless security at the Utah penitentiary—Simon was free to roam.

Once before, Simon had cleverly evaded Noble's grasp. It was seven years earlier, in 2009, when Noble organized a sting operation with his predecessor Hamilton Scott to capture Simon. As planned, it lured Simon to Florence, Italy to retrieve the last of his stolen funds—funds Noble had managed to syphon from his account at slowly paced intervals. However, Hamilton's race through the streets of Florence, and then through the famous Vasari Corridor, left him capturing an empty satchel—without the remaining money. Simon had disappeared once again.

Max burst into Noble's office in her usual brash manner and asked, "Did the senator agree to a meeting?"

"Don't you ever knock?"

Max ignored Noble's jibe.

"Yes, she agreed to meet on Friday at nine a.m. as I respectfully requested."

"Great!"

"I want you to join me in the interview and in the questioning."

"Me!"

"You can handle it. After all, Simon deprived you of an opportunity to interrogate him by escaping. Perhaps you'll uncover a clue that will put him back in his cell." He flashed a supportive smile, and then said, "Now, let's review the evidence. Start with the surveillance video showing the senator's visit to the prison."

Max anticipated correctly and had already queued up the video on the large multi-touch monitor. She hit the *Play* button.

Noble paid particular interest as the senator walked over to the table and sat down in the chair across from Simon, Noble's former Harvard classmate. He recalled sitting in the same chair three weeks earlier, when he spent six and a half hours interrogating Simon in a furious battle of wits. On the monitor, Simon again appeared to be comfortable sitting in the prisoner's chair, the one bolted to the floor. He was flashing his famous, unnerving Cheshire grin toward the senator—just as he had with Noble and any other undeserving soul. In a way, Noble felt as though he was still in that dim interrogation room illuminated by a single row of lights. Even in the video, they cast the same ominous yellow glow over the sparse furnishings, creating a sense of déjà vu.

Max observed intently, as well, but focused on the body language. Almost immediately, she paused the video. "Pay attention to the look on Simon's face when the senator lifts her handbag off her shoulder and places it on the floor," She reversed the video and then hit the *Play* button.

"His eyes are following her movements," he observed. "Wait a minute, he flinched."

"Right, I saw the same thing." Max reversed the video again. "Now watch, but this time pay attention to the senator's movement." She hit the *Play* button.

"I'll be damned. He flinched just as she returned upright after putting the bag on the floor. Simon must have felt her hand brush his ankle under the table, unless he was numb," he quipped.

Max hit the *Pause* button.

Then observing the scene more closely, Noble affirmed, "It looks like she slipped him something."

They both looked at each other and said aloud in unison, "xPhad."

The xPhad had become standard issue for the SIA. It was somewhat thicker than an iPhone, but when unfolded it transformed into a tablet matching the dimensions of an iPad. Both Noble and Max relied heavily on their xPhads and were well aware of its capabilities.

"It's circumstantial with a bit of speculation at best. We'll need more," Noble asserted.

They reviewed another video, this time showing Simon in his six-by-twelve-foot cell. He was sitting on a hard bed topped with a thin prison-quality mattress, positioned across from an unappealing stainless steel sink and toilet. Noble had inspected the same maximum-security accommodations the day before he entered the encampment. It was in anticipation of Simon's capture outside the Dugway Proving Grounds.

Max fast-forwarded the video and then hit the *Play* button. "Note the time on the video. It's after the senator departed."

Simon's cell was immersed in total darkness, except for a small beam of light emanating from under his blanket. The only illumination in the tiny chamber, they concluded, was from the tablet he was hiding underneath his bedcover.

They continued to watch the video, noticing the time-stamp. It was now 4:05 a.m. The station guard was nowhere to be seen as Simon walked through a series of gates. Then he walked directly out of the prison. From another surveillance video, they saw him as he slithered by the guard tower and ducked behind several cars as the revolving search light headed in his direction. Then he vanished from the scene.

Max and Noble shared the same sense of dread they felt when they first scrutinized the video together with the warden within hours of the escape.

"That confirms it in my mind," Max insisted. "He was using the xPhad the senator had slipped him to program his escape from his cell."

"We still need more evidence. Play the surveillance video you retrieved from the airport."

"Give me a sec." As Max fumbled through a series of folders, she harked back to Noble, "Remember the senator was to arrive at the South Valley Regional Airport in Jordan, Utah. Her jet pulled into the hanger at one-fifty p.m. Here it is." She hit the *Play* button.

They studied the video as the senator disembarked with her security detail in tow. From the various videos Max spliced together, they viewed her walking in a corridor and then entering a door to her right. The agents waited in the hallway.

"I guess the senator needed to powder her nose." Max smirked.

Minutes later, the senator returned to the corridor and the entourage continued out of the building. Parked at the door were three black sedans, the usual sinister looking cars with their opaque black windows. They escorted the senator to the middle car.

"Everything seems to square with what the secret service reported," Noble conveyed. "One of the agents reported checking the senator into the hotel and accompanying her to her suite. She requested not be disturbed for the evening and announced she would see them in the morning. Each agent had a turn standing guard outside her door."

"We have the prison's visitor logbook showing that she signed in at nine p.m. So how did she leave without them knowing and make her way to the prison?" Max asked.

"Good question. Get the surveillance video for the hotel corridor. View the section between the time she checked in until she had left the next morning to join her fellow envoys at the prison as scheduled."

"Fine, but I won't be able to get my hands on the tape until late tomorrow."

"We'll have to go into the meeting with the senator with what we have. Who knows? Maybe she'll give up something." Without warning, Noble felt the intrusive vibration from his xPhad. "Hold on. Let me take this call," he requested, holding up his right index finger.

"Burke, what's up?"

"We have a lead on Simon. It is possible he's heading west toward Reno. The day he escaped, he stopped in Mill City, Nevada at the 'Travel Centers of America.' Essentially, it's a truck stop, which includes a gas station, a restaurant, and shower facilities. The attendant on duty explained that he was responsible for cleaning the shower stalls after each use, replacing the towels and soap…"

Noble was furious and cut Burke off. "Why are we just hearing this now? That was two weeks ago!" he admonished.

Burke took no offense and explained calmly, "The manager returned to work yesterday after recuperating from emergency back surgery. He happened to be sorting through the *Lost and Found* bin. Evidently, it's typical to find articles of clothing, toothbrushes, et cetera, left behind by travelers. Guess what? A pair of white sweatpants and a white shirt found its way to the bin. Printed on the back of the shirt was Draper State Penitentiary Inmate. He called the local precinct and they called the warden."

Dialing down his ire a notch, Noble scoffed, "What gives with the attendant? He thought the owner would come back and claim them?"

Burke understood Noble's frustration and kept his cool. "The sheriff for the Nevada Highway Patrol interviewed him. The attendant remembered the clothing but he said they were folded, as if someone had planned to put them back into a travel bag. He swears he put them in the bin exactly the way he found them."

"Does he remember who they belonged to?"

"Yes. In fact, he recalled filling the gas tank for a customer who had just showered, but then the customer had departed before the attendant returned to clean the shower stall. Director, he identified Simon from a photo and he remembers the make and model of the car. Believe it or not, it's a 2012 Ford Escape."

"Escape!"

Burke could not resist a chuckle.

"I fail to see the humor," Noble interrupted.

"Harrumph." Burke cleared his throat and continued, "It's a blue metallic XLS sport utility model. From a surveillance video, we were able to identify the license plate. It was from Utah. The number is four seven zero, X as in X-ray, B as in bravo, A as in alpha. We ran the plates. Get this! The car is registered to a Hal Simmons."

"Dust for prints and get back to me A-S-A-P?"

Burke could tell from Noble's voice that he was exasperated. He tried not to prolong the agony. "Will do!"

However, Noble was not finished. "What time did he arrive in Mill City?"

"As viewed on the video, he filled the gas tank at ten a.m. That would be about right. It's a five and a half hour drive west on I-80 from the prison."

"Great! He escaped at four a.m. and by nine thirty—he was taking a hot shower. Thank goodness massages weren't available."

Burke had one last burning question. "The video showed the car leaving. Simon turned right on to I-80 continuing in a westerly direction. But why would he head west? You'd expect him to head south to the Mexican border or cross over north into Canada."

"He's not finished," Noble lamented. "There's a good chance he'll try to dump the car at some point. Update the APB with a description. Maybe, we'll get lucky."

"I'm on it."

"Burke, if you find the car I want you to run the prints. Only you," Noble cautioned.

Burke had come to trust Noble's instincts and did not question why. "Later, Director." He ended the call.

❧

Noble filled Max in on the conversation.

"Hal Simmons! Then the escape had to have been prearranged if he's using one of his aliases."

"I agree. But how the senator fits in to all this is what I want to know!"

"Maybe on Friday we'll get lucky and find out." Max tried to sound encouraging.

Noble's discouragement was transparent.

"Maybe you should call it a night, boss."

"You too—go home," Noble ordered.

❧

"Darling, you sound exhausted."

Hearing Amanda's voice gave Noble a momentary surge of energy. "I'm still at the office, but I'll be heading home soon."

"Would you like some company?"

"You know I love your company, but I need to get some sleep tonight." Noble missed the nights when Amanda stayed over, but this case had to take precedence. He needed to be sharp and stay focused.

"I understand sweetheart. Are we still on for dinner with the Ridges Friday night?"

"Of course, I'm looking forward to seeing them."

"Call me tomorrow."

"I will. I love you."

"I love you too. Now go home," she commanded.

Noble heard the click on the other end of the line and placed the receiver in its cradle. Then he looked over at the framed photo on his desk and thought about how much he loved Amanda. He was forty-seven-years-old and up until a year ago, he had avoided any serious relationship, preferring his work to the "getting-to-know-you" dating scene and all that followed. At times, he questioned his reluctance to engage in intimacy. Often, he reasoned that losing his parents at a young age might have aided his aversion. There was no question that *challenge* was his Achilles heel and left little room for anything or anyone. Then when he assumed the position as the director of the SIA, he became more driven in the pursuit of national security. He recognized his reticent personality had shifted and he had become more demonstrative in spite of his obsession.

Then something changed.

His brother-in-law Paolo introduced him to Amanda and his heart skipped more than a few beats. She was striking, with dark black hair and light blue eyes. She was also extremely intelligent. Noble decided at that moment to make an attempt at a relationship. From the start, he relished her company. An added bonus was that she tolerated his erratic, non-stop work schedule, which endeared her to him even more. Aside from her stunning beauty and charm, he admitted to himself there were other influences that caused him to take the plunge. As he looked again at the photo staring back, he reckoned the reasons were no longer important. His only thought was how happy he was to have Amanda in his new life. He ruminated a bit longer. Then noting the time, he packed up his briefcase, including the senator's files containing the evidence, and headed home wistfully to an empty bed.

3

LIGHTENING STRIKES TWICE

Director Bishop is here to see you," announced the senator's secretary, and then added, "He's accompanied by Deputy Director Ford."

"Direct them to my conference room. I'll be there momentarily."

The secretary left to comply.

Several minutes later, Senator Maryann Townsend, the former first lady, entered the conference room. She offered them a puzzled look as she had only expected to see Noble.

Both Noble and Max rose from their chairs.

"I understood this meeting was to be with you, Director," Maryann balked.

"I apologize for the confusion, Senator. However, Deputy Director Ford and I are working on the case together to recapture Mohammed al-Fadl. Her knowledge of the evidence is crucial to the questions we need to ask."

The senator displayed no expression and gestured them to be seated at the table. Then she sat down across from them. "Director, Deputy

Director, what is it you'd like to know?"

"We understand that the president appointed you as one of the envoys from the Senate Intelligence Committee to travel to Draper, Utah, to witness the interrogation of al-Fadl at the state penitentiary?" Noble asked respectfully.

"That is correct. Our role was to ensure that the prisoner's rights were protected."

"Why did you go alone to see al-Fadl?"

"You already know that I was asked by the president to be part of a delegation to ensure the prisoner's rights were upheld."

Max took the opportunity to interject. In a polite tone, she asked, "Excuse me, Senator. We are speaking about the night before, when you went to meet with the prisoner without the envoys. We have the logbook with your signature; you signed in at nine o'clock p.m."

"It was my duty to ensure that he had proper accommodations and of course, was not being *tortured* before the meeting with my colleagues."

"Why didn't you wait for the other envoys before going to the prison?"

"As I said before, I wanted to ensure that there was no evidence the prisoner had been mistreated."

Max was getting nowhere. She chose to move the conversation ahead. "Did your security detail drive you to the prison?" She knew the answer, but wanted to give the senator an opportunity to skirt the truth.

"Yes."

That went well, Max smiled inwardly. "We interviewed the prison guard at the entrance gate. He said that you asked him to call a taxi, but does not remember you arriving in any vehicle. All he recalls is that you appeared at the gate."

"Obviously," Maryann continued, "I had a car drive me with my secret service detail following."

Now we are getting somewhere, she really is lying. Noble sat back. He knew where Max was heading.

No further response came from Maryann. Her face remained deadpan.

"With all due respect Senator, we're just trying to clarify some details."

"Look, I simply left my hotel suite when the agent on duty stepped away for a moment. I called for a taxi and went to the prison on my own accord. I took a rare opportunity to be alone. It becomes very claustrophobic with people surrounding you constantly. Besides, no one even knew I was in Draper. I wasn't in any danger."

Max did not buy it. She sensed it was time to turn up the heat, but Noble quickly stepped in.

"Senator, we have you on a video camera while you were meeting with al-Fadl." Noble nodded to Max.

On cue, she turned the tablet toward the senator and hit the *Play* button. The video began.

Noble proceeded, "In this scene, it's clear to us that you are passing something to al-Fadl under the table."

"How dare you! I am a United States Senator! And I would be very careful with your accusations."

Noble ignored Maryann's outburst. "According to the logbook, you were there for ten minutes. Why spend so little time with him, if you took such efforts to see him in the first place?"

"I'm finished with your impertinent questions." Maryann leered, displaying an obvious heightened annoyance.

They had created the desired effect.

Maryann directed her attention to Noble, and in a condescending tone meant for an underling, she asked, "Is this an interrogation?"

"Consider it a conversation for now, Senator," Noble replied with spurious politeness.

As he sat across the table from Maryann, he found it surprising that he had never been in such close proximity to the former first lady, for any length of time. A quick handshake in a reception line, or a wave as she buzzed in and out of the Oval Office, was the full extent of their familiarity. When in her company she was always aloof. His mind drifted back to the past, as he imagined her twenty years younger, thirty pounds lighter, and with long black hair. Then the vision of her in a black mini skirt with bright red lipstick—seemed unreal.

Lightning struck. *No way! Maryann and Simon, it couldn't be,* he thought. In that instant, Noble suspected she was the "hooker" on campus at the Harvard Yard. The one Simon arranged to proposition Noble and then conjured up the campus police to play the heavies. Simon had bribed them to create the illusion of reality. Then he rode in on his white mount in time to save Noble from disgrace. All was planned by Simon in an effort to lure Noble into his web, which he resisted adamantly.

From the expression on Maryann's face, she began to suspect that Noble had uncovered Simon's ploy.

"Had you ever met al-Fadl before seeing him in prison at Draper?" Noble inquired with respectful directness.

He's figured it out, Maryann thought. "Seriously, I never made the connection between al-Fadl and Simon Hall, until I visited him at Draper. It was a terrible shock!" At first, Maryann deflected the precise question and began to talk briefly about her time at Cambridge as though it were a matter of record. Then at the end, she finally admitted to knowing Simon.

"It was a college fling," she blew off. "It ended after I graduated from Radcliff and entered DePaul University College of Law. Then for years, we maintained our friendship." She paused, and then asked hopefully, "I expect you'll be discreet, Director?"

Max was flabbergasted by Noble's question and even more astonished by the senator's answer, but she sat back and remained uninvolved during their repartee.

Noble chose not to persist further. He was still in shock by her revelation. But he allowed that it added an interesting twist to the case. "Senator, I thank you for your candor. Your past relationship with Simon is not germane to our case. You can rely on our discretion."

Maryann's outward sternness appeared to wane.

Noble felt it was best to conclude the interview. "We appreciate your giving us your time."

Maryann stood up briskly.

Noble and Max took their cue, stood up and walked around the desk.

Max was the first to offer a respectful handshake and thanked Maryann again for her time.

Then Noble took the opportunity also to shake her hand, but held it longer then he had ever had the opportunity in the past.

She eyed him with indifference and then walked out of her conference room.

Noble turned toward Max expecting an outburst. "Wait until we're back in my office," he cautioned.

4
GRIDLOCK

The moment they set foot inside Noble's reception area Max unleashed. "What are you crazy—making nice? We had her on the defensive. She would have answered our questions!" she fumed.

"Are you finished? She would only deflect the answers and lie when forced. Most important, we have a direct link between our senator and Simon," Noble affirmed and then filled Max in on Simon's devious hoax at Harvard.

"A hooker!" Max could not contain her laughter, shedding all signs of anger.

Doris continued to tap at the computer's keyboard, trying to remain invisible.

"Enough Max. We need concrete evidence. I know it's out there somewhere. Go find it!"

Max conceded, Noble was right. She picked up a symbolic piece of white paper from Doris' desk and ceremoniously dangled it in the air. Then she headed to the conference room to resume sorting through the myriad papers and forensics awaiting review. "Coming?" she called out.

"In a moment, I have a call to make."

"What was that all about?" Doris inquired.

"Never you mind, just please get Kramer on the line. And clear my schedule for Tuesday."

"Noble, you've already told me to keep your calendar clear for the week. I'll call him now."

"Thanks."

Within minutes line one was blinking.

"Hank!"

"Yes, Noble. What is it this time, kneecapping or the rack? Oh, let me guess, Simon again! And you need to see me in your office pronto!"

"Relax Hank, not pronto, Tuesday morning at eleven o'clock."

"Commuting between Chicago and Washington is becoming tedious. And it's President's Day weekend, travel will be a bitch."

"Make it happen."

"If I have to travel all that way, can't we at least meet for lunch?"

"Hank!"

"See you Tuesday." Hank slammed down the phone.

Noble held all the cards and Hank knew it, including his immunity agreement. So when Noble summoned—Hank obliged. In reality, the commute was not as troubling as the subject matter.

Max had previously scanned many of the papers and documents retrieved from the underground encampment, during Operation NOMIS. She transferred them to the SIA cloud and placed them in the folder titled NOMIS. In the same folder, she also stored the charts and blueprints found on the flash drive Simon accidently left in the indoctrination facility in the underground encampment—before he set off an explosion. For the better part of a month, she had studied all of the materials trying to make sense of them—to unravel Simon's ultimate plot. Moreover, spread out on the conference room table, were mounds of other training manuals they had recovered from the facility.

"Where do you want to start?" Max asked, as she waved the back of her hand over the evidence.

"Finding the proverbial needle in a haystack might be more inviting," Noble conceded. All the same, he had the utmost confidence in his deputy.

Max had diligently worked at his side ever since he brought her into the SIA in 2010. His selection was easy. Years before, they were not only colleagues at the CIA, they were also friendly rivals. Max was undoubtedly the best among the undercover agents and possessed the precise demanding qualifications for the job. She was tall and slim, with straight blond hair and dark hazel eyes, and considered by those with undiminished eyesight to be extremely attractive. Her beauty, however, was a deceptive veneer, disguising the tomboy within. Competing with four older brothers created a toughness in her that became a major asset. At times, she even placed Noble on the defensive. But aside from their obvious physical differences, they shared the same intellectual space. While Noble was brilliant, Max was not far behind. He knew that if there were a clue to move the investigation along, she would uncover it with her laser-like focus on the evidence. In the meantime, Noble would work from another perspective and focus on those people who could have any knowledge of the case.

"It's your show." He gave her the floor.

"Okay, let's review the key documents we discovered in the underground encampment."

The mere mention of the encampment gave Noble the chills. It did not go unnoticed.

Max, as well, could not erase the horror she and Agent Burke experienced during the explosion in the indoctrination facility. Sadly, two soldiers lost their lives by a grenade detonated as they opened the door—a door exiting the facility that entered into another underground tunnel. Simon had set the trap.

Refocusing, she pointed out that many of the manuals they uncovered were straight out of the al-Qaeda handbook. They were basic tactical maneuvers including rifle marksmanship, engagement skills, and situational training exercises. Then there were disturbing manuals one might not expect: *Cyber-terrorism, Unconventional Warfare, Propaganda, Insurgency, Intimidation,* and *Suicide Attack.*

"Wasn't there also a copy of the *SERE Instructor Training Manual?*" Noble recalled.

"Yes, there—right there," she pointed.

They both knew the importance of an intense military training program, an acronym for **S**urvive **E**vade **R**isk **E**scape that dealt with *Tactical Maneuvers, Explosives,* and *Special Forces.* That manual alone provided partial evidence that connected Simon directly to the bombs used in the attempted assassinations of the heads of state from France and Great Britain. It also connected Simon to the bullets that sprayed the stage in Germany, while the chancellor stood at the podium. All were staged on New Year's Eve, alarming the world and causing many countries to go on high alert. It was Simon who also orchestrated the assassination attempts to fail. It was Simon's way of head-faking Noble and his hounds when they became precariously close to discovering the underground encampment in far off Utah.

"Where are the booklets on preparedness?" Noble also recalled the other manuals that had been recovered from the facility.

"Right here." Max handed him a stack of various guides.

Noble panned through them at a rapid pace and then shook his head. "They're all published by FEMA. Where's the connection?"

"Remember that we also found organization charts in the facility?"

Noble nodded. He remembered that on one of the charts, there was a red circle around the box for the head of FEMA, the Federal Emergency Management Agency.

Max hastily retrieved each of the charts from the NOMIS folder and placed them side-by-side on the multi-touch monitor. On the various charts, also circled in red, were the boxes for the Office of the President, the Department of Energy, and the Department of Homeland Security.

Both Max and Noble stared at the monitor trying to make a connection.

Noble was the first to speak. "When we first analyzed the charts, we considered all key executive branch functional heads, including the president, as possible targets. But what if they're simply involuntary bit-players in Simon's drama? On the other hand, they could be fundamental to Simon's plot in some bizarre way!"

"Let me conduct an argumentation exercise to test our premises as we've done in past cases, to ensure we haven't strayed off course. We must take into account every possibility," Max insisted.

"I don't like the way this is starting to shape up—manuals on preparedness—the inclusion of FEMA. Get me all you can on FEMA's role in the event a national disaster occurs."

"What are you thinking?"

Noble, unsure himself, said, "Let's move on. Is there anything further on the blueprints that you found on Simon's flash drive?"

"Yes, as I expected, they're power grids—interestingly, they're U.S. power grids."

Noble understood the power grids' main function was to send power to over 3200 public utilities through a series of transmission lines, sweeping over 2.7 million miles. In addition, nine regional "reliability" councils manage the energy flow in North America that serve more than 300 million people.

"Do you have grids within all nine regions?" he asked curiously.

"No, only five grids." Max swiped the touch-screen, spinning the organization charts out of sight, and placed one of the grids on the monitor. "This particular grid is managed by the ISO, California's Independent System Operator Corporation, and distributes energy to about eighty percent of the state, serving over thirty million people."

"That's part of WECC, the Western Electricity Coordinating Council that operates most of western North America. It coordinates the grids for eleven states and two provinces in Canada: British Columbia and Alberta," Noble conveyed with a tad of concern.

"Remember the report a couple of congressmen released citing the vulnerability of the power grids. It showed frequent attempts were made to invade the control systems." Max added with equal unease.

"Yes, it was in 2013, and it stated that the cyber-attack methods ranged from phishing to malware infections. In addition, *The Wall Street Journal* ran an article citing the escalation of cyber assaults by Iranians—and their preferred hacking targets are energy companies."

"So can we logically suspect that Simon may attempt to disrupt the power grids by hacking the control-system software? This is not good news."

"Logic points us in that direction, but it looks as though Simon will have to compete with his fellow hackers." Noble countered.

"Which will make it more difficult to identify Simon's cyber-hacking among his cronies, unless we can determine his modus operandi."

"I regretfully agree."

"At least, if our assumptions are correct, he's only tinkering with half the country. Remember only five of the nine grids are accounted for." Max tried to give it a positive spin, but Noble was right. She pressed on, "ISO recently opened a control center in Folsom, known as Mission Critical, to manage the integration of renewable energy when it becomes available."

"Wait a minute! Wasn't Simon heading toward Reno, Nevada? That's only a couple of hours from Folsom."

"Shall I put them on alert?"

"And tell them what? As of yet, we have nothing tangible. Let's go through the rest of the evidence first."

Max began to place the next grid on the monitor.

"Stop! What does the number in the upper-right hand corner of the grid signify?"

"I wondered if you'd notice," she prodded. "It was something I also questioned. I thought it might refer to a page number, but I cross-referenced it with all of the manuals having to do with energy. Then I checked the Department of Energy manuals having to do with the grids. There was no reference to either. I came up empty handed."

"Do all the grids have similar numbers?"

"Yes." Max swiped the display, returning to the screen with the organization charts. "What do you see?"

Noble studied the screen briefly. "A number is written in the upper-right hand corner of the FEMA chart. It looks to be in the same handwriting."

"I noted it also. I'm stumped but determined to find the meaning behind the numbers."

"Keep working on it. That might give us our first clue. Let's get back to the next grid."

Max spun the display once more and placed another grid to the right of the one for WECC. "This is for ERCOT, the Electric Reliability Council of Texas, naturally covering Texas and twenty-three million Texans. It is also the Texas Interconnection. Their control center is in Taylor, Texas."

"All of these grids were on Simon's flash drive? I don't like the way this is shaping up."

"Sorry, boss. There's more and it's not encouraging." Max put the third grid on the screen. She explained that it was for MISO, the Midwest Independent System Operator, and controlled the energy supply for fifteen states and one Canadian province. "It is also part of the Eastern Interconnection and provides power to fifteen-point-one million customers."

"Where is their control center located?"

"Actually, MISO has two control centers that run parallel, one in St. Paul, Minnesota, and the other in Carmel, Indiana."

Max then placed the fourth grid on the monitor. "This covers a small area in SERC, the Southeast Electric Reliability Council, again part of the Eastern Interconnection. It services power to portions of Mississippi, Alabama, and Georgia, for four-point-four million people. The control center is in Birmingham, Alabama."

Noble noted the number scribbled in the upper-right hand corner and then waved her on.

"The fifth and final grid that we were able to locate is interesting. It is for the Northeast Power Coordinating Council, the N-P-C-C, and part of the Eastern Interconnection. It covers the greater part of the northeast and five provinces in Canada. What makes this unusual is that the control center is located in Mississauga, Ontario. It's not even in our country."

"It's across the *border!*" Noble raised an eyebrow.

Max removed the individual grids from the monitor and placed a map of the U.S. where she had circled the grids in question. "Here's what we are dealing with."

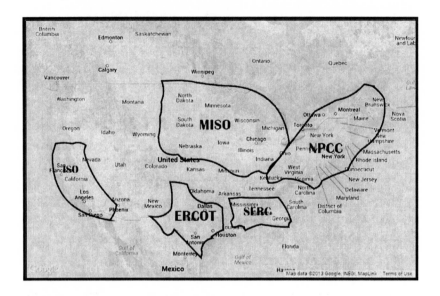

They both sat back and studied the map.

"It may only be half of the country Max, but any one grid going down would have devastating affects.

"I agree, especially in light of what happened in 2003." She recounted the events of the massive blackout that covered not only the Northeast, but also parts of the Midwest and Ontario. "I believe it affected over fifty-five million people. The cause was attributed to power lines that brushed against overgrown foliage. That problem first brought down the power in Ohio. With no failsafe system in place, and the inability to transmit power from functioning sectors of the grid to the troubled facilities, blackouts cascaded throughout the states within the overall grid."

Noble stirred uneasily in his chair. He interrupted, "I remember very well. I was in New York City at the time. Everything stopped: trains, planes, communication, including cell phones and television broadcasts. Typical in a crisis, most New Yorkers pitched in to help their neighbors, while others began looting. It was mayhem…" he stopped short, clearly intense.

"What is it?" Max began to feel a sense of urgency.

Noble, clearly struck by concern, stated slowly, "That one grid alone, despite the fact the trauma only lasted three days, cost upward of six billion dollars and contributed to at least eleven deaths. What if the five grids you identified were to shut down simultaneously?"

"It would be devastating!" Max rattled out a scenario of how commuting on trains and planes would cease. Traffic lights would not function. All travel would be brought to a standstill. Communication would be impossible when the backup power for the cellular sites failed. Pressure from the water pumps would decrease, causing contamination and sewage spill over into the waterways. Industries and corporations, along with the stock market, would halt.

"It would be total chaos—it would create a looter's paradise. Noble, there'd be panic on a national scale!" Max, in her own tense state, painted a picture of anything that came to mind, knowing she had only scratched the surface. Suddenly, she blurted out, "You really believe that Simon is planning a major strike against the U.S.? Max hesitated, and then answered her own question. "He's going to use the electrical grids as his weapon of choice."

Noble remained composed, even after having already considered the consequences. "Yes, all clues and logical implications point to Simon. What we know thus far carries his imprint. So whatever he's up to—we need to find out how he's going to carry out his plan—and the timetable." He let out a deep breath. "Put the individual grids back up on the monitor."

He stared again at the five grids and at each of the numbers scribbled in black ink, in the upper-right hand corners. *They are all written in the same style. It has to be a clue*, he pondered. "Let's keep working to find the purpose of the numbers."

Max stared at the screen, as well, attempting to decipher their plausibility and whether it supported Noble's inference. "It's virtually impossible for Simon to hack into each of the systems and individually shut them down. For years, hackers have been trying to plant *backdoor* codes into each of the grids for that purpose. But each attempted intrusion was thwarted and security was heightened through redesigns," Max acknowledged.

They both were aware that the backdoor is an undocumented method a programmer uses to access a program or a computer. Initially, it provided a way for the programmer to stop a program or computer gone awry. Today the backdoor is used for more nefarious reasons, providing a 'private entrance' for the hacker to enter a computer system.

"Max, the grids are still a patchwork quilt across the country despite these advances. The technology is antiquated by today's standards, and is vulnerable to invasion. These grids are comprised of overloaded transmission lines, unable to redistribute power as needed to grids in other areas. If one has a glitch, it can easily create the cascading effect you described. The 2003 blackout was the perfect example that can't be dismissed."

Max understood, but turned to another topic, no less curious. "I also found documents referring to the Tres Amigas Project called the *Superstation*. The project was designed to resolve past issues, by physically connecting the three main interconnections and control the transmission of power from a single main control center."

Noble nodded. "It's my understanding the two-point-five-billion dollar superstation has been stalled for years." He paused. "But I have a contact who might be able to shed some light on the reasons. It's possible the Superstation is a piece of the puzzle. Coincidently, I'm seeing that particular person tonight. Let me see what I can find out. In the meantime, I want you to alert the chairman of the Federal Energy Regulatory Commission."

"Why FERC? Why not the Secretary of the Department of Energy? Max interrupted.

Naturally, they were aware that FERC was an independent regulatory agency within the Department of Energy responsible for the review, approval, and regulation of the transmission of electricity, natural gas, and oil within the U.S. However, Max was curious as to why Noble would want to involve another agency.

"Because we didn't uncover an org chart with FERC circled in red," he pointed out. "My sensors tell me to deal directly with the FERC chairman. Ask him to contact the directors at each of the control centers and to inquire as to whether they've had any malicious cyber or physical breaches, either in their facilities or with their main operating systems."

"Do you want him to include the Superstation as well?"

"Yes, let's cover all our bases. In addition, I think we have sufficient information now to ask him to increase security at all facilities. Have him notify us immediately of any suspicious activity."

Max looked over toward the wall clock and noted the time. It was 7:30 p.m. "The chairman should be able to reach most of them, but Birmingham and Mississauga can wait until tomorrow. I'll call him right away. With any luck, I won't be too late for my dinner date. You're not the only one with a social life."

Noble missed her expression. He was already halfway across the room and heading out the door.

All Max heard him say was, "Great job with the grids."

5

THE SOURCE

There they are." Amanda pointed toward the bar where Nancy and Adam Ridge were standing. "Sorry we're late," she apologized while flashing a smile in Noble's direction.

"Not a problem. There's about a ten minute wait for our table," Nancy replied, as they each managed the appropriate handshake or air-kiss greeting.

Adam placed additional drink orders.

Adam Ridge was a lobbyist for the Oil and Gas Industry and Amanda's boss. Noble was well aware of his credentials. Before he became a lobbyist, he worked for the Department of Energy, the DOE, making him a key source of vital information.

The month before, Noble had met with Adam in a clandestine get-together on the premise that he may have information that would prove useful in tracking down Simon. At the time, Noble suspected that the government-owned land in Utah was an essential part of the case. Adam was able to clarify some of the activities that took place since Congress passed the Omnibus Public Land Management Act in 2009. As a result, the government had set out to claim a laundry list of land—including land in the area Noble had dubbed the *Dead Zone*. Their conversation also led them to a major regulatory case that involved Adam's clients, regarding the mining of beryllium within the same area. It was the same metal ultimately linked to an explosive device used in the London New Year's Eve bombing. The metal was traced back to Simon.

"Your table is ready," the waiter announced. "This way please."

The ladies followed the waiter, while the guys stayed behind to settle the bar tab. At this point, Noble took the opportunity to say, "Adam, I need to talk to you about your time at the DOE."

Adam appeared slightly shaken. "I'm leaving on a business trip tomorrow for a few days. Can it wait until I return?"

"How about tonight after dinner?"

"The gals aren't going to be happy. It's that urgent?"

"Depending on what you tell me it could be," Noble pressed.

Adam capitulated. "Okay, but let's have a pleasant evening of conventional small talk first. Then we can make our amends and go do our thing."

"Agreed."

They both walked toward the table, removing the sternness from their faces and saving it for later.

"What are you two whispering about?" Nancy cajoled.

"The weather," Adam teased.

She knew it was always business.

Amanda knew it was always business.

"And what were you two talking about?" Noble asked, reversing the inquiry.

"Actually, we were talking about the National Symphony's performance last week with Hugh Wolff conducting," Nancy explained.

Amanda added, "Dvořák's New World Symphony was marvelous!"

"This is Amanda's way of reminding me that I cancelled at the last minute," Noble quipped.

Adam returned a broad smile.

"You too?" Noble chuckled.

Adam nodded in affirmation.

The men surrendered and took their seats. The women had already perused the menu and had made their choices. Noble chose Amanda's main course, forgoing the appetizer; Adam chose both of Nancy's selections.

Noble insisted on ordering a bottle of Capannelle 50&50—his favorite Tuscan wine.

It did not escape Adam's attention that he was preparing the gals for a later disappointment.

Then at the end of a delightful two-hour dinner, the moment of reckoning arrived.

Noble made the announcement. "I'm afraid ladies I am about to tarnish a wonderful evening. I have urgent business to discuss with Adam and this is our only opportunity."

"Noble, how rude," Amanda carped.

Adam spoke in Noble's defense and stated, "I agreed. You two order a big fattening dessert and then, dear, call my car service and have them drive you both home safely. We'll take care of the check when we leave."

"You're not leaving?" Nancy inquired, feigning a hint of surprise.

"The crowd's thinning out. We're going to sit in the back in the corner booth where it's quiet and private." Adam was the first to stand. He leaned over and kissed his none-too-happy wife. "I'll see you at home."

Noble stood and kissed Amanda, and then whispered in her ear, "Stay at my place tonight. I'll get there as soon as I can."

"Sorry I had to screw up the evening," Noble apologized.

"Let me get home at a reasonable hour and all will be forgiven."

Noble wasted no time. "Tell me about your stretch at the DOE?"

Surprised by the question, Adam asked, "You want to know about me or about the department?"

"I'm interested in their current activities, but I have to admit I am curious as to why you left in the first place." Noble always wondered why Adam had left the government and joined forces with a lobbying firm that was constantly at odds with his former employer.

"You're aware that I was the Assistant Secretary for Fossil Fuel?"

"Yes, and you left in 2013."

"Are you familiar with the GAP Analysis?"

"Isn't it basically a way of mapping the distribution of various endangered species in our country?"

"Primarily. However, when President Clinton created the National Gap Analysis Program in 1999, the scope went far beyond mapping just species and ballooned into a program to preserve protected areas as deemed by the government. These protected areas handed the government open latitude, literally to seize vast tracts of land. Presumably, it was a plan for the long-term maintenance of our biosphere."

"You said deemed by the government. Who made the decisions?"

"It's a mélange of federal, state, and non-governmental organizations, along with private businesses and academic institutions. They call themselves a coalition. Of course, the Environmental Protection Agency, National Park Service, and the Bureau of Land Management are among them. The non-government entities are an assortment of environmental interest groups, including The Nature Conservancy and the GreenInfo Network."

Adam paused noticeably before continuing. "Remember during our last meeting, we talked about the systematic federal land grabs that were taking place in the West that delayed the discharge of drilling leases?"

"Yes, I remember it created an impossible situation for the mining companies with leases, who were unable to build roads or bridges through federal-owned land to access their own privately funded drilling sites. Also didn't the government begin to reduce the amount of federal land previously allocated for drilling by various means?"

"Correct. Back in 2013, they reduced the acreage from one-point-three-million acres to seven-hundred-thousand acres."

"Why didn't you bring this up during our earlier meeting?" Noble inquired.

"You seemed to be focused on Juab County and the surrounding areas in Utah. The importance of what I am telling you now is that it's my belief that the mapping that took place under the Clinton GAP analysis was the precursor to identifying land—land to be confiscated later in the name of preservation."

"I do recall that the former president released a roadmap for solar-energy development based on a joint study by the U.S. Bureau of Land Management and the DOE. Is that what you are referring to?"

"Precisely, the plan was to allocate two hundred and eighty-five thousand acres of federal-owned land to build twenty-three-thousand-seven-hundred megawatts of solar-energy capacity over twenty years. The Secretary of the Interior at the time said that the program laid out the next phase of the president's strategy, 'for rapid and responsible development of renewable energy.'"

"I assume that's an example of your land-grab theory?" Noble posed.

Adam nodded. "There are many examples, but my premise solidified a few years earlier in September 2010 when the CLEAR Act surfaced." He paused again, this time to make sure Noble was following along.

"You have my attention. Keep going."

"The impetus for the CLEAR Act was the BP Oil spill. In my opinion, it was a ruse and another land-grab scheme. Even Gohmert, a representative from Texas, supported my assertion when he stood on the floor of the House of Representatives and clarified the provisions of the Act." Adam explained that it called for the federal government to spend nine-hundred million dollars a year to purchase private land over the next thirty years, for a grand total of twenty-seven billion dollars over three decades.

"The Act passed into law?" Noble asked, quite surprised given the economic situation at the time.

"Unfortunately, the House passed the Act, but by a thin margin. Twenty-one republican representatives did not appear for the final vote, so I do not believe the president wanted to gamble that it would not pass the Senate. For all practical purposes, he turned the Act over to the United Nations for implementation. It was a complete end-run around Congress."

"The United Nations. I'm confused."

"Give me a sec." Adam began tapping on his smartphone.

At the same time, Noble realized he was sitting precariously on the edge of his seat. He pushed back and waited for Adam.

"Oh, here it is." Adam held up his right index finger as he resumed. "HR 3-4-3-5 states…"

> *To provide greater efficiencies, transparency, returns, and*
> *accountability in the administration of Federal mineral and*
> *energy resources by consolidating administration of various*
> *Federal energy minerals management and leasing programs*
> *into one entity to be known as the Office of Federal Energy*
> *and Mineral Leasing of the Department of the Interior, and for*
> *other purposes.*

"And for other purposes," Noble interjected with a dubious look.

"In short, HR 3-4-3-5 is called the Consolidated Land, Energy and Aquatic Resources Act of 2010, or the CLEAR Act."

"But there was no mention of the United Nations in terms of administration." Noble appeared to be mystified.

Adam took note. "Listen to this. In section 106 of the Act, titled Abolishment of Minerals Management Service, there's a provision in item (e) that states—hold on." He advanced the screen on his smartphone. "Here it is. It states, 'Executive orders, rules, regulations, directives, or *delegations of authority that precede the effective date* of this Act…'" Adam waved his right hand…yada—yada—yada…then he continued to read, "'Statutory reporting requirements that applied in relation to the Service *immediately before the effective date of the Act shall continue to apply*,'" he enunciated.

Noble flapped both hands in the air, "Now I'm thoroughly confused. I still haven't made the connection to the United Nations."

Adam pressed on; he was about to connect the dots. "Two months before the CLEAR Act passed in the House, the president signed Executive Order 1-3-5-4-7, titled 'Stewardship of the Ocean, Our Coasts, and the Great Lakes.' It specifically called for," Adam looked down and read…

> *America's stewardship of the ocean, our coasts, and the Great*
> *Lakes is intrinsically linked to environmental sustainability,*

*human health and well-being, national prosperity, adaptation
to climate and other environmental changes, social justice,
international diplomacy, and national and homeland security.*

"The Law of the Sea Treaty!" Noble was stunned.

"Bingo! The language in the Clear Act reverts back to the prior Executive Order that substantially mandates membership in the United Nations Convention on the Law of the Sea Treaty, or LOST, bypassing the two-thirds votes required to ratify it in the Senate." Adam was impressed that Noble had knowledge of LOST, the international agreement that defined the rights and responsibility of nations and their use of the world's oceans.

"It sounds a bit like global governance," Noble acknowledged.

"It sounds a lot like global governance. I also portend this Act will place a permanent roadblock to American energy, locking down our offshore drilling capabilities." Adam abruptly changed topics. "Are you familiar with the Tres Amigas Project?"

Noble was excited by the question and played along. He assumed it would all start to make sense. "It's a sort of national gateway that would connect the Eastern, Texas, and Western Interconnections and control the transmission of power to all states, with the exception of Alaska and Hawaii. It was in the news for a while and then there appeared to be no further mention. I just assumed it was one of those *shovel-ready* projects to nowhere. Why is it important?"

"They call it the Superstation and it is alive and well. It is still around and it is not just a *super-power-station*. The goal is to create a super power exchange, in addition to opening up markets for renewable energy. Investors and private placements fund the project."

Noble shifted in his chair. *Now we are getting somewhere*, he thought.

Adam went on to explain that while the project was still in the construction phase, it had been slow going. In 2009, the governor of New Mexico granted a ninety-nine year lease in the city of Clovis for the Superstation. In return, the state would receive approximately nine million dollars per year in revenue, once it is operational; it was originally slated for 2014, and then pushed to 2016.

"In fact, it wasn't until 2013 that FERC first granted approval to interconnect with the Southwestern's transmission system, allowing them to begin the first phase. Then they needed additional approvals from FERC for the other interconnections, and they're still acquiring the rights-of-way for transmission lines throughout the region," Adam clarified.

"I'm following."

"Okay, have you heard of Stronghold Management?"

"Of course, they've been awarded a multitude of government contracts. Primarily, they are consulting gurus operating within a multitude of industries, providing design, operations, and project management services."

"That's a simplification. They operate in sixty countries, with over thirty thousand employees, bringing in annual revenue of over seven billion U.S. dollars. One of their major projects is to manage the construction services for the Superstation."

Noble gave his undivided attention to Adam as his interest amplified.

"Bear with me," Adam cautioned, "it gets more interesting. Between the years of 2009 to 2012, the federal government granted Stronghold Management over two billion dollars of stimulus money from the *Jobs Recovery Act*. Their contracts were awarded to several governmental agencies, including the DOE."

Adam described how he scoured over 470 government quarterly reports on the government's recovery.gov website and reviewed the various Stronghold grants. The reports indicated that the total number of jobs created was slightly over 7300, but fifty percent of those jobs remained in the government and the other half fell into a category called *other*. He found that many of the reports indicated less than one job created, with a qualifying statement that read, *No jobs created, only retained.*

"It was hard to determine on this *transparent* website just how many jobs were created with the expenditure of over two-billion taxpayers' dollars."

Noble was stunned. "This is starting to smack of crony capitalism."

"It's not a smack; it's a straight-out head butt. By the way, did I mention that Stronghold Management reallocated upward of ten million dollars of stimulus money to manage the design of a defunct solar manufacturing plant in California?"

So we're using taxpayer dollars not only to build a company, which we know failed, but also to keep that company from going into bankruptcy.

"And the political peddling is even worse." Adam explained, "In one year, Stronghold Management's political donations totaled over six million dollars. Add that to another four million dollars for lobbyists; it takes their influence in Washington to new heights."

To Noble it sounded like a resounding climax, but he could not fathom how this would lead him closer to Simon. Even still, he found it fascinating and urged Adam to continue. "You never told me why you left the department?"

"I started to dig deeper and deeper into the Stronghold companies and the Superstation. Stronghold has a long list of infractions and disputes with the government, including timecard fraud and paid kickbacks."

"I thought you said the DOE and the other agencies continued to pay out stimulus money to Stronghold?"

"They did, and what I discovered was frightening. Stronghold's Remediation Company managed environmental cleanup projects. Remember when we spoke about one of my clients, a producer of beryllium?"

"Yes. I recall they were having difficulty accessing the drilling sites due to the surrounding federal-owned land."

"That's what I thought at the time. Now I believe it had more to do with environmental reasons. Stronghold was chartered with the cleanup of the beryllium by-product, the dust particles created when developing the metal used in the nuclear industry. They received hefty fines for not adhering to proper work restrictions regarding nuclear waste."

Adam's excitement had waned, but he continued to explain his predicament in a doleful manner. "After careful consideration, and even knowing what I had uncovered trailed back to the DOE, I decided to become a standard-bearer for whistleblowing. Out of respect, I first spoke with my boss, the newly appointed Secretary of the Department of Energy."

Adam was chameleonic with emotion, trading in calm for extreme agitation. "My boss reminded me who I was going up against! In his words, 'beware, they own the government, or at least aspects of the government.' I was not absolutely sure whom he was speaking about specifically and he wouldn't elaborate. Then I started to get mysterious veiled threats to both my family and me. The mention of my family was all it took. It was not a battle I wanted to fight." He stopped. Then with a touch of angst he stressed, "Particularly frightening—was that the only person I told of my concerns—was my boss."

Noble grimaced. "Based on recent events of what's happening to government whistleblowers of late you made the right choice. However, by confiding in me I feel compelled to pursue these matters fully." He noted Adam's discomfort. "It's a new administration. Do you want to speak to the president?" Noble asked.

"No. I'm not going down that road. Frankly, I don't trust anyone in the government."

"If you change your mind, I'll do whatever I can to help. But Adam, I'm still not quite sure what the link is between all of these events."

Adam began to fidget as he glanced around the room. Then straightaway with one hand, he reached for his pen, and with the other grabbed the cocktail napkin lying on the table. After a moment of hesitation, he scribbled something on the napkin and handed it to Noble. "Follow the trail—but be careful."

Noble looked down at the scrawling. "What!"

"It's late. I need to get home." Adam's agitation was evident.

"Go. I'll pick up the check." Noble remained alone in the booth. *Land grabs, United Nations, global governance, power exchange. Nothing seems to connect to Simon.* He rolled the words around in his mind. Then noting the time, he settled the bill and headed for his apartment.

6
DREAM DATE

Noble eased the key gently into the lock and turned it to the right. At the same time, he tightened his jaw, hoping his entry would not disrupt the silence. He crept through his apartment, removing his clothing along the way, and then he slithered in between the bed sheets.

"That was an enjoyable evening," mumbled the sleepy voice next to him.

Noble, pleased she was half-awake, rolled over for a goodnight kiss.

Amanda pushed back kiddingly, and probed, "Why did you and Adam have to conduct business tonight? That's not your usual style during a social evening with friends."

"I needed to discuss a critical issue with him," Noble whispered. "It's germane to a case I'm working on." Artfully, he diverted the subject, pulled her into his arms for a more passionate embrace, and cooed, "I love you. Now let's get some sleep."

∽

"Noble—wake-up." She rocked his shoulder several times to no avail.

His body continued to squirm about in the bed. "Noble—Noble." she uttered in a more forceful, but fearful tone.

Suddenly, he awoke from his fitful sleep flailing his arms, startling Amanda even more.

"Darling, are you okay?" she asked in a calming voice. She had never seen him so vulnerable. She refrained from commenting, but it caused her great concern.

At last, Noble sat up in bed and strained to slow down his breathing. Then he began to sound off. "I had a terrible dream! I was falling, falling deeper and deeper into a dark hole! My body became numb and I couldn't feel my legs!" His breathing again accelerated.

Amanda rubbed his back in an attempt to calm him down. "It's okay. You're with me. You're not falling."

"It was so dark! I realized I was surrounded by water! I was confused! I couldn't breathe! Then, as I gasped for my last breath of air—I found myself standing on a bridge—looking down into an abyss..."

"Darling, calm down please! You're scaring me."

"Let me finish!" He held her hand gently and in a steadier voice, said, "A face was staring back from the black water, but it wasn't my reflection." He gulped several times and then stared into her eyes and said, "It was his face."

"Whose face?" Amanda's heart ached to see him looking so helpless.

Noble refrained from answering.

"Honey, how long has this been going on?" Her expression was total wonderment.

He glanced away and admitted, "For a while. They are just more frequent." Then sounding natural as though the dream never happened, he looked once again into her eyes and said, "Amanda, when you think you're about to die, you search for a reason to live—you were the first reason that entered my mind." Noble took a moment, and then before he lost his nerve, he blurted out, "Will you marry me?"

Amanda was blown away by the question as she struggled to grapple with the events of the last several minutes. For the first time she was speechless.

"Does your silence mean no?"

Piercing through her fog, she cried, "Yes, yes, I will marry you. I love you so much."

"I love you, but…" Noble stopped mid-sentence, wanting to select his words with the utmost care.

Amanda retreated into silence again. She had expected a possible caveat, despite their intense romantic interlude. She also surmised any response would be useless.

"Much to my dismay we have to wait until this case is over."

"You mean Simon."

"Yes."

"Darling, you've spent the last nine years going after him. Before that, Hamilton spent another fifteen years. Simon has escaped twice. What makes you think it will ever be over?" Amanda realized she was pleading, but she could not hold back at that life-changing moment.

"I just know!" Noble shouted. "This time I will capture the S-O-B and close the case forever!" He despised the pain he caused Amanda and softened his tone. "I just need a little more time to seal his doom."

He kissed Amanda gently and apologized. "I regret you had to see me in such a foolish state." Then he allowed, "I do believe in the notion that dreams of falling are just an indication of feeling overwhelmed and anxious. It's good old fashion stress."

"According to Freud, it's an indication that you're surrendering to a sexual urge." Amanda glanced at him with a come-hither, twinkling smile.

Noble gently rolled her back into bed to seal the deal.

7

A MAJOR UPSET

It was President's Day and the White House was eerily quiet. The only real activity was taking place in Noble's lair. On his orders, many of his staff were in attendance.

At least it was quiet until Max rushed past Doris at her usual hurried pace.

"He's in with someone right now. You'll have to wait your turn."

"This is important."

"It's always important! He should only be a few more minutes."

Max began to pace back and forth impatiently gathering her thoughts.

"Max! Would you please stand still," Doris pleaded.

Without warning, the office door swung open.

"Max, what's with all the noise?"

Ignoring Noble's rebuke, she breezed past him into his office. The sight of Major Stanton caught her short.

The major stood tall in full uniform and donned a broad smile.

Noble took note and said, "Give us a minute." He gestured the major toward the conference room, "We'll join you shortly."

Stanton left and waited next door.

Noble closed his office door, putting Doris and Stanton out of earshot. "Rather rude," he chided.

"What's he doing here?"

"He's here to update us on the detainee interrogations. Meanwhile, I offered the major a reassignment."

"You what! Why didn't you tell me? I can't work with him!"

"Max, relax. It is not with the agency. The head of the president's secret service detail is retiring and the president asked if I would recommend a replacement. He appears to be the leading candidate."

"Why Stanton?"

"Why all the fury?" Noble had an inkling of their relationship, but he would let Max squirm a bit.

Max, ignoring his question, only flushed as she repeated, "Why Stanton?"

"He has a sterling record, and also the major is one of the few who knows the entrance to the encampment. In a crisis he is the best equipped to shield the president. You know as well as anyone, if Simon is planning a strike on a national scale, the president will need protection."

"Why is the entrance to the encampment such a secret anyway?"

"That's one secret I can't disclose. Let it go, Max."

When he used that serious tone, she had learned it was time to close the book.

Noble stood firm by his promise to the president to protect the location of the *Presidential Lair*—a promise he would never break.

The underground encampment Simon used for a terrorist training camp was a bunker that in 1953, President Eisenhower decommissioned by executive order. Subsequently, it was removed from the military roster. At the time, the president had seen the end of a devastating war and the beginning of the Cold War. The bunker was to be a place of last resort, should the enemy discover the other established safe havens.

Total secrecy of the bunker was essential.

The reference to the underground encampment's existence was in the *President's Book of Secrets*—a book passed on exclusively from president to president. Out of forty-six United States presidents, there are only seven alive who know the location of the facility, tagged the *Presidential Lair*. The book contained the blueprint and the location of the bunker. However, someone callously ripped the page out of the book. It happened during the Baari Administration—after Simon learned of its existence. Noble logically concluded the person most likely to have access to the book and the blueprint would be Baari's chief of staff and Simon's accomplice, Hank Kramer.

"While we're on the subject, I've also asked to have Agent Burke reassigned to head up the D.C. bureau. The FBI Director is in accord."

"He knows the location too," Max chimed in sarcastically and then relented. "I admit I don't understand why, but I do understand you want to keep us all close until Simon is collared. They're both good guys and have proved their capability and their loyalty."

"All of you have!" Noble emphasized.

"I'm aware the feds and the SIA are oftentimes in a power struggle, but Burke worked heroically by my side during Operation Nomis. He's proved his worth." Max caught Noble's demeanor change. "What's the matter?"

"I just had a flashback of you being knocked out by the blast in the indoctrination center. You scared the hell out of me!"

"How do you think I felt? Enough on the subject, I give up! Both Stanton and Burke may prove to be helpful, especially on this case."

"Now that we're in agreement, would you like to join the major and me?"

"One more thing first, the FERC chairman spoke with each of the directors from the control centers. The Birmingham facility was the only one to report any kind of unusual activity. According to protocol, the director of the control center called the Department of Energy. The DOE sent in someone from their geek squad to check it out. Everything proved to be okay. It was just a blip. Nothing has occurred at the Superstation; their computer system has not gone live yet. Evidently, they have internal measures for testing the system." Max had something else to spring on Noble, but she wanted to hear what Stanton had to say first. She took a deep breath, put a smile on her face, and said, "May we go?"

⟋⟋

Max, looking unnerved, followed Noble into the conference room. "Hi Major, nice to see you again," she greeted, and then took her place on the opposite side of the table.

Noble took the lead. "Before you arrived, the major explained that all of the hundred and nine detainees had been interviewed. However, several had been cordoned off from the others, and held for further interrogation."

"By the way Director, I want to confirm how long the captives can be detained if it's determined that they are enemy combatants?" Stanton asked.

"I'm sure you are aware that the National Defense Authorization Act was signed by the president, during the prior administration. Therefore, it does not run out until December of this year. The controversial provision regarding *Counter-Terrorism* is still in effect."

"So if we suspect our prisoners are involved in terrorism, they can be detained indefinitely in military detention?"

"Correct."

"And that would include U.S. citizens arrested on American soil."

"Yes, Major." Noble was curious as to why the major should need clarification. Certainly he understood the law.

"All detainees are American citizens," Stanton reported.

"What!" Max exclaimed, interrupting the conversation. "How is it possible Simon was able to round up that many young Americans to fight for the jihadi cause?" She remembered seeing the Special Forces capturing the prisoners in the encampment. Many were young women.

"That's what's confusing, as well as alarming. It's apparent from the documents and manuals we recovered, along with the evidence from the encampment, that the training was geared toward terrorist techniques." Stanton continued to explain that in the absence of any identification, they processed the detainees utilizing retina scans and fingerprinting. Then he had them confined to their cells, while awaiting identification.

"Meanwhile, as we waited for their records, my men and I conducted a cursory interrogation with each individual detainee. All we were able to ascertain was the mumblings of a mantra. It was the same chant repeatedly. It was as though they were giving their name, rank, and serial number—and nothing more."

"What exactly did they say?" Noble inquired.

"Whew, I heard it so many times I can repeat it verbatim..."

> *I start from where the world is,*
> *as it is, not as I would like it to be.*
> *That we accept the world as it is,*
> *does not in any sense weaken our desire*
> *to change it into what we believe it should be.*

Max wide-eyed, blurted out, "They quoted Saul Alinsky!"

"It gets stranger. Once we identified each of them, we conducted a second round of interrogation." Stanton explained that they elicited bits and pieces from each detainee. "But whenever we asked them about their mission, they repeated that damn mantra." He looked over toward Max, "Excuse me, ma'am."

Max had calmed down. It was obvious he was mocking her.

Both Stanton and Noble knew her sarcasm could rival theirs any day.

"Major, no offense taken. But what did you derive from your interrogations?"

"Each detainee reported receiving hoards of rap music over the Internet, either through their social networks or by direct mailings. It was political rap promoting social revolution. They mentioned names like Grandmaster, Public Enemy, 2 Live Crew, 2pac, et cetera. I listened to a few of their songs. Pretty heavy stuff."

"I'm more interested in the effect you think it had on the prisoners." Max asked in a serious tone.

"They took to it. That was the point. It's the same technique al-Qaeda used first to grab the interest of potential recruits. They call it 'Jihadi

Cool,' utilizing pop culture to inspire. It is the first step to radicalization when recruiting for the cause. They would use other media as well, video games, comic strips, et cetera, anything. In al-Qaeda's case, it would portray a positive spin on Islamic fundamentalism." Stanton shook his head. "You won't believe their number one rapper. He has received over twelve million hits on YouTube and it has been downloaded to millions of computers worldwide. Listen to this crap." He pulled a piece of paper out of his pocket and read the lyrics.

> *Peace to Hamas and the Hezbollah,*
> *OBL pulled me like a shiny star,*
> *like the way we destroyed them two towers ha-ha.*

In disgust, Stanton crunched the paper in his fist and tossed it into the trash receptacle nearby. "It's called 'Dirty Kuffar' by Sheikh Terra. Kuffar means nonbeliever."

"Is the political rap you listened to as horrendous?" Max asked, a bit wary of the answer.

"Let's just say if you wanted to start a social revolution—it's the way to go."

Noble had remained silent listening to Stanton, but at that point he was perplexed. "What about in this case in particular? How were our detainees recruited?"

"It's unclear. They reported that they had been invited into various chat rooms and blogs, but thus far, they have not been forthcoming as to which ones. Director, information-gathering is a slow process given the *lack* of interrogation techniques at our disposal."

Noble chose not to react and urged him to continue.

"These methods allow the recruiter to observe the activity of the recruits, watching their comments in a forum of like-minded individuals. Once they're engaged and identifying with the ideology, the recruiter moves on to the next and final phase, the weeding out process, identifying the willing and able. It appears from what information we've derived, the al-Qaeda 'handbook for recruiting' was followed to a tee."

Max chimed in, "I remember a report generated by the New

York City Police Department that studied how terrorists utilized the Internet to recruit. I recall specifically a statement referring to these online arenas as 'virtual echo chambers that act as an accelerant to radicalization.'"

"Scary thought," Stanton observed.

"Where do we stand now?" Noble asked.

"Director, I need more time. I lie awake at night with the damn chant in my head. That's all they keep repeating. It would appear they are following instructions given to them on the off chance they were captured. But whatever their mission is—they haven't given the info up."

"So what's your next step?" Max took an opportunity to cut to the chase, as usual.

"Many of the recruits are from low-income homes, dysfunctional families, or just your textbook misfits. They are the perfect candidates to suck into a cause. But there's another group that didn't fit the profile. They're college educated, articulate, with stable families and jobs. But their responses are identical—that damn mantra." Stanton looked Max's way and smiled. "Like I said, I need more time." At last, he displayed discouragement at his current lack of success to obtain more information.

"Did that handful of 'brainiacs' happen to include our four cyclists?" Max inquired.

"Yes, along with a group of techies. I also think we've identified those responsible for the deaths in the Dead Zone. But as I said, I need more time to clarify this hodgepodge."

"And Agent Darrow's murder?" Max asked.

"Yes."

Noble's brow furrowed a trifle upon hearing the Dead Zone mentioned. The name he had given to the location of his investigation centered in Utah months earlier, although it seemed like a lifetime ago. The mysterious deaths at several abandoned mines south of the Dugway Proving Ground were still fresh in his mind. In particular, the murder of Agent Darrow that led them to the underground encampment and the capture of Simon was especially prominent. In the beginning, the cases appeared totally unrelated, as the pursuit of

Simon had become cold. Once again, Noble found himself embroiled in another investigation pursuing Simon, which ultimately proved to be nothing but a stalled continuation of the first pursuit.

Noble cast a glance in Stanton's direction and stated, "Major, I have no clue as to how much time we have. Simon has disappeared, but he has not evaporated. Of that I'm positive." It was evident he was disturbed by the paucity of information. "We need to start processing the detainees and bringing in counsel to represent them. First, put all of them through another round of intense interrogation. Use *whatever means* necessary. Find out what the hell Simon has planned."

Max glared toward Noble at the mention of the words "whatever means" and guessed, *he is referring to waterboarding.*

Noble caught her eye. "Max, do you have anything relevant to add to the case?"

"Nothing pertinent," she replied, shrugging her shoulders.

Noble stood. Stanton took the cue.

As they shook hands, Noble stated, "I'll need your answer on the other matter we discussed by the end of the week."

"Yes, Director."

Stanton walked out of the conference room.

Noble remained behind and flagged Max to do the same. "There's something I need you to do."

"There's something I need to tell you!" she retorted.

Noble ignored her wordplay for the moment and asked, "Find out everything you can about this, pronto." He handed her a cocktail napkin. Written on the napkin was the word, *Agenda,* followed by the number *21.*

"You think this connects to Simon?" she asked, wrinkling her nose.

"It's a long shot, or it may have more to do with my source's agenda. Just find out what you can."

Noticing a name imprinted in the lower left hand corner of the napkin, Max inquisitively asked, "Oh, is this where you had dinner the other night?"

"Jealous?" Noble smirked, cocked his head, and noted, "Yeah, great restaurant." He knew she was prying and allowed, "I met my source later in the evening after my dinner guests had left." *I don't think that raises to the level of a white lie,* he reflected. "Now, what do you need to tell me?"

"Agent Burke found the Ford Escape. It was abandoned just outside Newcastle, California, about sixteen miles from Folsom. The car had been torched, but thanks to a torrential downpour that must have occurred shortly thereafter, they were able to pull some fingerprints."

Baffled, Noble noted. "You could've discussed that in front of Stanton."

Max shook her head and said, "No—I couldn't. Burke ran the prints."

"Whose prints? Simon's?"

"Nope—the former first lady, Senator Maryann Townsend."

Noble reacted, "She's been lying through her teeth!"

"They found prints on the glove compartment and on the underside of the latch in the trunk," Max explained. "The only other thing they found was a partially scorched CD that was still in the player with Simon's print. Evidently, he's an admirer of Bach."

"So she was in the car with Simon?"

"Either that, or she was careless wiping down the car before leaving it for him outside the prison. It wasn't a rental, because we know it was registered to Hal Simmons. Burke is trying to trace its origin to find out where it was purchased. Are you planning to *respectfully request* a meeting or haul her back in?"

Noble thought for a moment and then without answering, asked, "Did you receive the surveillance tape from the hotel?"

"Yes, it arrived this afternoon, but I haven't had an opportunity to run through it."

"Review both that video and the one from the airport. Then meet me first thing in the morning, and I'll answer your question. Remember, I have the meeting with Kramer at eleven."

Max pouted. "Another nighttime assignment."

"Don't worry Max; I have my own homework assignment. By the way, I proposed to Amanda."

"You what?"

Noble smiled. He knew she hungered for the details, but he abruptly did an about face and left for his office.

8

GOTCHA

Noble enjoyed arriving at his office early, pre-Doris. It gave him an opportunity to make a pot of coffee and ease into the day before she began nagging about his schedule. Although, on the nights Amanda slept over, he preferred to share his first caffeine fix of the day with her, but that was not the case last night. In fact, she had not stayed over since the night he proposed. *She is giving me a wide berth. It is now in her best interest that I capture Simon, as soon as possible*, he calculated.

He ventured to the kitchen next to his conference room, filled the pot with water, and hit the button. While waiting for the drip, drip, drip of java, he noticed an illumination from under the door. Thinking the cleaning crew had left the light on the night before, he opened the door and reached for the light switch. "Max, when did you arrive?"

Startled by his announcement, she whipped her head around and quickly glanced his way. Her hair was mussed and her wardrobe appeared to be identical to the one she had worn the day before.

Noble grinned.

"It's not what you think! I've been here all night. I slept on the sofa."
In a milder, less defensive tone she said, "Noble, you're not going to
believe what I uncovered."

"One minute." He thrust his hand in the air to halt her exposé.

Moments later, Noble returned with two cups of eye-opening
coffee and sat down across from her at the table. "Now, what's so
unbelievable?"

"We've got her!" Max exclaimed. She reviewed in general terms
what she had discovered on the surveillance tape sent by the hotel.
It revealed exactly as the secret service agent had described. On the
video, she was able to view Maryann arriving at the hotel and checking
into her suite at 2:45 in the afternoon. "That squares with her arriving
at the airport at one fifty p.m. and driving a half hour to the hotel. I
fast forwarded the video to nine o'clock, when we know she was at the
prison based on the sign-in log."

"And?"

"The senator never left her hotel room."

"How's that possible?"

"I asked the same question. The single conceivable explanation is
she actually arrived at the hotel after she saw Simon." It was clear Max
had Noble's attention. While he sipped his coffee, she continued. "I
went back and reviewed the video when the senator was at the airport,
before she left with her security detail and drove away in the black
sedan."

"Watch this!" Max queued the video showing the scene on the
large display and they both sat back and watched the video for the
second time. As before, Maryann walked down a long corridor with
her security close behind. Then she stopped and made a trip to the
Ladies' Room. Four minutes later, she walked out and continued down
the corridor and out of the building.

"That's what we saw before," Noble stated, but with increased
impatience. From Max's demeanor alone, he deduced she was on to
something.

"Watch this. I'll slow it down."

Again, they watched Maryann walk down the corridor, enter the
Ladies' Room, and then return to the corridor.

Max paused the tape. "Look right there." She pointed toward the senator's feet.

Noble studied the screen. "Back it up—stop—I still don't get it!"

"The senator walked into the Ladies' Room with her signature pair of one-inch-square heeled shoes, peering from under her pant legs. Her decoy walked out wearing a pair of two-inch spiked heels appearing below the hems of identical pant legs."

"Un-be-liev-a-ble!" Noble let loose. "The change of the shoes compensated for their difference in height."

"Brilliant deduction my dear Watson." Max snickered. She was openly proud of her discovery, but puzzled as to the senator's carelessness. "Surprisingly, the senator forgot to specify the specific shoe style!"

They both focused at the monitor in silence as they watched the decoy walk down the corridor with the former first lady's security detail in procession.

Noble took a deep breath, followed by a sigh, and asked, "So where did our senator skip off to?"

"I went back to the original surveillance videos from the airport that I had spliced together to follow the senator's trail. I watched beyond the point when the decoy reentered the corridor. Moments later, the senator emerged from the Ladies' Room wearing identical clothes, including a pair of square-heeled shoes. She then exited the airport and hailed a taxi."

"Were you able to get the name of the car service or a license plate number?"

"Naturally, I have both." It was obvious that Max was delighted with her investigative prowess, one aspect of the job she most enjoyed. She related to Noble how she had been on the phone all morning, tracking down the senator's trail. "The taxi made two stops, first to Mail Boxes Etc., and then to a used car lot. The taxi driver said she was only inside Mail Boxes Etc. for a few minutes, and then returned with a large envelope."

Noble was about to ask about the second stop but held back and smiled. *Max of course would have the answer.*

She predicted his thought and grinned as well. "I got off the phone with the owner of the car lot an hour ago. A woman arrived wearing the clothes I described from the video, but she had long red hair and she was wearing sunglasses. He said she was there to pick up the car she had purchased. He didn't recognize her as the woman who originally paid for the car, but she had the key and the registration. So he released it to her."

"And the car was a blue metallic Ford Escape XLS sport utility model."

"Precisely, and the plates matched." Max took a half-bow.

"So now we know that she left the car somewhere outside the prison grounds and Simon used it as his getaway car."

"And that the envelope must have contained the key and registration for the car."

"And the xPhad." Noble sat back and began to ponder his next step. Max left him to contemplate.

"I'll call the senator," Noble announced. "This time she is coming to us. If she does not cooperate, I'll threaten her with a Senate committee hearing. I will also encourage her to bring counsel. We're handling this one strictly by the book." Noble paused, and then queried, "I just have one nagging question. How did she get back into her hotel suite without the secret service agents knowing?"

"Good question—hold on." Max queued up the video from the hotel and fast-forwarded to nine o'clock p.m. They sat back and watched the scene play out in the corridor. One of the senator's agents was sitting in a chair outside her door, flipping through a magazine. Max moved the video forward at a slow speed. An hour on the video had passed and the scene had not changed. Max and Noble persevered. She paused the tape. "He appears to be taking a call on his smartphone."

"Where's he going?" Noble was aware of the protocol. He was not to leave his post.

"Look!" Max exclaimed. She paused the video again. Coming out of the exit door was Maryann scooting toward her suite. Max hit the *Play* button. They watched as Maryann knocked on the door and the door opened. She slid inside the room and then closed the door shut. Moments later, the agent returned with an ice bucket and several Diet Cokes. He knocked on the door to the suite. Max and Noble continued to view the scene in utter amazement as Maryann opened the door dressed in her bathrobe and reached for the ice bucket. The door closed once again and the agent returned to his chair and magazine, none the wiser.

"Mystery solved!" Noble scoffed in jest, and then said, "Good job, Max."

"Thanks boss. Now, how did your homework assignment go?"

"I found two more grids."

"What! That's impossible. I scoured through all the manuals pertaining to the Department of Energy."

"They weren't there. I found them folded between the pages of the FEMA's *An In-depth Guide to Citizen Preparedness*. One was for the Florida Reliability Coordinating Council, and the other was for the Northern Tier Transmission Group. What was odd, other than the fact they had been separated from the other grids, was that no number appeared in the upper right hand corner of the page."

"Noble, I don't know how I could have missed them. I swear I went through that manual as well. Do you think they're significant?"

"It appears Simon is avoiding those grids for now. Interestingly, the Northern Tier controls the energy supply to Utah."

"That would make sense. He, of course, wasn't expecting that we would discover the location of the underground encampment. It's obvious Simon would've planned to rely on the power."

"Also, let's not forget it's about two hours away from Camp Williams near Bluffdale."

"You mean the location of the four-billion-dollar project, housing the National Security Agency's Data Center? Their data mining activities are mindboggling. I suppose it could be a target, but it is also heavily fortified including its own police force. I doubt if Simon were to create a national disaster that location would serve a purpose."

"But I understood the NSA uses a cloud technology that allows other agencies to access the data bank remotely. Simon's a hell of a wily creature; perhaps he's discovered a vulnerability."

"What are you suggesting?"

"I'm not sure. This case is getting weirder by the day." Max tossed up her hands as if she were giving in, and asked, "Incidentally, why avoid

Florida? It would affect close to five million citizens."

"Not sure. Let's not discount either grid for now." Noble glanced at his watch. "Kramer's showing up soon. What did you find out about Agenda 21?"

"I've been a little busy." The minutes the words left her mouth, she realized it was not the desired answer. "I'll get right on it."

"And I'll have a conversation with our unscrupulous senator. I suspect she'll meet with us willingly. It's a better cover here than in her office."

Max let out a deep breath and asked, "Noble, don't you think it's time to bring in additional resources? We're all stretched pretty thin." She was not as concerned with herself, but it was obvious the case was taking a toll on Noble. She did not understand why they had to tread so cautiously.

"With all honesty—I'm afraid of what we might discover. I'm not sure who we can trust. For now, I only want Stanton and Burke involved and to a limited degree." Noble paused. "This may prove to be bigger than all of us. I haven't even informed the president of these latest developments."

"Boss!"

"I will—soon. But let's give it a little more time."

Max could tell by Noble's demeanor that it was best to change the subject, at least for the moment. "I assume you don't want me to sit in on the meeting?"

Noble shook his head with the familiar *no*.

Max anticipated the answer but thought she would give it a shot. She remembered her conversation when they first started to trail Simon. It was a rare moment when Noble stepped out of character and divulged the name of one of the members of *La Fratellanza*—a direct connection to Simon. It was Hank Kramer. He never revealed the others and she suspected he never would. She agreed with Noble that Kramer would speak more freely without her being present.

9

THE PLAYERS

Noble noted the time. He had twenty minutes to make a few mental notes and prepare for another round with Hank Kramer, a member of La Fratellanza, and the linchpin joining Abner Baari and Simon Hall.

Years earlier, while Hank played the conduit between these two, the other members of La Fratellanza busily worked in the background unbeknown to Baari. They prepared his lesson plans that Hank later imparted, and organized in advance to prepare for his election campaigns. At the behest of Hank, Baari later hired the same La Fratellanza members to organize his campaign for the Illinois State Senate. Ultimately, Baari appointed them to his administration in the White House, again based on Hank's recommendations.

Other than the members themselves, Noble was the only one aware of their involvement. During the course of the Baari Administration, each member under investigation had resigned from his post at Noble's bidding. On the other hand, Hank stubbornly hung in until the day Noble's investigation forced Baari himself to resign.

Noble still found it inconceivable that a group of Harvard scholars could devise a plot to place their "Chosen One" in the office of the president of the United States. In their defense, he believed this group of intellectuals had never conceived at the time that their actions would trigger events leading to a banking crisis and open the door for a terrorist to infiltrate the U.S. Treasury and steal its funds. Clearly, they did not have the vaguest notion that Simon, their fraternal brother and self-appointed leader of the group, was Mohammed al-Fadl.

Unlike his most recent confrontation with Hank, Noble decided to try the "attract more with honey" routine to elicit his support. He suspected Hank had pertinent information, but was still holding some cards close to his vest. Moreover, Hank had convinced himself that the game had ended. However, Noble believed the game was in the late innings but had not finished. He thought if Hank, in a constant state of apprehension, were to learn that the ball was still in play, he would surely want to distance himself from Simon. Noble contemplated his approach as he scribbled a few points on his note pad and readied himself for what he anticipated to be a long and confrontational meeting. He glanced at his watch in reaction to the intercom buzzer.

Hank was prompt.

"Send him in, Doris."

Noble stood up and walked over to greet Hank. His gesture was as friendly as he could muster. "I appreciate your coming in," he said as he extended his hand with a faux, but convincing smile.

Hank, a tad grumpy, was not buying it. "Like I had a choice."

"Let's sit over there, it will be more comfortable." Noble walked toward the overstuffed chairs on the other side of the room.

Hank followed.

Noble did not trust Hank, and he always had difficulty keeping Hank's trademark bluster on point. But he needed Hank and he would tolerate his pontification, painful as it might be.

"I apologize for the grilling last time, but I was in the midst of a crucial case and believed you had information that would be helpful, and it was. Now I have a series of other questions and I trust you will be as forthcoming." Noble sensed Hank might be softening his demeanor, so he began his restrained inquiry. "Have you had the occasion to speak with Senator Townsend recently?"

Hank attempted to hide his nervousness as he recollected his last encounter with the former first lady, punctuated by thoughts of Simon. The whole affair had exhausted him. Nevertheless, he tuned into Noble's technique of asking questions, knowing in advance he had a hint of the answer. Hank yielded. "Yes, she asked to meet with me a couple of months ago."

"For what purpose?"

Hank shifted slightly in his chair, and then looking squarely at Noble, answered, "She had a message from Simon."

"The senator and Simon?" Noble feigned surprise.

"It wasn't until our meeting that I had my confirmation. I always suspected they had met before."

"Under what circumstances?"

"Simon suggested that Baari needed a wife before running for his U.S. senatorial seat. In fact, he already had selected whom he considered the perfect candidate. I doubted his convenient selection for the future first lady." Hank explained that based on the suspicion he harbored, he felt it prudent to vet Maryann. In the course of his inquiry, he discovered she had attended Radcliff at the same time the members of La Fratellanza attended Harvard, including Simon.

"Over time, I never made the connection until she passed along Simon's message, which startled me. Then I remembered Simon's bedroom was always off limits, even though he gave us free reign of the rest of his apartment. All of us suspected that it had its uses, though we were not privy to the details. We would snicker over the possibility that it accommodated a parade of women. Bear in mind that oftentimes, when you joined us for drinks or dinner, Simon would create an excuse and slip away. He did it quite often, which naturally played into our guessing game."

"At last we understand why." Noble smiled, trying to ease the tension. "What was Simon's message?"

Hank shifted in his seat again and answered sheepishly, "He wanted me to leave my pager on. He complained and then reminded me that I was to be available at all times."

Hank had revealed to Noble in a previous conversation that Simon had configured his pager to receive alphanumeric messages, but limited his responses to a *yes* or *no*.

Noble remembered the conversation well. Simon left specific instructions for Hank to deliver a message directly to Noble. His exact words were "back off or the world will be sorry." *It still gives me pause, imagining what Simon had in store*, he pondered.

Hank caught a glimpse of Noble's reaction. "The last time you summoned me to the White House, the security guards confiscated my electronics. They returned my smartphone and pager when I departed. It was at that moment that I decided I wanted no more contact with Simon. There were imposing inherent risks, but I didn't care."

Hank took an irate tone unexpectedly. "Then I get the message from Maryann forcing me back in the game! I was hoping to stay on the sidelines. Having no choice, I passed along Simon's message to you, knowing you'd dangle the immunity agreement! But oh no, you kept me in the game, forcing me to stay in contact with Simon! I remember your threat if I defied your orders, 'you'll put me away for a very long time. I'd go down alone.'" He stopped abruptly. It appeared his blustering had run its course. Hank clasped his hands, stared at the carpet and retreated into silence.

Noble gave him a momentary time-out session.

Then Noble proceeded with added calm, and questioned, "After each of you signed the immunity agreement, I advised you to extricate yourselves from Baari's Administration. The others responded, but why did you stay to the end? You knew it was only a matter of time before the walls would come tumbling down."

"I couldn't leave. The Chestnut Foundation was my baby that I built from the grassroots and we were being attacked from all angles. The right flank was coming at us constantly no matter what we did. The left flank wanted more from me. With all sincerity, I only wanted to give a voice to a segment of the population that was downtrodden. Alinsky had it right. Community organizing gives the power to the people. I admit we pushed it to the edge at times, but it was for the greater good of our constituency." He paused. "I hung in because I needed the protection that the office of the president offered."

Noble did not buy his bleeding heart argument. He remembered the numerous accounts of voter fraud and voter intimidation pointing to the Chestnut Foundation. He suspected in part that Simon pressured Hank to stay close to Baari.

"The day you forced Baari to resign was the worst day of my life," Hank lamented.

"Looks like you got the short end of the wishbone."

Hank looked back at Noble with a dubious stare. "Simon is still on the loose and you need my help. What do I get in return?"

"Once Simon is in custody, I will modify the immunity agreement. It will give you more latitude and restrict the means by which you can be prosecuted."

Hank shook his head with skepticism, though he felt an odd sense of partial relief, until reality set in. It was clear his life was in even greater peril, as long as Simon continued to roam free. He sank back into the chair.

Noble almost felt sympathy for him. "Deal?"

"Deal."

"What else did the senator divulge about Simon?"

"Nothing, other than she had no idea what was going on and didn't want to know. She said she was simply doing a favor for a friend."

So the prison was not the first time she made the connection. She lied again. Noble thought, and then posed, "a friend, who she knew was a terrorist!"

"She said she only made the connection, when al-Fadl stole the money from the Treasury, and then both he and Simon disappeared at the same time."

"Did she know about Baari's true identity?"

"Not until you went to the press," Hank noted irritably. "Then she figured out later that I was in the thick of the plot. Needless to say, she was furious."

"Has she spoken to Baari since he disappeared?"

"I asked her the same question. She swears all she knows is what's been flowing in the rumor mill and bits and pieces from her own sources."

Within a month of Noble making the announcement to the press, exposing the true identity of President Abner Baari, stories started to swirl around the Beltway like a cyclone. Various sources reported that he had fled to Libya to work on their National Transitional Council. After the ousting of Qaddafi, the council had failed miserably in their attempts to restore some form of government. In fact, several dictatorial leaders who stepped in following Qaddafi met the same fate. Baari's arrival was convenient timing and coincided with the council's desire to institute a quasi-democratic regime.

"Last she heard was that Baari had reverted to his birth name, Hussein Tarishi, and had been appointed president of the Senate in the Libyan parliament," Hank informed.

"And there has been no other contact?"

"Not to my knowledge. Why all the questions about Maryann?"

"I'm trying to understand all the players. What legislation did Baari try to push through during his first term?"

"You mean other than trying to change the constitution allowing for a third term," Hank quipped.

Noble smiled. He remembered a representative from New York had submitted a bill to the House of Representatives to repeal the twenty-second Amendment that imposed a two-term limit on the office of the president.

"No, something more in line with Baari's ambitious, but futile effort to resolve our energy dependency on foreign and fossil fuels."

Hank cocked his head.

Noble gave him a moment to contemplate.

"In June, the year our *dear* former president first took office, he established a task force to develop a national policy to ensure the protection of our natural resources and enhance their sustainability. Three months later in September, the task force submitted the *Interim Report of the Interagency Ocean Policy Task Force.*"

"What's the significance?"

"It was the impetus for a bill he submitted to the House the following year, H-R 3-5-3-4, referred to as the Clear Act," Hank responded.

"However, there was more than meets the eye," Noble alleged and then followed up. "When it narrowly passed, the president signed Executive Order 1-3-5-4-7, bypassing the senate and surreptitiously opening up the mandate to sign the Law of the Sea Treaty with the

United Nations."

Hank was aghast.

"I've been reading up on the subject," Noble smiled. "What else?"

"So you're aware that the Clear Act paved the way to set aside more land for government ownership for the purpose of preservation. It also halted all forms of drilling for energy supply in an effort to force support for renewable energy."

"Tell me about Tres Amigas."

Taken aback for the second time, Hank paused. Then he slowly began to answer, "The Superstation…" and then stopped.

"What is it you want to say?"

"It's more of a question," he stammered. "What do you think Simon was planning?"

Noble remained silent as he second-guessed his chosen methodology. But there was no other way. He had to confide in Hank.

"What I am about to tell you—will never leave this room. The stakes are too high for both of us," Noble confided.

The expression on Hank's face was one of disbelief. He could not believe he was about to be brought into the inner sanctum and accorded trust. *Noble needs me,* he mused with an inner swagger, momentarily forgetting his fears.

Noble remained steadfast in his pursuit. "Remember the deal. The immunity agreement stays intact until Simon is in custody. I already have evidence that you've violated the agreement and not only in spirit. At any time, I can hand you a *go straight to jail* card. Do you understand?"

"Yes, Noble," Hank responded with unaccustomed politeness.

Noble was pleased, although surprised. *Hank's on board,* he thought, and then pressed forward. "We believe Simon is planning some disaster on a national scale. We believe it has something to do with our energy transmission. Is there anything you can tell me that will help us figure out what he's planning?"

Hank's face paled. "Oh hell, I never thought it would go this far." He was obviously agitated.

Noble reeled him back in. "Explain."

"It's no secret that Baari ran on the ticket that handed open largesse to the environmentalists' lengthy menu of demands. It was one of his leading campaign promises. It was all Simon's idea. He thought it had the most bang for the buck." Hank talked about how Baari was an enthusiastic and dedicated exponent of Saul Alinsky's playbook and how he appealed to the masses in his campaign rhetoric. "It was simply community organizing on the national scale and over the next several years, Baari seized every opportunity to recite Alinsky's quotations to the masses. He'd often repeat a well-known Alinskyism. 'It is necessary to begin where the world is if we are going to change it to what we think it should be.' Working at Baari's side, I concluded he was using the word *world* in another sense." Hank feared Baari was no longer content organizing a national community and that he had set his sights on going global, concerns he shared with Noble. "And along the way, he got on this sustainability kick using the environment as his springboard. The redistribution of wealth is the very crux of the plot."

It's the same mantra Simon's recruits chanted, Noble recalled. A point Hank did not need to know. "I'm not making the connection," he pressed.

"Global warming was great for campaign-speak, but even Alinsky said, 'I could never accept any rigid dogma or ideology, whether it's Christianity or Marxism.' But Baari started to believe he was sempiternal. His messiah complex enveloped him. He was no longer satisfied with just transforming America, as he promised during his campaign. Then in 2013, when the Arab Spring turned into protests for all seasons, Baari started to dip his toes in the water, giving the appearance he was about to dive in and solve the problem. Moreover, while his verbal response was supportive, his actions were lukewarm. Eventually, world leaders began to realize he never intended to get wet above the knees. You saw how he handed the Syrian conflict back to the U.N."

"Maybe the former governor from Alaska was correct when she said, "Let Allah sort it out!"

Hank ignored the barb. "Remember whenever the scandals heated up, Baari headed out of Washington. Many said he was leading from behind."

"I recall once he traveled to South Africa and spoke to a group of students in Johannesburg. Didn't he say something about how the planet will boil over?"

Hank forgot his angst for the moment and smirked; he remembered it well. "Yes, he said that if people in Africa are allowed to attain air conditioning, automobiles, and big houses, the planet would boil over unless we find new ways of producing energy."

"While he cast aspersions on America's way of life, he neglected to mention that he was about to pour three hundred and twenty million dollars into Detroit, one of his own cities, to save it from bankruptcy."

Hank agreed, but would not admit it other than to acknowledge, "He would refrain from discussing any U.S. problem that could be directly related to his administration or its policies."

"Apparently, the weight he placed on environmental and climate issues was out of balance with our nation's problems, including the economy and foreign affairs agenda," Noble espoused.

"Something like that." Hank hesitated and then his ire returned, but it was not directed toward Noble. "He was sacrificing jobs, and more important he was sacrificing his job! During a second term, you would expect him to become a lame duck. But that duck, as I said before, had a messiah complex he couldn't shake."

"Why do you believe his behavior was meant to be destructive?"

"I have no evidence, but I believe Baari's shift to more radical policies, and jumping on the environmental bandwagon during his first term, came at the behest of the Godfather. Once he appeared on the scene, Baari acted as though he was about to ride a wave—one of tsunami proportions."

"Wait a minute, the Godfather! What, Baari was following a new guru?"

"You've got it. A few months before the first election during the financial crisis, the polls were soaring in Baari's direction. The unbelievable was in our grasp. We understood it, and so did two wealthy backers who entered the picture wanting to attach their purse strings and personal agendas to his coattails. Simon, of course, was thrilled that *Uncle Rob* no longer had to fund future campaigns." Hank jeered.

Noble was acquainted with Uncle Rob, the name of the slush fund used to finance La Fratellanza's plot to elect Baari. Simon's hacking talents had accumulated those funds, syphoning small amounts of dollars from various banks over a multitude of years.

"Who were the backers?" Noble was not sure he was steering the conversation in the right direction, but he let Hank's story unfold.

"I don't know for certain. Baari started to play the *anonymous backer* game. In fact, when Simon disappeared, I think the backers moved in and took over as his handlers. He referred to one of the billionaires as the Godfather, and the other as the Financier. After they signed on board, hoards of 501(c) (4) groups starting cropping up, organized to promote the *progressive movement* and aimed at attacking the opponents. The IRS paved the way with favorable tax treatment. Then his foreign policies in the Middle East appeared to work against U.S. interests and its support for Israel waned." Hank appeared even more annoyed.

Noble did not want to lose him at that stage. "Take it slow! But is this going to get me any closer to Simon? I need to find out what he has planned."

Hank inhaled. "It will!" He took another moment before continuing, and then explained, "During Baari's second term he was haunted with scandal after scandal. There were so many leaks during those first few years there weren't enough Dutch boys in all of Holland to plug the holes." He smiled briefly at his own metaphor.

Noble remained stoic.

"There were times I thought some of the scandals were leaked as intentional diversions. Then during the hullabaloo, Baari called me into his office. He demanded to know the identity of his original, anonymous supporters. He said, 'the ones who provided me with the keys to the kingdom.' It was strange. In the early stages he had stopped asking, finding it unimportant as long as his purposes were served. Then all of a sudden out of nowhere, he became more inquisitive."

"How did you handle it?" Noble was a little on edge, afraid of what Hank might have unleashed.

"I promise you, I didn't mention La Fratellanza. I told him Simon was the sole benefactor. That he was the mastermind behind the plot. That was all Baari needed to hear. He insisted he meet with Simon in private—without me."

"That had to hurt."

"Of course it did! I'm the one who traveled to Florence to find Simon's *Chosen One*. I befriended him. I brought him to Chicago. I spent countless hours teaching, grooming, and preparing him for political office. He wouldn't have been sitting in the Oval Office if it weren't for me. How dare he!"

Noble ignored his outburst. "Did they meet?"

"Yes! And neither one will tell me what they discussed." Hank's eyes lit up as he conjectured, "You think Simon and Baari are working together?"

Noble looked disapprovingly at Hank, but thought it best not to waste time castigating him. Not alerting him to the meeting between Simon and Baari was a clear violation of Hank's immunity agreement. He put the question back to Hank. "Do you think they're working together?"

"I was just the facilitator. To my knowledge, they never met again. But after their meeting Baari became distant and unreceptive to my ideas."

"Let's get back to the Superstation."

Hank shifted into a more defensive stance. "Baari's in Libya. There's no point."

"No point in what?"

"One day I was meeting Baari in the Oval Office. It was when all of the scandals were spiraling out of control and his poll numbers dropped precipitously. Baari was in a highly agitated state. In the midst of a sentence, he blurted out, 'what we need is a national disaster to calm things down.' I assumed he was venting his frustration, but we insiders know he was the master of diversion."

"You think Baari wanted to destroy the Superstation?"

"No. Baari was in full support of the project. It is exactly what he needed to push his renewable energy agenda. Nevertheless, there were delays in FERC approvals, lining up industrial revenue bonds, and agreements with transmission lines. There appeared to be one battle after another."

"Perhaps, he thought some sort a blackout would force the need for the Superstation to go operational?"

"But it's a moot point. Baari is no longer in the picture."

Noble's mind churned, thinking back to the time when he and Hamilton interrogated La Fratellanza. Each member revealed a major critical task he had performed for Simon, unbeknown to the other members. *Baari had been playing the same game*, he surmised.

"Noble, what are you thinking?"

"You may have only one part of the picture. I'm going to bring your fellow brethren in for a chat."

"What!" Hank spouted in a raised voice.

Noble held up his hand to silence him. "As far as anyone is concerned this meeting did not take place. You and I have not spoken. I'll inform your La Fratellanza brothers that I'm working on a case that may stem from actions that took place during the Baari Administration. If you truly want Simon out of your life—you'll play it my way."

Surprisingly, Hank remained silent and attentive, and then he muttered, "Whatever you say."

"I'll be back to you in a day or two. Be prepared to return to Washington, and keep your pager on."

"Like I have a choice."

10
STRONG SUSTAINABILITY

Max arrived in Noble's reception area just after Hank Kramer had departed.

"Go on in, Max," Doris said, giving her the all clear.

Unlike her usual intrusions, Max felt that given the circumstances, it was prudent to knock. There was no way to anticipate Noble's frame of mind after meeting with a member of La Fratellanza. Admittedly, Hank was the only member's identity to which she was privy. Nevertheless, she found the entire affair deliciously clandestine and hoped one day Noble would entrust her with the names of the other members. She did not pry; she understood his reasons.

"Have a seat, I'll be right back." Noble brushed by her as he headed out of his office to speak with Doris.

Max sat back and waited, trying unsuccessfully not to eavesdrop. Noble did not attempt to lower his voice. *It is not as though he were passing along some grave secret*, she told herself. Then she saw him make a turnabout and return to his office.

"You're bringing in members of the Baari Administration? You think they may know something?"

"Does your snooping ever go dormant?"

"Sorry, but you really think spending time with Baari's cohorts will lead us to Simon? Didn't you tell me that Baari didn't even know Simon?"

"Yes—but he did."

Max looked askance.

"So what happened with Kramer?"

Noble proceeded to fill in Max on the salient points of his conversation with Hank.

"The Godfather and the Financier! This is starting to sound like a *Three Stooges* movie. So you think Baari's campaign finance director, communications director, and documentarian have information connected to Simon's plot?" Max asked with skepticism.

Noble nodded affirmatively. "Possibly inadvertent. I'll also be calling Kramer back."

"Kramer, a member of La Fratellanza?"

"Yes. And your understanding is that he was solely Baari's Chief of Staff," he cautioned.

Max ceased her inquisitiveness and veered off topic. "By the way, I received confirmation from Senator Townsend's office. She's in her pet city Chicago for a series of events, but she's agreed to be here on March sixth at one o'clock."

"Great. Now tell me what you found out about Agenda 21?"

Max grit her teeth as she faked biting her thumbnail. She eyed him pensively.

Noble noted the apprehensive expression; it was not a good sign.

"Follow me, boss."

They both headed for their stomping grounds with the technical paraphernalia.

Noble sat in his usual place and announced, "You have the floor."

Max remained standing at the table and began as though she were conducting a class. "Agenda 21 is a three hundred and fifty-one page document that was introduced at the United Nations Conference on Environment and Development in Rio de Janerio, Brazil in 1992." She explained that leaders from more than one hundred and seventy-eight countries signed the document adopting its tenets. President George H. W. Bush signed for the U.S. Then she paused for an instant while she fumbled with her notes. "Here it is—the opening preamble to Agenda 21."

> *Humanity stands at a defining moment in history. We are confronted with a perpetuation of disparities between and within nations, a worsening of poverty, hunger, ill health and illiteracy, and the continuing deterioration of the ecosystems on which we depend for our well-being. However, integration of environment and development concerns and greater attention to them will lead to the fulfillment of basic needs, improved living standards for all, better protected and managed ecosystems and a safer, more prosperous future.*

She paused to make sure Noble was following.

"Keep going. So far it seems altruistic."

"Listen to this. It ends with 'No nation can achieve this on its own; but together we can—in a global partnership for sustainable development.' The rest of the document is complex and comprehensive—and its history is quite fascinating."

"Sustainable development—isn't that part of the global warming debate?"

"In part, but it also dictates land management."

Noble's ears perked up. "Go on."

"It further states in chapter ten, point five…"

> *The broad objective is to facilitate allocation of land to the uses that provide the greatest sustainable benefits and to promote the transition to a sustainable and integrated management of land resources.*

"They really like using the word sustainable." Noble grinned, and then a look of curiosity illuminated his face.

Max took note. "For some that word implies totalitarian control, eventually leading to depopulation, as a means to preserve the sustainability of the world's resources."

Noble's grin dissipated as his curiosity turned to unsettling clarity.

Wasting no time, Max turned and touched the large touch-screen monitor; instantly an organization chart displayed. This one, however, did not resemble any of the charts from the U.S. government. "We need to go back a bit in history to understand its genesis." Using a laser pen, she pointed to the upper left-hand box. Inside the box was the name Gro Harlem Brundtland. She continued, "In 1987, Brundtland, the first woman Prime Minister of Norway, chaired a commission for the United Nations, referred to as the World Commission on Environment and Development, or W-C-E-D. The findings from the commission were detailed in a published report entitled, *Our Common Future*. Brundtland's report opened by stating, 'A global agenda for change.' The report went on to state…"

> *The challenge of finding sustainable development paths ought to provide the impetus—indeed the imperative—for a renewed search for multilateral solutions and a restructured international economic system of co-operation. These challenges cut across the divides of national sovereignty, of limited strategies for economic gain, and of separated disciplines of science.*

"So, sustainable development—is the core of Agenda 21!" Noble declared.

"Exactly! Brundtland then returned to the U.N. in 1998 as the Director-General of the World Health Organization, reporting to Secretary-General Kofi Annan. In 2007, the then-Secretary-General Ban Ki-moon appointed her special envoy on *Climate Change*. It was reported that Ban personally saw climate change as a global challenge and it was number one on his list."

Max pointed to the box on the right and then explained, "The architect of the document *United Nations Sustainable Development Agenda 21* is a Canadian who made his billions in oil. He is commonly referred to as the '*Godfather* of the Environmental Movement,'" Max stated with a raised eyebrow.

"That's an illustrious title given to many. Move on Max," Noble cautioned.

Max capitulated for a moment. "He was also a commissioner for W-C-E-D and in 1992, he was appointed Secretary-General of the *UN Conference on Environment and Development,* best known as the Earth Summit.

Noble interjected, "Ah yes, I vaguely remember the Summit."

"Here's one statement that the Godfather made at the Summit." Max read again from her notes:

> *It is clear that current lifestyles and consumption patterns of the affluent middle class, involving high meat intake, consumption of large amounts of frozen and convenience foods, use of fossil fuels, appliances, home and work place air conditioning, and suburban housing are not sustainable.*

Max caught an odd expression on Noble's face. "What's the matter?" she asked.

"That statement from 1992 is incredibly similar to the statement the president made in South Africa in 2013. Hank reminded me of the president's 'earth boiling over' speech this morning during our meeting." He lightened up a tad and chuckled slightly at the seeming coincidence, and then refocused on the monitor. "What's the connection between the rest of your featured players?"

Max moved the pointer to the next box with the name Mikhail Gorbachev. "In 1993 Gorbachev, then a private citizen following the fall of the Soviet Union established Green Cross International, a non-profit, to focus on sustainability as a follow up on his work at the Earth Summit. He and the Godfather are close friends."

"So their common ground is sustainability?'

"Yes, and another friend of both men was also instrumental in helping to shape the agenda for the Summit. His name is Albert Gore Junior, the former Vice President and *self-accredited earth scientist.* Gore's relationship with the Godfather goes farther back to when he was a senator. According to the Godfather, Gore was instrumental in the political process for the U.S. to endorse the Summit."

"Why Gore? Bush was the president at the time."

"Evidently, Bush was reluctant up until the eleventh hour. It was the then-Senator Gore who convinced him to attend."

"Interesting circle of friends," Noble noted.

Max smiled as she highlighted the pointer onto the next box that contained the name William Jefferson Clinton. "The year following the Earth Summit, President Clinton issued Executive Order 1-2-8-5-2, establishing the *President's Council on Sustainable Development*, bypassing Congress."

"Why did he have to bypass Congress? Bush Senior participated in the signing ceremony at the Summit."

"Agenda 21 is not a treaty as such, and therefore is non-binding. However, Clinton's Executive Order mirrors Agenda 21." Max noticed Noble demonstrating impatience. "Take a deep breath. This will all start to make sense." She refocused on her notes. "Clinton's National Security Advisor, Richard Clark, ousted an unofficial pact named *Operation Orient Express*. It was organized by some members of the Clinton Administration to convince the members of the U.N. Security Council to block Boutros-Boutros-Ghali's appointment to a second term as Secretary-General of the U.N. The major objective was to engineer the appointment of Kofi Annan, which they did successfully. Annan then created a position at the U.N. for an Under Secretary-General for UN Reform."

Without missing a beat, Noble picked up. "And lo and behold, he appointed the Godfather to the position."

"And, as I mentioned earlier, Annan also brought the *Queen of Sustainability*, Brundtland, back to the U.N. in 1998."

"This all seem rather incestuous."

"It ain't shuffleboard. Wait, it gets more titillating. In 2005, the Godfather left the U.N and headed for China, making Beijing his new home."

"China?"

"Yes, there were allegations that he was involved in the Oil-for-Food Scandal at the U.N that implicated Kofi Annan's son. You recall the U.N. ostensibly permitted Iraq to sell oil to feed its people, despite the ongoing war, and much to the surprise of many thoroughly versed in the issue. Paul Volker's Commission investigated the scandal, but appeared to negate the evidence and exonerated the participants. The commission never leveled charges, but the Godfather's departure to China raised suspicions. Interestingly, he operates his businesses from an office in the Tayuan Diplomatic Residence Compound in Beijing. It is the same compound as three other U.N. agencies: the Industrial Development Organization, the Population Fund, and the High Commission for Refugees."

"So he's still playing footsy with the U.N.?"

"Not in any official capacity. However, in 2012, the Godfather made a rare appearance as a special guest of honor at the Rio 20 + Summit, the twenty-year anniversary of the Earth Summit. The United Nations Development Program in Beijing paid for his round-trip ticket, along with hotel and living expenses, based on the examination of the travel documents. Why is it the billionaires always get the freebies?" Max did not expect a retort and walked back to the table to grab another document.

"This guy's a real man of mystery," Noble observed.

"Well, whatever the scandal, the Godfather pops up in good company unscathed, including U.N. secretary-generals, world leaders, and other luminaries who continue to seek his counsel. His last official post with the U.N. was special envoy to North Korea appointed by Kofi Annan; it ended in 2005."

Max quoted from her paper a tribute from Annan on the Godfather's website that read:

> *If the world succeeds in making a transition to truly*
> *sustainable development, all of us will owe no small debt*
> *of gratitude… whose prescience and dynamic presence on*
> *the International stage have played a key role in convincing*
> *governments and grassroots alike to embrace the principle…*

She placed the document back on the table, shaking her head in disbelief. Noble, with equal frustration on his face and in his voice, asked the inevitable question, "Who is this Godfather?"

"He's been called everything derogatory from the 'Father of

America's Destruction' to 'World Enemy Number One.' CBS reporter Ann-Marie McDonald described him as a cross between Machiavelli and Rasputin. Conversely, he has been a guest of honor at state dinners around the world and the recipient of multiple awards. He even received the prestigious *Four Freedoms Award* from the Roosevelt Institute. Despite all these labels, he prefers the title, 'Citizen of the World.' All viewpoints aside, he's a self-described socialist, capitalist, and a staunch environmentalist."

"An interesting mix of dogmata," Noble postured.

"The Godfather clearly states that his belief in socialism go so far as it provides an economic base to meet the social needs of the people, and capitalism as a means to create and manage wealth to meet the socialist needs."

"It sounds like redistribution of wealth."

"It's textbook socialism," Max averred, and then added, "The other side of the Godfather's coin is an assortment of notable capitalistic business ventures, some failed, and some questionable. In any case, he's managed to sustain his status as a billionaire. You'll love this tidbit. Have you heard of China's Chery Automobile?"

"A trifle, didn't it bomb?"

"It never made it to the U.S., even though it's one of the largest Chinese automobile manufacturers that exports to over thirty countries. A plan was underway by Malcom Bricklin, founder of Subaru of America, and notable for importing the Yugoslavian car the Yugo."

"The Yugo! They were considered the worst cars on the road and he went bankrupt on that venture."

"Well, he tried again, along with partners, to flood the U.S. market in 2007 with as many as two-hundred-fifty-thousand Chery cars made on the cheap, and directed toward the low-end market. He established the company Visionary Vehicles. The Godfather was on the board of directors."

Max paused to ensure she lay out the events in an accurate sequence. "In 2005 and in 2006, Chery automobile had two major recalls due to faulty wiring. Again, in 2006, General Motors filed a lawsuit citing the piracy act against Chery for developing a knock-off of South Korea's Daewoo's Spark, GM's partner in the U.S. market. And, in the midst of it all, the Chinese found a better offer, much to Bricklin and his partners' ire."

Max paused. She was about to send up another flare and shed some light.

Noble caught her expression. "There's more?"

"Fasten your seatbelt. The plan had all the earmarks of a fast buck scheme—the environment took a back seat. In the end, the suit squelched Bricklin's and the Godfather's ambitions, along with their partner who invested two-hundred-million dollars—they call him the Financier." Max smirked.

"The Financier!" Noble exclaimed, almost bowling over in his seat. "You're not suggesting he is Baari's Financier. The same billionaire that pours money into U.S. liberal and social agendas?"

"Boss, it can't be a coincidence."

Noble heaved a few deep breaths and announced, "This is all fascinating, but I don't see a connection between the Godfather, the Superstation, and Simon. My source, a former insider, wouldn't have mentioned Agenda 21, otherwise."

"Boss, the Superstation, on the surface, appears to be a phantom company, although it's very real. Even the Navajo tribe invested one-point-five-billion dollars. Strangely enough, this multibillion-dollar undertaking to create what is billed as America's first renewable energy transmission hub isn't all over the U.S. news. If you were to ask any person on the street, he or she, in all probability, would have no clue as to what it's all about."

"Who's handling their PR, ghost whisperers?" Noble quipped.

"Real or not, this consortium will have their collective hand on the master switch. You would think the public would at least take an interest in who controls the transmission of all their energy. The same energy supply needed to recharge their electronic gear and to watch their favorite TV shows."

"In all seriousness, if Simon is planning to take down our U.S. power grids or use the Superstation as its control point, it has to be part and parcel of Agenda 21. We must connect all the dots before we can move in for the kill. Find the connection, Max.

11
NO WAY OUT

Director, it wasn't necessary for you to allude to the possibility of a Senate committee hearing. You just needed to ask politely," Maryann invoked with uncharacteristic graciousness, as she eyed Noble.

"Thank you, Senator, for agreeing to meet in my office. You are acquainted with the tools at my disposal and they will be necessary to present our findings. Senator, I also suggested you be accompanied by counsel."

"I'm here alone on my own accord. May we begin?"

"Certainly, please have a seat." Noble walked toward the head of the conference room table and motioned Maryann to the seat on his right.

Max was still standing to his left with her back to the large screen monitor.

Considering the cogent evidence, Noble decided to forgo the usual string of questions and instead reconstructed the crime for the senator's edification.

Max queued up the surveillance tape.

"Senator, please focus on the video," Noble requested.

The scene showed Maryann disembarking the plane at the South Valley Regional Airport in Jordan, Utah.

Max hit the *Fast-forward* button and then hit play.

Maryann continued to watch coldly as she viewed the decoy leave the Ladies' Room. Then she saw herself on the screen leaving the building and hailing a taxi.

Max paused the video.

"Senator, we know the taxi stopped at a Mail Boxes Etc. and that you returned to the taxi minutes later with a large envelope. The taxi driver then drove you to a used car lot, where preparations had been made for you to pick up a Ford Escape anonymously." Noble methodically laid out her moves.

Maryann remained steadfast as she focused on the screen.

Max advanced the video to the scene in the interrogation room at the Draper Prison.

"You signed the prison visitor's log at nine o'clock p.m." Noble confirmed.

Max paused the video once again.

"Pay particular attention to the expression on the prisoner's face when you sit upright, having just placed your handbag on the floor."

Max hit the *Play* button.

As Maryann watched the video she flinched in unison with Simon— an obvious silent signal.

Max hit the *Pause* button.

"What are you implying?" Maryann asked, directing her question to Noble.

"It is our opinion that you passed an xPhad to Simon—one he used to program his escape. We know for a fact that you left the Ford Escape outside the prison grounds and Simon used it as his getaway car."

"Pure supposition! You have no proof," she stated belligerently.

"On the contrary, a prison guard testified that he called a taxi for you when you were ready to leave. He had no memory of your arrival in a taxi as you previously claimed. In addition, we found the Ford Escape abandoned in a bordering state rather carelessly disposed of, since the attempt to burn the vehicle failed. We were, however, able to lift fingerprints. The prints are yours." This time Noble evidently rattled the senator.

Maryann appeared somewhat off balance.

Max hit the *Play* button without delay.

Noble maintained the pressure.

Maryann reluctantly watched herself on the screen as she exited the stairwell to enter her hotel suite. Seconds later, she saw herself open the door to receive the ice bucket from her secret service agent. "So what do we do now?" she asked in an imperious tone.

"I ask the questions and you answer honestly. First, I advise you again to ask your attorney to be present. We can postpone the questioning for now."

"I'd prefer to deal with this situation on my own without others involved. But I demand some form of immunity."

"We'll talk immunity after you answer some pertinent questions," Noble insisted.

Up to that point, Maryann had remained stoic, but unexpectedly her demeanor shifted to a supplicant one. "He threatened to kidnap my daughter and take her to Libya. He said I would never see her again. I had no choice!"

"Simon threatened you?"

"No, it was Abner."

"Baari was helping Simon escape?" Noble pressed.

Suddenly, tears began to well up in her eyes.

Max stood by and watched the byplay; Maryann was unconvincing.

Noble tried to be avuncular. "Would you like a moment alone?"

"Yes."

Noble moved the pitcher of water and a glass from the sideboard and placed them on the table in front of Maryann. Then he and Max left the conference room.

"Do you really buy the crocodile tears?" Max tested.

"They look genuine."

"I'm not so sure, Noble. Call it a woman's intuition. She's getting her revenge on Baari for betraying her."

"It had to have hurt. Don't be such a hard ass, Max."

"Suppose she's setting up Baari as a deflection, while helping Simon. As far as we know, Baari's sitting pretty in Libya, pulling strings in all directions. It would make no sense that he would run the risk and come back to help Simon. It doesn't compute."

Max had made valid points. But to be certain, Noble requested, "Delve into the possibility of Baari's undercover return with the Immigration Agency. Also try to trace any phone calls that may have transpired between Maryann and Baari, or with Simon."

She furrowed her brow, but for a different reason. "Are you really going to give her immunity? She lied before. How do you know she is not lying now?"

"Yes, to your first question, under certain conditions. I've discussed it thoroughly with our in-house counsel and given the prevailing circumstances, I have the authority. To answer your second question, she might be lying but I'm also convinced she could be useful in the capture of Simon."

Noble had pondered the issue for several days. As a first lady, he felt Maryann was recognized as weak, and while he did not subscribe to her political ideology, as a senator she was considered responsible. He took into account his part in the downfall of Baari, recalling it also caused the end of her marriage. In its wake, a nine-year-old daughter may have been used as a bargaining chip. Noble could not bring himself to destroy the child's mother as well. In the final analysis, Maryann was still viable in the chase for Simon.

Noble turned and headed back to the conference room. Max followed.

He knocked on the door before they entered the room and they then returned to their respective chairs.

"Can we now talk about an immunity agreement?" Maryann appeared to have returned to her typical regal manner.

"May I ask you once again, would you prefer to have your attorney join you?" Noble asked earnestly.

"As a lawyer, I'm perfectly capable of negotiating my own agreement. I do not need to be surrounded by the usual minions. Proceed." Maryann's back stiffened in her chair, along with her unyielding verbal posture.

Noble obliged. "We still have a few unanswered questions. I've asked Deputy Director Ford to proceed, since she has firsthand knowledge of the matters at hand."

Maryann nodded acceptance toward Max.

"Thank you, Senator." After the earlier crying jag, Max decided to change her role and play the good cop. "Is Baari in the U.S.?"

"I received a call from him. From where he was calling, I have no idea. It was during that conversation when he gave me the instructions on where to pick up the envelope—after I conceded to his abduction threat. He assured me everything had been prearranged for my protection in the event Simon was captured."

Max still doubted her story, but moved on. "We're almost there. Just a few more questions Senator. Why go through the effort of purchasing a used car and not simply rent a car?"

Looking at neither Noble or Max, Maryann continued to stare at herself on the large monitor. "All rental cars have built-in G-P-S systems. I am sure you are aware of that fact. It would be like painting a bull's-eye on my back."

"Did Simon purchase the car or did someone else?"

"I really don't know. The registration, keys, and an address for the used car lot were in the envelope. I was only instructed to pick up the car."

"Why were your fingerprints found on the glove compartment and on the underside of the latch inside the trunk?"

Maryann's increased discomfort was evident.

Noble and Max could not decipher whether she was angry with herself or with Simon. One of them had been sloppy when it was time to scrub the car.

"I opened the glove compartment to place the registration and keys inside." She inhaled, giving her a moment of pause. "I was stunned to see there was a gun. I was petrified to touch it. I left it alone." She redirected her eye contact to Max. "Then I became curious as to what else Simon had arranged to be planted in the car. So I opened the trunk."

"Did you find anything?"

"A duffle bag."

Maryann listed the individual items.

Max jotted them down on a pad of paper: clothes, toiletry kit including shaving equipment, contact lens case with a bottle of solution, toothbrush, and toothpaste.

"And," Maryann hesitated. "There were also two passports, one for the U.S., and one for..." She wavered again, "...the other one read, United Nations Laissez-Passer. There was also twenty thousand dollars in the bag."

Noble was pleased Max held back her reaction to Simon possessing a new U.N. diplomatic passport with enhanced security features and moved on. "Did you count the money?"

"There were twenty stacks of one hundred dollar bills. Even a SIA agent can figure it out," she answered curtly.

"Do you remember the names on the passports?"

Maryann remembered one of the names, the one on the passport for the U.N. Max jotted it down; it was not a familiar alias.

As Max was about to ask the next question, Maryann interrupted, and added, "The passports had names but no photos." From the look on her face she thought it was strange, but both Noble and Max understood the reason why and moved on.

"Did you notice any driver's licenses?"

"Not that I recall."

"Did you give him the xPhad?"

"Yes."

"And you left the car outside the prison gates?"

"Yes."

"Do you still have the burn phone that you received from Simon?"

"Yes."

Naturally, the senator knows about throwaway phones, the prepaid cell phones used for illegal activities, Noble thought.

While Max continued to question Maryann, Noble half-listened as he contemplated the specific terms of the immunity agreement. It was to be a balancing act. They had to be severe, but acceptable to the attorney general. The president wanted the entire affair to be handled discreetly, with as little fanfare as possible. Moreover, Noble still needed her cooperation. He interrupted, "Max, do you have any other questions for the senator?"

"We have the videos and the senator's testimony supporting the evidence. No more for now," she replied. Maryann had been forthcoming and Max was confident she had garnered all the needed information from the senator.

Noble was ready to take it to the next step and Max was not thrilled—but it was his call. He shifted the tone of the conversation. "Senator, you will be given full immunity for your actions in aiding and abetting the escape of Mohammed al-Fadl, along with related charges. While they are unconscionable and reprehensible, the national security of the country holds greater sway. The terms of the agreement include resigning from Congress within ninety-days from the signing of the agreement. We will script your resignation to dilute the effect. You are not to seek public office in the U.S., whether it is local, state, or federal. You are to contact me immediately should either Simon or Baari try to reach you. Any breach in the agreement, I will revoke your immunity and you will be prosecuted to the full extent of the law. Do you understand?"

Maryann glowered at both Noble and Max. Obviously, she was contemplating her options with disdain. "I will need time to consider your terms."

"Out of respect for your position, you'll have until the end of the month, Senator. I expect an answer by the close of business on the thirty-first."

Maryann stood up. "Am I free to go?"

"I'll await your call."

Maryann headed to the door unescorted.

❧

"That went well," Max groused.

"She'll take the deal. She knows we have enough to destroy her reputation. I also think she's afraid of Simon or Baari or both of them."

"Well I still think Simon prearranged everything. He most likely deciphered that you would send him to Draper, being the nearest maximum security prison."

"You may be correct, but we can't ignore the possibility that Baari is in the midst of this puzzle in some way."

"Noble, do you remember when you used the Locator App to track the text message Simon sent? He sent it from Salt Lake City, probably while he was arranging for his prospective escape. When you interrogated him at Draper, he admitted luring you back after the death of Agent Darrow. Simon doesn't make a move without a backup plan. What we don't know is his plan."

"However, what we do know is that Simon is desperate. He has lost his recruits and his financing, and he is on the run. Hank and Maryann are panicky. Something has to break soon."

"Wait, aside from discovering Simon possessed a diplomatic passport, there's something we didn't touch on. Remember Maryann said she didn't see any driver's licenses in the duffle bag. They could have been hidden among the clothes, but anyone renting or buying a car is required to have one. You think that's why he left the passport photos blank?"

"A standard 1-0-1 CIA tactic."

Max understood. Simon would change his appearance and then seek out a readily available counterfeiter to produce both a fake driver's license and add the photos to the already forged passports.

"And the fraudster will never be aware of Simon's true identity, nor would he care."

Max followed through. "I'll call Burke and have him head to Folsom. He can get a list of the usual suspects from FBI files and then weed them out. Someone has been helping Simon."

"Also, extend the APB to all used car lots in the vicinity."

"Why didn't he just steal a car?"

"It would be reported. And as odd as it may sound, I don't believe Simon would commit a crime unless it was vital to his plan. No detail usually escapes him. For him everything has to have a purpose."

"What, he has a code of ethics?"

"Sort of." Noble smiled and headed back to his office.

12

ALL THE FORMER PRESIDENT'S MEN

Chase Worthington, the first to arrive, was the campaign finance director for both presidential campaigns, but he never accepted a post with the Baari Administration. After each campaign, he returned enthusiastically to his chief executive officer's position at the National Depositors Trust Bank in New York. He still suffered pangs of guilt for his role in causing the 2008 financial meltdown. He sat back and watched as the rest of his fraternity brothers strolled into the reception area and took their seats, foregoing their usual warm hugs. Their relationships were not fractious, but given the circumstances, they thought it prudent to remain at arm's length. Chase waited with nerves on edge—for a meeting he was sure to dread.

A few minutes after Chase arrived, Seymour Lynx and Paolo Salvatore entered.

Seymour was the campaign communications director and subsequently the president's documentarian who had enjoyed his stint in the administration, until it all collapsed. Soon thereafter, he returned to Los Angeles and dabbled in political documentaries. Then finally, he was welcomed back into the Hollywood inner circle when the Academy nominated his film *The Framework* for best picture.

Paolo was the campaign speechwriter and later the communications director and speechwriter for the president. Coincidently, he was the same Paolo who introduced Amanda to Noble, his brother-in-law. After the president's forced resignation, Paolo worked strenuously to repair the damage to his marriage because of the fallout resulting from his complicities. In the end, with a happy family in tow, he established his own consultancy and began to work as a freelance speechwriter in the private sector, catering to the Washington elite.

The last to arrive was Hank Kramer.

All members of La Fratellanza had been accounted for—except for Simon Hall. Each eyed the other in silence, recalling when they sat in a different reception area at the CIA headquarters in Langley, Virginia— waiting to enter the interrogation room.

All seemed to be lost in thought when Noble startled them upon opening the door to his office. "Good morning guys. I appreciate all of you being here." He offered each of them a warm handshake, a little chatter, and then invited them into his conference room.

Upon entering the room, they were surprised once more at the sight of Noble's deputy director standing at the end of the table.

"You've all met Max?" Clearly, it was a rhetorical question.

Each nodded in her direction and grunted a polite response before taking their seats.

Noble, remaining true to form, wasted no time. "Max and I are working on a helluva complex case. Some of the evidence leads us to believe that certain key events that could affect the outcome took place during the Baari Administration. You may have crucial information that can be helpful. That's why I've asked you to join me today."

"Why is Chase here? He was never part of the administration." Hank challenged.

"Hank, please, I'm asking the questions." *Great start,* Noble thought. "I'm looking for any unusual activity regarding energy resources or renewable energy supplies that you may have encountered." Noble detected pained expressions on their faces.

Hank took his cue with Noble's tacit approval. He reiterated much of the conversation he had in his earlier meeting with Noble, as if it never happened. He talked about the CLEAR Act, the executive order, about the delays plaguing the Superstation, and even about the Godfather and the Financier. In the course of the dissertation, Hank complained about how he felt unjustly displaced by Baari's new handlers. His pontification lasted close to thirty-minutes, which was a piece of cake for Hank.

As he spoke, Noble and Max spent the time studying the group's body language. Most seemed nonplussed. They were aware of it all, having worked closely with Hank in the Baari Administration, except for Chase, who was his usual uneasy self.

Then Hank surprisingly changed his tone and referred to a day when Baari was highly agitated. "And he blurted out, 'what we need is a national disaster to calm things down, so I can get control of the wheel.' I assumed at the time he was only venting his frustration."

Paolo and Seymour looked at each other wide-eyed and pale. Chase broke out in a nervous sweat. Hank sat down. He had created Noble's desired effect.

Noble was confident at that point that they had some knowledge, but were reluctant to speak with Max in the room. The group's behavior led him to conclude that it somehow involved Simon.

"Max, I need you to check something out." Noble scribbled something on a piece of paper and handed it to her.

"Now?" she asked with a surprised expression, having read his note.

"Yes, please. It can't wait."

He obviously has his reason, she thought, as she headed out the door reluctantly.

The others in the room scrambled to figure out what Hank had said that caused Noble to send Max on an urgent mission. All Noble jotted down was an abrupt LEAVE.

"I'm sure you'll recall that during the interrogation, it was uncovered that each of you had performed an individual and isolated vital task for Simon unbeknown to the others." Now with the afterburners in full flame, Noble asked, "Is there any specific major event or earth shaking act that Baari asked you to do in confidence?"

They were mute as they exchanged glances.

Noble waited them out.

Paolo broke the silence and said, "Many of the speeches I wrote were directed toward one of his favorite themes, the environment. Baari, disenchanted with the usual party line, wanted to change the message and to place more emphasis on global warming."

Paolo explained that in 2009, when the New York Times reported the hacking of a server at the University of East Anglia in the U.K., everything started to cool down—literally. Email exchanges between the university and the National Center for Atmospheric Research refuted a study they had conducted recording the earth's temperatures over the last two millennia.

"Initial reports posited that the temperatures were cooling, not warming, and that the numbers had been fabricated." Paolo scanned their expressions, and then continued to elaborate. "The whole affair..."

"That's all poppycock," Hank blurted out. "Global warming exists no matter how you size up the numbers."

"Excuse me Hank. Wasn't it you who suggested to the president that he change the terminology to *climate change*, a phenomenon that cannot be challenged?" Paolo asked, obviously perturbed at the interruption.

"Remember the ice age, Hank? That was climatic," Seymour quipped.

"Hey—hey guys, let Paolo finish," Noble requested.

"As I was saying, the whole affair was coined *Climategate* and there was never any real resolution as to the true meaning buried in thousands of emails that had been hacked. At the same time, other critics of global warming popped up. Brian Sussman, a journalist and meteorologist, also reported that the North Pole had recorded the coldest summer on record and that the Arctic sea ice was the most expansive it had been since August 2006."

Hank interjected Paolo's diatribe once again. "I recall a science reporter for the BBC News reported the opposite. In fact, he said by 2013 the Arctic would be free of ice."

"Correct, but back in 2013 it was reported that the ice in the Arctic increased sixty percent. That prediction alone sent the

U.N. Intergovernmental Panel on Climate Exchange, the I-P-C-C, scurrying to Stockholm in September of that year for a pre-summit. They published their fifth assessment report the following month. The report substantiated their findings that humans continued to cause global warming."

"It appears politics is trumping scientific evidence," Chase chimed in, seeming to enjoy the discourse between Hank and Paolo.

Hank, still steamed, stated, "At least that's something both sides can agree on."

"Ah, even you Hank, would have to admit that the succeeding reports were rather milquetoast in quoting the statistics. Naturally, the I-P-C-C explained that after adjusting the computer climate models to measure more accurately the increase in CO_2, additional years of testing would be required before issuing conclusive evidence of global warming," Chase mocked.

"Get your facts straight, Chase," Hank challenged.

"Boys, this is not Old Home Week, let's get back on track," Noble scoffed. "Paolo, how did Baari react?"

"He ignored all the reports and simply redefined the issue under the rubric of sustainability." Paolo paused and looked in Hank's direction. "Then he asked me to write an entirely different speech for him. It was to be his response in the event of a national emergency. He swore me to secrecy. Baari said, 'Including Hank.'"

"Son-of-a-bitch," Hank mouthed in a muffled tone, but loud enough for all to hear.

"A clever son-of-a-bitch," Seymour chimed in. "He asked me to create a video portraying a rolling blackout, which was the figment of his imagination based on past events. I first touched on the blackout that occurred in 2003 in the Northeast and then triggered cascading blackouts across the entire country. He insisted on showing pictures of the aftermath. And he even suggested I cut and paste scenes from disaster movies to punctuate the damage inflicted." Seymour shrugged his shoulders, "I didn't have a clue what he was thinking. I told him he would come across as a fear-monger and I opposed it as a bad idea. He told me he would use it only if necessary, but would not share what *necessary* meant. Like Paolo I was sworn to secrecy." Seymour glanced at Hank.

With a sense of despair in his voice, Hank divulged, "Baari was concerned that the Superstation was getting caught up in red tape. The project was scheduled to go operational in 2014, and then the schedule was further delayed until 2016. To this day, there is still no specific end date." He stopped for a moment and then said, "My suspicion was that he was being pressured, by whom I don't know."

Paolo interrupted. "Wait a minute. Was Simon still pulling Baari's strings through you, Hank? We've surmised for some time that you never really cut your connections with either of them." He looked at Seymour and Chase for confirmation.

Noble focused on Hank.

"Wait a minute!" Hank shouted, "I have nothing to do with any of this. It was all between Simon and Baari. I was out of the picture." The moment the words left his mouth, he gauged it was a huge mistake. He sat back and gave each Paolo and Seymour an opportunity to react, expecting them to vent their spleen. Surprisingly with no retort he meekly stated, "I never told Baari about any of your special arrangements, I swear. I convinced Baari that it was Simon who planned all the events, starting from bringing him to the U.S. to placing him in the White House."

Everyone remained silent for a moment. Noble let it rest, having already taken his toll on Hank when he strayed off the path. He sat back as Hank's brothers took their pound of flesh. Throughout the interplay, Chase continued to stare straight-ahead, clasping his hands, hoping they would forget he was in the room.

No such luck.

"Chase, have you anything to add?" Noble commanded, more than requested.

"Shit! Baari asked me to conduct a feasibility study."

"So what," Seymour interrupted. "That would have been before Baari took office."

"No it wasn't." Chase huffed, "He asked me during his second term. He wanted me to work on it out of Washington—out of the White House. Moreover, no one was to be involved, except Hank. He was to provide whatever information I needed."

Everyone turned and glared toward Hank, especially Noble.

"What?" Hank asked incredulously. "I was never let in on the secret. Baari told me to supply Chase with whatever information he requested, so I did. It never occurred to me that it was part of Baari's disaster plan or any other plan. I was only a conduit."

Noble ignored Hank's outburst and refocused the group's attention, sensing he was gaining ground. "What was the purpose of the study?"

"It was to determine how long it would take the country to recover from a national disaster and be able to sustain our country and its resources."

"And what were your findings?" Noble asked, masking how he truly felt.

Chase, resuming his straight-ahead stare and absent eye contact, stated, "It would require years to recover with permanent damage to the economy and our infrastructure. It would be—unsustainable."

Everyone froze. It was as if an Arctic wind had swept through the room. As the thaw set in, the members of La Fratellanza once again began to fidget.

Noble had his confirmation. *I have to stop Simon,* a thought that only added more dread. "Chase, what was Baari's response when you delivered the final report?"

"He shook my hand, thanked me, and then reminded me that I was sworn to secrecy. I said I understood and I left. It was the last time I set foot in the White House," Chase paused and looked at Noble, and then said, "Until today. Please make it the last."

Noble always thought Chase was a bit of a sook, but he had sympathy for him and no more so than he did at that moment. "I hope it will be the last time I will have to call any of you."

As Noble was about to wrap it up, Hank reemerged from his snit and said, "I have no idea if this is important, but one of Baari's last appointments was the Secretary of Homeland Security, who in turn replaced the head of FEMA."

Noble was all ears, but he gave no indication of its possible importance. Then without further reponses emanating from the former president's men, Noble said, "Once again, many thanks for appearing with little notice to help me with the investigation. The information you've provided has been invaluable."

The members of the now defunct La Fratellanza began to ease themselves out of their chairs, uncertain as to how they helped Noble's case. Then each of them shook Noble's hand warmly and left the conference room.

Max was waiting in the reception area for their departure.

13
DAY TWENTY-NINE

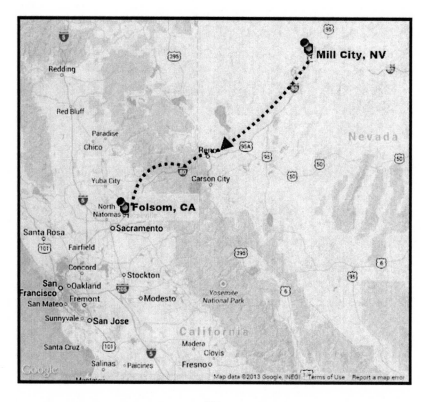

He had memorized the different twists and turns through the dark alleyway. One more left and he would be there. Up ahead, he noticed the dilapidated building with the four steps leading down to a basement apartment. He rang the buzzer three times as required.

"Who's there?" spoke the voice on the intercom.

"A customer."

"Do you have any ID?"

"What?"

A man opened the door and chuckled. "Everyone falls for that line."

"I fail to see the humor."

The two of them walked into the back room.

"As I said on the phone, I need a set of photos for driver's licenses and passports."

"Can do. May I see the documents?"

He opened his duffle bag and presented only a driver's license. "Take care of this first."

"Aren't we being careful," the shop owner said, noting the tape over the name.

The first photo was taken and the license was properly prepared and returned.

"Would you step out of the room for a moment?"

"Excuse me?"

"You heard me."

"You're the customer!" The counterfeiter obliged and waited patiently outside the door. Seconds later he heard a voice say, "Come back in."

"As I said before, aren't we being careful." The counterfeiter had seen a lot, but the changes were miraculous. No one could tell he was same person.

"Just take the photo. Here, it goes on these."

The counterfeiter snapped the camera and produced another photo for another license and a passport. He noted again the tape covering the names. "I know, I know." He stepped out of the room one more time and waited.

"Ready," he heard minutes later. Again, he was taken aback by yet another masterful disguise. He followed the same steps as before, but this time he held the license and passport firmly in his grip. "As we agreed on the phone, payment up front." He held out his other hand in a *give-me* motion. Then he counted as the one hundred dollar bills were peeled off and placed in his palm. With a satisfied smile on his face, the counterfeiter said, "Here you go sir. It's a pleasure doing business."

"One more thing."

"Oh, man, come 'on."

"Give."

Reluctantly, the counterfeiter clicked open the compartment on his camera and handed over the memory card.

The last sound heard was the front door creaking, then closing shut.

14

ASPIRATION VERSUS DESPERATION

Y ou look like it's the end of the world. What the hell happened?"
she asked impatiently.

"Baari was preparing for a national disaster to preserve his own
sustainability, if you'll pardon the expression."

"What!"

"And if it had occurred—it would have been unsustainable." Noble
then proceeded to fill Max in on the rest of the revelations he obtained
from the former president's men.

"Don't tell me you think Simon picked up the cudgels—where Baari
left off?"

"It appears that's where our loose ends meet." Noble answered with
caution. "Hank said that the Superstation was getting some pushback
from various opposing factions, so the construction phase continued
under wraps without public fanfare. There was little transparency so it
was easy to keep the project under the radar."

Noble continued to explain that according to Hank, Baari assumed
with the onslaught of scandals, in particular the NSA surveillance

scandal, that the U.S. citizens were on edge. He believed they were questioning the overreach of governmental power and the growing cavalcade of presidential executive orders.

"So it made it difficult to sell the Superstation at the time," Max conjectured.

"Yes, and Hank said Baari was cognizant of the public's increasing energy savvy and that it was greater than ever. He alleged Baari's plan was to create a national emergency. Perhaps, if the power grids *shutdown*, Baari would be forced to sign an executive order, ostensibly to cut through the red tape, which would give the Superstation a green light."

"With a thankful public at his feet!" Max opined with a hint of sarcasm. She did not expect Noble to respond and did not hesitate to add, "On another point, I checked with Immigration and there is no record of Abner Baari or Hussein Tarishi, either leaving or entering the country. And with Libya in perpetual turmoil, I wasn't able to confirm whether Baari still had a seat in the Parliament. Given that, I venture to say either the senator received a call from Baari in Libya or she was lying. I'm still waiting for the phone records." Max shifted the focus. "On the good news front, we might be getting closer to finding out Simon's tactics to execute his plot. I had an encouraging conversation with Stanton."

"Please, give me something to bolster my spirits."

"Stanton was putting one of the prisoners through another round of interrogation. He said there was something about one person that didn't compute. The prisoner swears he was recruited to install the command center in the encampment and set up a virtual private network, a VPN, in a cloud. All communication was to be undetectable and secured." Max sniggered, "Guess whose satellite he chose to attach it to?"

Noble offered a curious response. "I give."

"The SIA. You have to love the irony. In addition, he has no clue as to the words of the mantra repeated by the other suspects. Stanton happened to mention the guy's IQ appeared to be off the charts." Max dangled a carrot. "He's a Harvard grad."

"What year?"

"1997, the same year you graduated."

"Do you have a name or a photo?"

"Give me a minute." Max rapidly tapped the screen on her xPhad texting Stanton, asking him to send her the recruit's record. Within minutes, she received a response.

"Here he is. Check this out."

Noble was shocked. "I know this guy." He filled Max in on the particulars, at least those he could recall. "Go to Dugway. I want you to interrogate him in person."

Max grunted at the idea of another trip, and reluctantly texted Stanton again. **Stand down major. I'll handle this one. Be there at 1700 hours.** "Done!" she said as she looked up from her touch pad. Then unexpectedly, she flashed a huge grin as she realized she had taken a big bite out of the major's ego.

Noble sat back amused. He suspected what she was thinking.

About ten minutes into the continuation of their earlier conversation, his xPhad vibrated. It was Paolo. "Give me a sec."

❦

"What's up?" he asked, curious as to the timing.

"We need to talk."

"You could've stayed behind. We could've talked here."

"Not in the White House. Can you meet me at the usual place? Noble, this is important," he pleaded.

Noble glanced at his watch. "I'm in the middle of a meeting. Give me an hour."

"Thanks."

❦

"What was that all about?" Max probed.

"I'm about to find out." Saying nothing more on the subject, he took a moment to review certain aspects of the case when a second interruption arose.

"Director Deputy Ford," Max responded to the caller. Yes— When?—Why wasn't I alerted before?—Thank you. Please call if there is any other unusual activity—I will—Goodbye."

"What was that all about?" It was Noble's turn to inquire.

"That was the FERC chairman. After he called the director at the control center in Taylor, Texas, the director went through his logs going back a few months and evidently, there was a security breach to their operating system. It occurred on the sixth of January. The system was only down for about ten minutes. They notified the DOE and followed the protocol. The incident was then reported to Homeland Security's National Cyber Security Division. A techie was sent to investigate and it all proved to be nothing."

"Has the chairman heard anything from the other centers?"

Max nodded. "Zilch. I'll follow up with him again, before I leave for the Beehive State. I'm on the two o'clock flight."

"Report in as soon as you finish grilling my fellow alumnus," Noble ordered. "With any luck, we'll get a lead. Simon didn't fall off the face of the earth!" In a calmer tone he said, "I have a few things of my own to tie up."

"Like sanctioning an immunity agreement?"

"The senator has a few more days. She'll capitulate."

"I surrender." Max headed for the door as she waved her typical backhanded high-fiver.

15
FAMILY TIES

Noble walked into the Blackfinn Saloon and waved to Paolo as he walked over to their usual booth in the back corner.

"What's so important that you couldn't tell me earlier?"

"*Ciao fratello,* would you like to sit down first?" Paolo asked in a curt manner.

Noble unbuttoned his jacket and took a seat.

"You're going after Simon again?" Paolo asked, although he was aware Noble could not talk about it, but his reaction was enough.

"What's so important?" Noble repeated.

Paolo took it slow. "During our little reunion this morning, Hank mentioned the Godfather and the Financier. He appeared to be unaware of their identity. Admittedly, at the time, none of us were aware. But Hank was the last man standing, so I was surprised to find out he was clueless."

"What's your point?

"*Ho il maleocchio.* I am cursed. The point is—I discovered who they are. When I did, I wasn't taking any chances, so I resigned. Baari was way over his head and I didn't want to be any part of the fraud I thought was happening."

"Paolo, you're not making sense. Who are they?"

"*Aspetta*, hold on, first things first. A while back, Baari was scheduled to speak to an environmental group. He asked me to write a speech on the benefits of cap-and-trade. You know me, I research my subject matter thoroughly for every speech or communications directive I release. I discovered some interesting facts along the way. Have you heard of the Chicago Climate Exchange or CCX?"

"Vaguely, something about carbon trading in an effort to reduce greenhouse gasses."

"You're correct. Companies that produce clean renewable energy emit less greenhouse gasses or GHG as they call them, and earn credits. Then they can sell those credits to companies that produce too much GHG, essentially the polluters. It is akin to selling your frequent flyer airline miles to infrequent travelers."

"Which is the basis for cap-and-trade?"

"Yes, to limit or cap the amount of emissions a company can produce. Then it allowed them to market any surplus emission to companies that need to produce more than their allotted share."

"Something that can only function in a global warming frenzy!" Noble exclaimed.

"*Bravo*, but it's more complicated. The Exchange was a viable entity with over four hundred members, including major corporations, universities, and unions. Its startup cost came from the Joyce Foundation, a philanthropic group that provided over a million dollars for the initial funding for CCX. While their mission was to provide grants for improving the quality of life for those in the Great Lakes area, that specific grant was diverted to Dr. Richard Sandor, an economist at Northwestern University. The grant was to determine the feasibility of a cap-and-trade market."

"Paolo, where is this leading?" Noble was already working on overload after the meeting with La Fratellanza and had reached his limit of speculation for one day.

Paolo ignored Noble's impatience and eased back with a slight smirk. "Get this. A young senator from Chicago sat on the foundation's board during that time."

"That young senator didn't happen to become a U.S. president?" Noble did not expect an answer. He simply shook his head.

Paolo continued. "In 2003, Dr. Sandor founded CCX and trading operations commenced. The predicted gross annual income was ten trillion dollars. It was heavily predicated on the passing of cap-and-trade legislation in Congress. In 2004, former Vice President Al Gore and former Goldman Sachs executive David Blood founded Generation Investment Management, or GIM, based in London. Both GIM and Goldman Sachs jumped on the bandwagon and became two of the largest investors in CCX."

"So that's why Baari pushed so hard for a cap-and-trade bill. It was essential to the success of CCX."

"But that wasn't the only obstacle. Remember the server that was hacked at the University of East Anglia? That event, plus the cap-and-trade legislation that had stalled in the Senate, caused CCX to virtually collapse."

"Virtually, I don't understand?"

"These are smart guys. In 2005, they launched the European Climate Exchange and the Climate Futures Exchange. Then in 2006, they established the parent company Climate Exchange PLC to operate all of these entities. Dr. Richard Sandor was Chairman. Following?"

"I'm still waiting to see how they virtually collapsed," Noble interrupted.

"Fratello, here it is—*hanno vinto la lotteria!* They hit the lottery. In 2010, the Intercontinental Exchange in London, an international clearinghouse for multi-asset based companies, acquired the Climate Exchange PLC for over six hundred and four million dollars, based on the currency rate at the time. Records showed that Sandor made ninety million dollars on the sale for his sixteen percent share. GIM and Goldman Sachs each owned ten percent."

"So, which one of these smart guys is the Godfather? I assume that's where you're leading."

"None of them."

Noble's face was a mixture of confusion and frustration.

Paolo noted and picked up the pace. "The man who propelled the global warming movement, referred to as the 'Godfather of the Kyoto Protocol,' the international treaty that sets a binding obligation by country to reduce gas emissions—is one of the insiders who sat on the board of CCX and admits to being the one who helped Sandor set up the company from the beginning."

"He is also referred to as the Godfather of the Environmental Movement?" Noble was incredulous.

"Yes, and it is possible he may have met Baari during his community organizing days."

"That far back?"

"*Si*, but Hank never told us. It became evident over time that someone else was pushing the presidential agenda and it was not the president's staff. After Simon disappeared, we concluded we were no longer in control. Interestingly, global warming was never a subject in any of our theses at Harvard when it all began. It was clearly Baari's obsession."

"This is amazing." Noble shook his head, lacking any other means of expression, as the web of players spun in his mind. "Whether or not one believes in global warming, the fact remains these people have turned a prominent public issue into a cottage industry. Whoever entered the game early made billions of dollars to line their own pockets."

Paolo agreed. "They adopted a holier-than-thou demeanor as they cashed in. This is hardly a *Walden Pond* support group. Coincidently, if you look at many of the player's personal investment portfolios, for example Al Gore's GIM, you'll find essentially no green companies, but plenty of profits."

"Who is he, the Environmental Dr. Strangelove?" For the first time, Noble started to realize the absurdity. Then on a more serious point, he stated, "The Superstation was vitally important in the push for renewable energy. That could explain Baari's agenda in wanting to find a way to railroad it through."

Paolo sighed. "All said and done, you can see why I needed to distance myself. I couldn't keep writing speeches promoting an issue where the American people had no influence. Therefore, I resigned. I should have done it sooner as you and Natalie had suggested."

Noble left Paolo alone to cogitate. Nevertheless, he was still curious about the second part of his story. "Who's the Financier?" he asked. Unexpectedly and ill timed, his xPhad vibrated. It was a text message from Max. It read: **breach at folsom - simon**. Noble texted back, **in 10 my office**. "I've got to go. Thanks for the info, it could be helpful."

"Noble, in answer to your last question—follow the open society. *Ma occhio però.*"

Noble learned enough Italian to know Paolo was warning him to watch out. "*Grazie* fratello." He gave his brother-in-law a hug and dashed out of the restaurant.

16

HEADIN' EAST

Noble rushed into his reception area and looked over toward Doris. "Is Max in the conference room?"

"She just arrived."

He entered the inner sanctum and closed the door behind him. "What have you got?" he asked in an excited state, hoping it would lead them closer to Simon.

"After you left, the FERC chairman called back. There was another breach, this one at Folsom on the seventh of March. The director from the control center followed the usual procedure and called the DOE. They sent a techie to investigate."

"So what makes you think it's Simon?"

"Because at both the Birmingham and Taylor facilities, the systems were shut down for ten minutes. The Folsom system was brought to a halt for close to an hour. I asked the chairman to have the directors from the three control centers send me the photo identification for each of the techies who were dispatched."

Max used the virtual keyboard and tapped at the various keys.

Within seconds, three visitor's photo badges appeared on the large touchscreen monitor.

Noble was amazed. "So Birmingham and Taylor were hacked by the prisoner you're about to interrogate at Dugway. He is the one responsible for setting up the command center in the underground encampment—and he's a former Harvard classmate." Noble's shock quickly transformed into anger and he sputtered, "Which means our genius was a mole operating inside the Department of Homeland Security." Toning down his ire, he said, "Hank mentioned that Baari's last appointment before stepping down was the Secretary of the DHS."

Max raised a brow and intoned, "Very interesting!"

Noble shook his head in disgust. "What about the other guy? The one sent to Folsom."

"He's legit; a fifteen-year veteran with the agency and a clean record. In fact, I had an interesting conversation with him. He said that the hacker left behind some code. It is characteristic hacker code, used to destabilize the system long enough to raise havoc. Typically, the hacker removes the code before exiting the system leaving no trace. But this time it was left behind."

"Hmmm." Noble pondered for a moment, and then theorized, "The Folsom breach occurred after the mole was captured on January 31. And unlike the other breaches, their system was down for almost an hour."

"The Birmingham and Taylor systems were only down for ten minutes," Max reiterated.

"That's because the mole accessed the facilities and the main computer systems directly. He was able to then quickly alter the code."

"That's why I think it is Simon. Whatever he's doing to each of these control centers, he'll now have to perform himself. Moreover, not being able to access the facility directly, he'll have to manage his handiwork from the outside and within range of the control center's network. Simon is either in or heading toward Folsom. That's our confirmation."

"First, you need to interrogate the mole. We need more than guesswork."

"I agree. We need to find out his role; one Simon may have apparently assumed after the mole was captured. This could be our breakthrough." Max barely got the last word out of her mouth before Noble's phone rang.

"Agent Burke on line one," Doris announced.

Noble hit the appropriate button and then the one for the speakerphone. "Burke, I've got you on the speaker. Max is with me. What's happening?"

"I think we have a lead on Simon. Two young males picked up a hitchhiker a mile out of Newcastle and dropped him off in Folsom. They said at the time they had no clue who he was until a week later when they saw Simon's photo on a TV screen in a local bar."

"Where exactly did they drop him off?"

"At the bus station."

"Son-of-a-bitch." Noble's voice echoed through the speaker.

"Director, I have a feeling it was intentional. Simon is covering his trail. So I made calls to several of the local used car lots. And we got lucky!"

"Burke, what?" Noble was becoming encouraged. He needed the slightest break.

"The dealer said the customer vaguely resembled Simon's photo, except he had gray hair and a beard. I'm bringing in a sketch artist to draw up a composite."

"Any luck finding the guy who finished off Simon's false IDs?"

"We are still looking for him. You can't imagine how many counterfeiters set up businesses in and around the Folsom area—and not far from the prison grounds."

"Keep me posted. With any luck, we might be getting closer. Back to the dealer, what caught his attention?"

"He became suspicious when the customer became impatient, demanding he move the paperwork along, and he paid cash in crisp one hundred dollar bills."

"And the make and model?"

"He purchased a 1996 White Ford Bronco. The temporary California plate number is J as in Juliett, A as in Alpha, F as in Foxtrot, 4-2-8."

"Max, bring up the grids," Noble asked.

"Excuse me, I didn't hear you."

"Hold on a sec, Burke. I have Max putting something on the display monitor."

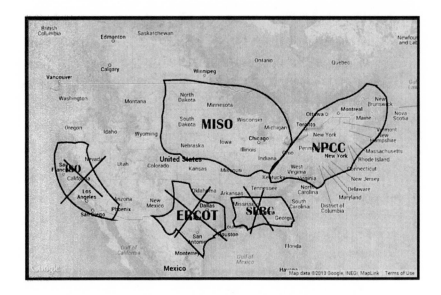

Max and Noble stared at a map of the country. Earlier, Max had circled the five grids where they had data leading them to conclude the control centers were the targets. Then she crossed off the breached facilities one-by-one. They took a moment to study them as Burke waited patiently on the other end of the line.

"Burke, he's heading toward the Midwest."

"Where in the Midwest?"

Noble explained that Max would be heading to Dugway to interview one of the prisoners. "We have evidence that this guy hacked two of the electrical grid control centers and are fairly positive Simon hacked the one in Folsom. We have identified three other centers as targets. One is in Minnesota, one is in Indiana, and one is in Mississauga."

"In Canada?"

"Yes. Whatever Simon has planned will happen after he crosses the border or perhaps, even leaves North America."

"Max, bring up a road map and identify the possible routes from Folsom to St. Paul, Minnesota."

She tapped rapidly until a map appeared with two possible routes.

"Burke, it looks like he could take Route 80 East, but that would put him back in Utah and straight thru Salt Lake City. Risky at best."

"Can he circumvent Utah?"

"Hold on. He could take Interstate 395 North, then Route 84 Southeast, and pick Route 80 on the other side of Salt Lake City near Ogden and continue east. It would take him roughly thirty-one hours."

"I suspect he'll stop along the way, which will slow him down. It's also possible he'll only drive at night," Burke concluded.

"Update the APB and get helicopter support."

"We'll find him Director."

"I want to know the second anyone lays eyes on him!"

"Yes, sir."

In a calmer tone, Noble said, "Good work Burke. Later." He hit the button on the speakerphone and disconnected the call.

"We'll get him," Max echoed. "But we still need to find out specifically how he's going to bring the grids down and dismantle his plot. I'm sure I'll get something out of the mole." Max tried to sound encouraging, but the skeptical look on Noble's face remained.

"It's time for me to have a face-to-face with the president. Go catch your flight."

"I'll call you directly after the interrogation. Hang in there boss." Max touched his shoulder gently on the way out of the conference room.

Noble remained in his chair and stared at the map for a while, until he could no longer ignore the inevitable. He reached for his phone. "Doris, I believe the president is in the house. See if I can get an hour with him today." Noble knew he did not need to say more. The president understood. Noble only required time when it was for the utmost importance. Throughout this case in particular, he had kept the president informed through a daily missive, for his eyes only. As Noble continued to focus on the map he did not hear the buzzer, but he noticed the blinking red light.

"He can see you at two o'clock."

It was twelve forty-five. "Thanks Doris. Would you order me the usual and hold all my calls?"

"Right away." Doris knew his favorite sandwich was turkey on whole wheat with lettuce, tomato, and lots of black pepper. She also knew *hold my calls* did not include Max, Burke, or Stanton.

With an hour to go, Noble began to jot down specific events that had led him to his bold assessment.

17

PRESIDENTIAL ENLIGHTENMENT?

M r. President, thank you for your time," Noble said as he shook the president's hand. Then they walked across the room and sat down facing each other on opposite sofas. "Sir, I trust your trip to the Middle East was satisfactory?" he asked, trying to mute any tension in his voice.

The president sensed that would be Noble's only softball question and obliged, although there was not a softball answer in reply. "As well as can be expected. Although, I seem to have spent more time mending fences than building bridges. Perhaps, I should have been a farmhand and stayed out of political office," he quipped. Though unplanned, he aired his frustration. "You'll never hear me express this outside the Oval Office, but my predecessor left the Mideast in utter turmoil. The Syrian debacle alone, with his famous redline diplomacy and waffling, put our authority in lasting jeopardy. He gave strength to our enemies and severely damaged relationships with our rapidly declining number of friends. It is my hope that we will at least be able to repair the trust lost with Israel. It was unthinkable that he would have contemplated bombing Syria to stop Assad. The Muslim Brotherhood, whose goal has always been to destroy the U.S., supports the Assad government, so we opted to give support to the rebels fighting alongside al-Qaeda against Assad, who also wants the destruction of the U.S. In the meantime, he created a situation that left Russia and Iran lolling in the spectator stands waiting for the U.S. to self-destruct." The president was openly angered by the chaos handed to him by failed policies of the prior administration. "It has cast an unfavorable light on our country globally." Then, in an equally serious tone, he turned the question to Noble. "You're not one to waste time, yours or mine. What's happening with the case?"

Through weekly briefings, the president was aware of the security breach at the control center in Taylor, the abandoned car outside Newcastle and the ongoing interrogations at Dugway—and that Senator Townsend agreed to the immunity agreement earlier than expected, which the president was about to sign on the advice of the attorney general. Hence, Noble spent his initial time to provide an update.

"We've had two more cyber-attacks reported. One in Birmingham that occurred last November that had gone unreported until now, and more recently at Folsom. Max is heading to Dugway to interview one of the prisoners who we know was the hacker in the first two breaches. It appears our clever intruder was a mole working inside the National Cyber Security Division."

"Brilliant," the president scoffed.

Noble concurred with his disdain, but he had more troubling facts to reveal. "What we have uncovered thus far, leads us to suspect Simon was responsible for hacking into the system at Folsom. From all the evidence, it is our best assessment that he is planning to disrupt the power supply of the country—in an attempt to create a national disaster. The reasons are still unclear."

At the words, *national disaster*, the president sat upright. "Are you certain?"

"Yes, sir. That's my conclusion as the facts suggest," Noble replied, while inwardly hoping to hell he was wrong. Then slowly and deliberately, he proceeded to fill the president in on his conversation with Baari's former staff.

The president was furious. "Even if Baari made that statement about the need of a disaster, and even if he said it in a moment of frustration, it's reprehensible. He took an oath to protect the people, not to destroy them!" In a calmer tone, the president asked, "You mentioned a feasibility study to gauge the nation's ability to recover from a disaster. What were the results?"

Noble hesitated and then answered, "Unsustainable."

The president was shaken for a moment as he contemplated the horror, before he challenged, "Three control centers have been hacked, and to date nothing of consequence has happened."

"Sir, Simon's a notorious hacker and adept at programming. It is highly possible he's inserted backdoor codes to allow ease of access at a later time. We'll have a better idea after Max speaks with the mole." Changing his expression slightly, Noble asked, "This may seem like an unrelated question, but can you give me an update on the Superstation?"

The president appeared surprised at the sudden shift. "You think there's a connection?"

"I understand there have been a series of delays since announcing the Superstation in 2009. Although, it's slated to go operational any day now, do you foresee any further delays?"

"I'm currently having FERC's prior approvals reviewed. It is important to ensure that the Superstation does not create a power monopoly for energy transmission. I question the reliability of the project and whether in the end the consumer will end up paying more for power. There is also concern that the EPA never conducted the required environmental impact study. I have yet to find one on record. It seems to have taken on an immoral life of its own. So yes, I could delay it further. Noble, what's the connection?"

"This is only a premise, sir, but if there was a rolling blackout affecting major cities across the country—could you be forced to authorize the Superstation to go live without the final governmental approvals, as a matter of national interest?"

"Of course, I'd have no choice, if the Superstation holds the solution."

"It is highly possible that is Simon's intent. He is carrying out what we surmise to have been Baari's original plan for a staged disaster had he remained in office. It now would provide Simon a ready-made vehicle to create his own national disaster he longs to achieve for presumably different motives."

"What's in it for Simon?"

"In all honesty—I don't know." Noble asserted evenly, but then he asked another leading question. "What can you tell me about the man referred to as the Godfather of the Environmental Movement?"

"Where are you heading?" the president asked cautiously.

Noble was forthcoming and divulged all he had discovered about the mysterious wealthy environmentalist. "Last week, I spoke with one of my sources, formerly from the DOE. When I asked about the Superstation, he became seemingly edgy. He dodged the question but he handed me a napkin where he had scribbled a word and a number, Agenda 21. When I pursued my inquiry our discussion came to an abrupt end."

The president listened intently, and then in a neutral tone he explained, "The Godfather is a powerful businessman, having held a string of positions in the United Nations, dating back as far as 1974. However, his tentacles reach beyond the U.N. to a multiple of business enterprises. He hobnobs with the international power elites, including five U.N. secretary-generals, U.N. functionaries and numerous heads of state, many of whom seek his advice. His influence peddling is well known in their inner-circle. And he uses that influence to push the concepts of global warming and the sustainability of Mother Earth."

"So the Superstation and its related renewable energy agenda are vital to their cause?"

"It would be an important cog, although the Godfather's interests are not limited to reducing gas house emissions." Then in a surprising and rare moment, the president changed his tone and shared his personal views. "There is science on both sides of the global warming argument. But it's a Potemkin village. Clearly, the sanctimonious message it carries makes it more palatable for our citizens to digest, and provides a diversion from the real issue. Sports fans would consider it a head-fake. But behind the smokescreen, is a group of powerful people who hold the view that as industrial societies prosper, they will consume an excess of the earth's resources to an unsustainable level, if not managed on a global basis. They believe the citizens are incapable of managing our planet's resources. They preach that sustainable development can only be achieved through the worldwide redistribution of wealth and imposition of global governance." The president stopped, as he observed the expression on Noble's face.

"Sir, are you referring to Agenda 21 as the real issue?"

"Indeed. Agenda 21 basically states that America is becoming overly affluent and our standard of living should be lowered, by sharing our wealth with poorer countries." The president took a noticeable pause before making his next statement. "Have you heard of what's referred to as the *Covenant*?"

Noble was stumped. "No, sir, I haven't."

"In 2010, the International Union for the Conservation of Nature and Natural Resources, referred to as IUCN, and the International Council of Environmental Law, ICEL, drafted a document and submitted it to the member states in the United Nations. The document is titled International Covenant on Environment and Development—or, the Covenant."

"Sir, is this similar to Agenda 21?"

"Some have described it as Agenda 21 on steroids. And while Agenda 21 is non-binding, if the Covenant is adopted by the U.N. it becomes enforceable through the International Criminal Court."

Noble was clearly distressed at the thought. Considering the dire implications, he challenged, "That would create an oppressive system of global governance that would claim authority over the environment for the entire world!"

"Your observation is correct. But what they are not emphasizing is that the road to redistribution of wealth means the sacrifice of our national sovereignty as a country over our land, oceans, and our atmosphere. Part of this transformation is to forfeit many of our individual rights. As you are aware there have been a number of erosions of our sovereignty, deftly handed to the UN without consulting our electorate, and with virtually no transparency." The president hesitated once again, as he heaved a sigh.

Noble took note of his intensity, but continued to absorb his words with great interest.

"The devious methods that cloak the issue of global governance are my primary concern. The push for a new world economic order is already underway. My responsibility is to protect the sovereignty of our nation. While it is not my wish, if global governance is our destiny, the implementers of the Covenant must be transparent about their strategy and intent. They are playing a bait and switch game with the American citizens, without giving them a say in the process—if renewable energy is a cornerstone it should be evolutionary, not revolutionary." The president paused. Then for the first time, he spoke fervently, "In no case should it be controlled by a few wealthy power brokers who seem to profit at every turn!"

Noble fretted, "So, if they achieve the goal of the Covenant the United Nations becomes the governing body of the world. A frightful thought when you consider the example of Europe's inability to unite fully since the Treaty of Rome in 1952. What hope is there for a new world order?"

"I concur. They have done nothing for Tibet, by way of another example. The despotic nations that have chaired the Human Rights Commission would be laughable, if not so serious. And God forbid we find ourselves forced to go to war again to protect our country—and Cameroon has the deciding vote," the president added.

Taking into account the magnitude of their actions, both the president and Noble managed a smile. They chatted about the U.N. resolution to support the invasion of Iraq and the absurdity that the vote rested on a tiny country on the African coast. They also discussed the time in 2013 when China and Russia, allies of Syria, consistently vetoed any resolution, as the Syrian President Assad continued to gas his citizens.

"When they finally passed a resolution to remove the gas, there was no enforcement mechanism," the president alleged.

"These are sad examples of the decisions that have come out of the U.N. Security Council," Noble observed.

"The implications only get worse." The president expounded, "For a very long time, various activities have been underway at the U.N. to promote the outcome of global governance. But in recent history the momentum has accelerated."

The president explained that in 1995, a U.N. Commission on Global Governance was established and at one of the conferences on disarmament, a report incorporated a worldwide objective to control all firearms.

"I recall in 2012, when then-Defense Secretary Leon Panetta testified at a committee hearing, and stated that the U.N. and NATO should have supreme authority over the actions of the U.S. military," Noble observed. Then he acknowledged, "There appears to be a pattern that connects back to the United Nations."

"Worse yet, the connivers would have us lose our permanent seat at the U.N. Security Council. Through a reorganization plan already sanctioned by the U.N. Commission on Global Governance, it would castrate the United States of its position of power. It would be the coup de grâce for the U.S.'s influence internationally."

Noble cocked his head, confused by the president's last statement. "Sir, how is that really possible?"

"One of the major reform efforts that came out of the U.N. Commission on Global Governance was to remove the five permanent members and replace them with two from industrial countries and three from the larger developing countries. Currently, we pay twenty-two percent of the U.N. budget in annual dues. The second largest contributor is Japan, paying ten-point-eight percent. There was no mention of a reduction in dues for the U.S."

"This will fundamentally transform America!" Noble exclaimed.

"One sidebar you may find interesting. The OIC—the Organization of Islamic Cooperation—is a collective voice of fifty-six member states and the Palestinian authority. This coalition is comprised of twenty-three member nations represented within the U.N. and twenty-four additional nations with an Islamic population of over fifty percent, not including Iran. They are the largest international organization outside the U.N., but operate somewhat within the confines of the United Nations. OIC's Secretary General Ekmeleddin Ihsanoglu stated, 'I think there should be a seat for OIC in the Security Council.' He makes his case for being the largest collective voice of the Muslim world, while other nations are also jockeying for a seat on the council.

"I can only imagine some of the countries that may hold our fate?"

The president added to Noble's concerns. "What frightens me the most is how they are attempting to accomplish their goal. The Godfather has verbally stated that he does not believe in global governance. He has even said that it is not feasible. However, he was not only the architect of Agenda 21, he was also involved in writing the final report for the U.N. Commission on Global Governance, and he is a patron of IUCN, the organization that drafted the Covenant. He is the same man who was quoted saying, 'Frankly, we may get to the point where the only way of saving the world will be for industrial civilization to collapse.'"

Noble's intensity rose again. "That's the connection! Simon and the Godfather! They both strive for the destruction of western values, albeit from different perspectives and dissimilar goals—however, the result would be the same. Mr. President, your insights have been extremely helpful."

Noble paused to absorb the gravity of his revelation.

The president took note.

"Tread easy, Noble. You are making a giant, deductive leap. All of what we have discussed has not been proven," the president cautioned. Although he was confident that Noble understood the gravity of his observations, there was nothing more to add. He glanced at his watch and then asked a final question, "Do you need more resources?"

"Sir, we're fine for now. Confidentiality is of the essence. Max and I are pouring through the evidence looking for a clue on how to deconstruct and stop Simon's ultimate plot. I have Agent Burke and his men following Simon's trail and Major Stanton and his B Team are still gathering vital information from the detainees. Admittedly, we are stretched to the limit, but we can manage. By the way, both Stanton and Burke agreed to their new assignments, but I'd like to keep them on the case until we corral Simon, or at a minimum foil his scheme."

"Of course—and thank you Noble. I understand your reasoning for wanting to bring them to Washington."

"Thank you, sir. I'll keep you informed of any pertinent events."

"Be careful," the president warned again, with added concern. On a lighter note, he admitted, "There are days I feel like the captain of the Titanic."

"And the Covenant was the iceberg you didn't see coming?"

"What is frightening is that I did see it. Conrad Black, a foreign observer from the U.K. saw it as well. He has been quoted saying that, 'Not since the disintegration of the Soviet Union in 1991, and before that the fall of France in 1940, has there been so swift an erosion of the world influence of a Great Power as we are witnessing with the United States.'"

"Sir, one might conclude that the Syrian uprising was a giant step to move us closer to global governance when the former president transferred the decision making to the Russian leader and to the U.N."

"You are alarmingly correct. It certainly set the stage for world governance to fall under the U.N. aegis. Nevertheless, I am mindful of my responsibility to stay positive for the sake of the American people. We are a resilient country and we shall survive—in spite of the United Nations."

After a solemn pause, the president stood up.

Noble followed suit. He offered a cordial smile as he shook the president's hand and made a hasty retreat.

18

THE MOLE COMES CLEAN

The man stood and saluted from behind the desk, "Welcome back, Max."

During Operation Nomis, Max insisted the military officers address her informally. She never was comfortable with the stodgy deputy director title and used it sparingly as a source of intimidation. It also put the *uniforms* at ease around her. "Thanks, Sergeant." She returned his smile and then asked, "The prisoner?"

"Second door on the left. Major Stanton is with him now."

Max turned and quickly headed down the corridor. As she opened the door, she observed Stanton standing in the corner of the room. She nodded in his direction maintaining her stern demeanor and then she glowered at the mole. Without delay, she opened her briefcase and retrieved a large stack of papers. She slapped the top three sheets of paper in a row in front of the prisoner. They were photocopies of ID badges.

Stanton was impressed. *Nice touch*, he thought, as he looked at the daunting stack of papers. But he knew this was her show and his role was to be an observer.

Max pointed her right index finger emphatically at the first photo. "This is you entering the control center in Birmingham, Alabama on the seventh of November, three days after a security breach was reported." She used her left hand to brace herself as she leaned over the surface of the table and towered over the prisoner. Pushing her index finger onto the next photo on the table, she stated, "This is you entering the control center in Taylor, Texas on the ninth of January, again three days after a breach." Moving her finger to the final photo, she maintained her directness. "This is one of your colleagues entering the control center in Folsom, California, on the tenth of March, coincidently, three days after a breach." She then plumped down in her chair, startling the mole. As she gave him a moment to digest the photos, she prepared herself to record some notes on her tablet.

The mole stared eyelevel at Max and responded, "And your point is?"

He is not going to make it easy for you Max, Stanton thought as he smiled inwardly.

"We know you were a classmate of Simon Hall at Harvard, between the years of 1995 to 1997. We already have proof that Simon hacked each facility I mentioned causing the security breaches intentionally, so your department head at the National Cyber Security Division would assign someone to investigate."

On the face of it, the mole was impressed that Deputy Director Ford had made the connection. But he also knew another classmate of his was her boss and the head of the SIA.

"What was your role?" Max probed in a raised voice.

"I refuse to answer your silly questions. I have rights; I want to speak to a lawyer," the mole demanded.

"Wrong answer. In accordance with the National Defense Authorization Act, we have the right to hold you indefinitely in a military prison, if we suspect you've committed terrorist acts against the U.S..."

The mole attempted to interrupt.

Max shot her hand in the air to restrain his words and then completed her statement. "...even if you are an American citizen."

The mole sank into his chair. His expression changed ever so slightly displaying some concern. "I was to enter each facility, identify the program that contained the failsafe code and send a snapshot to the cloud…"

Max cut him off. "The cloud you set up in the encampment when you established the VPN?"

"Yes. I executed a program that downloaded Simon's backdoor code. It was designed to attach itself to the facility's operating code." He looked down and fidgeted for the first time. Making no eye contact, he muttered, "When I was finished, I reported to the director that it was just a blip in the system and everything checked out."

"Why were you always sent in three days after the breach?"

"Typical protocol. The DOE received a call the day after the breach. I assume because they tried to resolve it themselves. Then the DOE called Homeland Security and they sent the request to us. It took us a day to get out there. No big mystery."

Max was not a hundred percent sure. "How could you or Simon be assured that the local techie couldn't resolve the issue in-house?"

"Typically, a hacker would weaken the Internet protocol, the IP, creating a distributed denial-of-service, or D-Dos to disrupt the website and to establish the means to disrupt the system at a future date. It would leave the facility vulnerable to an attack."

"So why couldn't the techie identify the D-Dos attack? It's pretty standard hacking code."

The mole, seemingly impressed with Max's Internet acumen, bolstered, "There's nothing standard about Simon's code. I've never seen anything like it. The local techie would never be able to detect it and naturally would be forced to call us."

"Why didn't Simon hack the system and place the code there himself?"

"The security's tight and he needed more time to modify the failsafe code. It's different for each facility. Later, he would use the backdoor and replace the code without raising any red flags."

"Why the failsafe code?"

The mole casually added, "The failsafe code is designed to reallocate power from a healthy grid to one that is experiencing a power outage. It happens at warp speed and the power is restored immediately. Without that capability you'd have a blackout."

"What exactly was he modifying?" Max asked.

"The code! He would trigger an override of the failsafe code on a programmed date," he paused, "causing the entire grid to shut down."

"What date?"

Max unnerved him with her aggressive tone. "I don't know! I never saw the modified code!"

"Why are there months between breaches?"

"As I said, he needed more time; each facility's code was different. And he didn't want to raise suspicion."

"You were captured on the thirty-first of January, so your colleague had to go to Folsom in your place. How many of Simon's moles are working at the National Cyber Security Division?"

"Only me!"

"How can you be sure?"

The mole pointed to the picture with the photo of his colleague. "I'm positive this guy knows nothing. How long was he at the facility testing the system?"

Max was surprised at the question, although she sensed he did not expect a response.

"I was there for less than an hour. It would usually take me that long to locate the failsafe program. Each facility had a different program name. Basically, I was in and out as instructed."

Max had learned from the directors at each facility that the mole was accurate about his timing. She also knew that the techie sent to Folsom was there for over four hours. She concluded that Simon had to have been hacking Folsom from outside the facility, keeping the system down for close to an hour and piggybacking on the techie's time. Thus far, the mole seemed to be forthcoming.

"How could you be sure you'd be given the assignment when the security breach was reported?

"I knew the dates Simon would hack. I passed along my other assignments to my colleagues to ensure I'd be available on the key dates."

"Which other control centers are to be hacked?

"I was assigned only two other centers, one in Minnesota and one in Indiana."

"You mean at Carmel and St. Paul."

"Yes, they run parallel, operating the same grid, but their failsafe codes are different."

"When is Simon scheduled to hack the system to cause the next security breach?"

"It's scheduled for May ninth in St. Paul.

"There's one other grid you didn't mention," she challenged.

"That's all I was assigned to do!"

Max remained silent. She sensed that he was about to come clean.

Stanton wondered why she did not push harder as he thought, *its perfect timing. You have him on the defensive.*

"Simon…" the mole began to say.

"Simon what?" she pressed.

"He planned on handling the last one himself."

"Which one?" Max sounded gruffer with each question.

The mole shifted in his chair with each answer.

Stanton tightened his jaw, resisting his urge to be part of the interrogation.

"Mississauga!"

"Beautiful! That puts him over the border, in a country that won't extradite for capital crimes," Stanton volunteered without invitation.

Max glared at Stanton for an instant, then picked up where she had left off. "So that will leave you here to take the rap." She frowned. "When is he scheduled to hack the system?"

"July fifth."

"Not the fourth?" Which seemed logical in her mind.

"No. The fifth."

"Are there any other grids? Any others Simon has talked about?"

"None! Just the five."

Based on the grids that she discovered in the encampment, she was confident he had told the truth. Nevertheless, there were still a few questions that plagued her. "How did you pass security with the code? The procedure at all facilities is to turn over all electronic equipment, briefcases, et cetera. You're only allowed to enter basically with your knowledge." Max noticed Stanton was also curious for an answer.

After a slight hesitation, the mole revealed, "My wristwatch."

"Your watch?"

"The watch contains a *Quick Response*, or QR code, a mosaic square that functions similar to a bar code. I used the reader on the touchpad to scan the code. Simon programmed the QR code to first embed the backdoor code into the systems operating program, and then to access the cloud. I would locate the failsafe code within the operating system and upload a copy of the code to the cloud," the mole stated matter-of-factly.

Both Stanton and Max were aware the touchpad was multi-functional. Not only was it used for fingerprint security access, it also functioned as a QR reader to scan the QR code.

"Why did you need the watch? You said you downloaded the backdoor code from the cloud."

"I lied." He smirked. "I only had access to upload, not download."

"Where's the watch?"

"I assume he has it." The mole glanced toward Stanton and shrugged his shoulders.

"Major, would you please retrieve this man's personal belongings?"

Stanton did not want to leave the room at that point. "Let me call the sergeant?"

Max remained silent while he placed the call and the mole stared at the photos.

"He'll bring them in a moment," Stanton announced.

While they waited, there were a few more questions Max wanted to ask. They were not directly pertinent to the case, but she thought the answers could shed further light. "Why did you return to the encampment after Taylor?"

"Simon only gave me one QR code at a time. He changed the backdoor code for each facility. I had just received the one for Folsom when I was captured. That's the one in the watch."

"Why did you go along with Simon's plan in the first place?"

The mole seemed the most hesitant to answer that specific question. But after pondering and reasoning he had nothing to lose, he unleashed a response. "While attending Harvard, Simon caught me changing grades for students in the database in exchange for tuition money. He agreed to say nothing, but promised one day he'd call in the favor. Years later, to my misfortune, I was contacted by Simon; he reminded me of the outstanding IOU."

Max thought back to Noble's tales of La Fratellanza and how Simon had used similar ploys in the past. Remarkably, it was how he engaged the U.S. Secretary of the Treasury. Simon ultimately landed a position in the Department of Treasury commissioned to design the TARP system. It provided Simon the perfect opportunity to misappropriate billions of dollars that he manipulated for his cause.

"And then what?" she persisted.

"He soured the pot."

"What does that mean?"

"He made an offer I couldn't refuse. He found out somehow that my hacking days weren't over and that I was siphoning funds from some unsavory characters. Let's just say I'd rather wrestle with you guys than end up in a meat grinder. Anyway, he said he was going to get me a job with the Department of Homeland Security in their National Cyber Security Division, and I was to sit tight until he got back in touch with me. Shortly after settling into my new assignment—Simon called in the IOU. The rest you know," the mole responded glumly.

There was a knock at the door.

Stanton answered and retrieved the bag handed to him. He walked over to the table, turned the bag upside down, and emptied its contents.

The mole attempted to reach for the watch, as Max held up her hand to stop him.

"Tell me where the code is stored."

"It's under the sliding panel on the back of the watch face."

Max turned the watch over and slid open the panel. Displayed inside was a mosaic square. "Ingenious," she said as she handed the watch to Stanton.

While Stanton perused the evidence, Max stared at the mole. She envisioned him out of the fatigues he was wearing and in place, black pants and white shirt with a black pencil tie. *Definitely, a nerd*, she thought, *this is not your average terrorist. He is telling all he knows.*

Stanton looked up from the watch and asked, "Deputy Director

Ford, I'd like to ask a question."

"Certainly, major." At that point, Max had extracted all she could from the mole. Unquestionably, the information validated their concerns.

"From my earlier interrogation, you denied knowing the other recruits and their assignments. Do you hold to your statement?"

"Yes, except for the other techies. We were cordoned off from the others. Each day the same recruit would escort us back and forth from our dormitory to the command center. He would remind us that our work was highly classified and unknown to the others. So we were forced to take our meals in the dormitory and not in the mess hall and we had a separate courtyard for recreational activities."

"So you never heard the others talking?"

The mole took a moment to compose his thoughts. Then he admitted, "On a few occasions we'd overhear conversations as we passed by a group. They'd talk about how they'd fight to keep their country safe. I thought it an odd statement—they were all Americans."

Max turned to Stanton. They exchanged looks to acknowledge they had enough information.

"Please have the prisoner returned to his cell," Max ordered. She quickly returned her stack of papers to her briefcase and left the room. At the end of the corridor, she encountered the sergeant and inquired, "I need to use one of the offices for about an hour."

"Sure thing, Max. Follow me."

19
WATCH FOR THE WATCH

Noble, we have our confirmation. Simon is heading east, first to Minnesota, then south to Indiana. And you were right that he's hitting Mississauga last, assuming he stays his course."

"Slow down Max. It's great news, but do you know when and how?"

Max explained the results of her interview with the detainee. She elaborated on the mole's task to download and install the backdoor. Then she explained how he would locate the program containing the failsafe code and proceed to upload a copy of the code to the cloud. Simon would later modify the code, if all went according to plan.

Noble could not help but wonder why Simon did not try to recruit the mole at Harvard, to join La Fratellanza, rather than try so hard to coax him. *Perhaps, he was a backup candidate, but that was then.* "You said that the code was in his wristwatch?"

"Yes, you'd have to admit it's quite ingenious."

"Quite." Noble had a mind's eye view of the gold watches Simon had presented to each of his La Fratellanza brothers. Each watch stored a copy of their thesis on a microchip. "Yes, Simon is quite ingenious."

"The mole also said that Simon was scheduled to hit the St. Paul facilities on May ninth and then four days later change the code at the Carmel facility. Mississauga is scheduled for July fifth."

"July fifth?"

"Yes, I questioned the date as well. He swears it is the fifth. So at least we know we have time on our side."

"I'm not so sure. Simon is on the run and he might become desperate. He still has to hack into three systems, plant his backdoor, steal a snapshot of the failsafe code, and return later to install his bastardized version. He'll need time. He could also accelerate the timing. We can't be sure of the dates anymore. But why did he originally schedule lapses between breaches over several months?"

"The mole said he didn't want to raise suspicion and have it look like sabotage, triggering an investigation. Noble, he also said Simon modified each failsafe code to include a specific date designed to shut down the grid. Those dates must already be hardcoded in the three control centers he has already compromised. Nothing has occurred thus far. It has to be a common date, or at least within proximity of each other, to inflict the greatest damage when the grids are shut down."

"Brilliant, Max. I'll have the FERC chairman gain me access to the individual operating systems at the facilities and to identify the location of the failsafe programs."

"If anyone can crack the code, it will be you. You'll find the date, boss. Then we'll know exactly how much time we have to stop him."

"I hope you're right. Burke is already in hot pursuit of Simon, although up to now the leads are not definitive.

"At least we know that the New Year's Eve bombings in Europe were a diversion."

"We can't be sure of that either. They still could be trial runs for future attacks. I spoke with Enzo earlier and he reported that they've souped up security, and thus far no activity."

Max knew that Enzo Borgini, the executive director of police services for Interpol, the International Criminal Police Organization, had been tracking Simon down for nearly as many years as Noble. First, he worked alongside Hamilton on the sting operation in Florence and later he worked closely with Noble in Lyon on the European New

Year's Eve assassination attempts, ultimately making the link to Simon. He has as much at stake as Noble does in wanting Simon put away permanently.

"I need to call Enzo back and pass along the descriptions of the other disguises and the names Simon may try to use."

"You mean if we fail to capture him and he attempts to enter Europe."

"I don't want to contemplate that scenario. It's almost certain Simon is planning to take down five major sections of the national power grid—creating a national emergency in the U.S." Noble shuddered at the thought. He quickly switched gears. "How's Stanton doing with the rest of the interrogations?"

"He has a few more to wrap up. I really haven't had time to discuss it with him in detail. I am meeting with him later today. We can review his reports when I return tomorrow."

"No Max, I want Stanton here tomorrow prepared for a full debriefing. Have him bring the watch with him."

"Noble, I can bring the watch. I'll be back in Washington in the morning."

"There is something else I need you to handle. I want you to fly down south and interview Simon's mother."

"Down south, where?"

"She is in a nursing home in Orlando..." Noble stopped in midsentence. "Maybe that's why Simon's not hitting the Florida grid."

"You're trying to tell me Simon has a heart?" Max snickered.

"Of course, he has a heart. It's slightly tepid, rather than stone cold."

"That's more of a reason for you to interview her, not me. Noble, seriously, I need to be in Washington. We need to continue pouring over the evidence. We must stop Simon."

He listened to her plea, but then insisted, "Max, she'll be more receptive to you. Years ago, after La Fratellanza implicated Simon, Hamilton sent me out to Berkeley to interview the parents. It was a full-court-charm-press but nothing they told me was helpful. All I got from them was the usual. 'My son leads a busy life...he travels a lot... he calls occasionally...we don't know much about his business.' I had a feeling at the time there was something they weren't telling me, but nothing tangible enough for me to pursue further. Now she's older, feeble, and alone, maybe you can get something out of her."

Max succumbed. "How did you find her anyway?"

"Burke tracked her down."

"What, Burke works for the SIA now? I thought he was going to head up the D.C. bureau."

"Of the moment, Federal Agent Burke is on our team. He has been extremely helpful and he is one of the few people who are acquainted with the details of this case."

"Noble, do you always have to play it so close to the vest? I understand it's Simon, but you employ hundreds of minions who can do some of this work. Why is it always you, me, and Burke?" Max sounded tired.

Noble reacted calmly. "Look, we admittedly don't have all the pieces. It may have to do with our national security. It may have to do with other rogue elements in the government. We need to be the first to learn what is going on, without diluting our efforts. We can handle this on our own for now, Max."

"Burke found her, let him interview her." It was not working. Max dug in her heels.

So Noble tried the opposite approach. "Max, we don't know what the hell's going on! Simon could be some Islamic fanatic or simply an Alinsky disciple! In either case, he's dangerous!"

"Perhaps, he's both." Max answered in a calmer manner.

Noble lightened the conversation and quipped, "It's starting to feel like a British bedroom farce. I can't tell who's sleeping with whom anymore."

Max finally capitulated. "I agree we can't comprehend what he's planning if we don't understand the underlying motives."

"Go talk to his mother. You'll only be gone one day. Two hours down. Two hours back. Leave first thing in the morning, you'll be home by dinner."

Max changed her tenor. "So tell me about her?"

In a paternalistic voice, Noble explained that Ann Hall was an investigative reporter for Emit Magazine, and later became a Professor of Journalism at Berkeley. Simon's father died several years ago of a heart attack and Ann suffered a stroke that left her partially paralyzed. She now resides in the Guardian Care Nursing & Rehabilitation Center in Orlando.

"That's all I know, except that I can count on you to find out the rest. And Max, go easy on her, she has a heart condition."

"Great, now I'll have to handle her with extra-soft kid gloves."

"Thanks Max, my instincts tell me she has one of the missing pieces."

"Are we finished?" She asked as she looked at her watch. She had fifteen minutes; she did not want to be late.

"Don't forget to tell Stanton I want him in Washington tomorrow afternoon. And make sure he brings the watch."

Max smiled as her mood softened. "I won't. Good night, Noble."

20
A MINOR INFRACTION

Max drove slowly looking for the address. She noticed the flashing neon sign on the right that read BAR and pulled into the nearest parking space. She sauntered into the saloon and walked over to the bar stool on the end. Without warning, she found herself caught in a warm embrace, one she admittedly enjoyed, although rarely.

"Hey, what can I get you?"

"A beer, please." She puckered her nose as she perused the joint. "Why have you picked this place?"

"To be off base."

Max flashed an impish smile. "Or to be on third base?"

Stanton shot back a mischievous grin and then changed the drift. "You were really great today. I had spent hours whacking at that guy and got nowhere."

"I guess I had the advantage of solid evidence."

"Well, it's blatantly clear that Simon was provisioning the encampment for his protection—while in the process of attempting to paralyze our country."

Max did not share her thoughts about Baari's possible role, according to Hank, or that Baari could have set the stage for Simon's plot. Stanton, and for that matter Burke, only knew that they were pursuing a notorious terrorist attempting to disrupt the electric grids. "What's important is to stop him before he carries out his plan."

"We did obtain some bizarre information from the other interrogations but the mole corroborated what we uncovered. I suppose the key element—is the code."

"I filled Noble in. He'll take it from here. Trust me, he's the best." Max veered from the subject. She no longer wanted to discuss the case. She had something else occupying her mind. "Are you really going to sign on to the president's security detail?"

"Yeah, it will be a nice change. After three tours, I was reassigned to Dugway as a training instructor. It was a good gig, but now it's time to move on."

"You'll be putting your life on the line every day for the president." Max observed with genuine concern.

"I put my life on the line every day for my country. It's the least I can do. Besides, I'll be closer to you." Stanton smiled and leaned over for a kiss, but he was too late.

Max pushed him back and warned, "Not too close." Then she leaned in and retrieved the kiss she had craved. She was still waffling between entering a relationship and giving up a slice of her independence, not convinced she could manage both. Then there was her career that had always taken precedence.

"When do you have to go back to Washington?" he asked.

"Actually, Noble's sending me to Orlando to speak with Simon's mother."

"He thinks she knows something?" Stanton quizzed, somewhat surprised.

Max explained that Noble had interviewed her years earlier, but he felt she might be more willing to speak now that so much time had passed. "And she's quite ill. It may be our last opportunity to uncover another piece of Simon's puzzling life."

"And he thinks you can add a woman's touch." he chided.

Max feigned a pout. She despised the excuse used to send her out on a case, but she admitted to herself that it usually worked. Her expression slipped back to her deputy director mode. "I may be going to Orlando, but you are going to Washington." Max reached into her pocket and said, "Here, Noble wants you to deliver the wristwatch to him. And be prepared to brief him fully on the interrogations."

It was Stanton's turn to pout. "Then we'll have to cut our evening short. I still have a few questions for our elite group of detainees."

Max looked at her watch. "And I have an early flight."

"Can you give me a ride back to the base?" Stanton asked.

"How did you get here?"

"I walked. It's only three miles."

"What, were you planning to walk back or were you planning to get a ride to my hotel?" Max played the interrogator.

"I had hoped for the latter." He moved in for another kiss and then whispered in her ear, "I'll make it up to you in Washington."

"Pay the tab, Major."

21
A MOTHER'S TORMENT

Max eased the door open gently and peered inside the room. Still, the noisy hinges were enough to awaken the elderly woman lying in the bed. Ann Hall was in her late seventies, although she appeared frail and much older. Her silver hair, pulled in a tight bun behind her head, provided no frame for her face, a colorless face that blended into the starched, white pillowcase. The pale blue eyes that gazed in Max's direction provided the only color.

"Come in," she spoke in a robust voice, belying the body.

"Mrs. Hall?"

"Yes. They told me I was to have a visitor today, but not one so young and attractive. Please sit down my dear."

Max walked toward her, but stopped short to move the chair placed next to the wall closer to the bed. As she sat down on the seat, positioning herself at face level, she found it perplexing that the lovely woman was Simon's mother.

"Mrs. Hall, my name is Maxine Ford. I'm Deputy Director at the States Intelligence Agency and I'm here to ask you some questions about your son."

"Call me Annie, dear. However, I'm afraid there is not much I can tell you. I haven't seen my son for years. Although, he still pays the bills for this place for which I am grateful. I honestly don't know how I can help."

"Do you know about your son's activities?"

"I've heard he'd been accused of committing horrific acts. Someone from your agency came to speak with my husband and me years ago. Even now, I find it impossible to believe Simon is involved. I don't know any more now than I did all those years ago. I'm sorry, but I don't think I'll be able to help you," she answered in earnest, but in a softer tone befitting her age.

"Excuse me Annie, but you look awfully uncomfortable. May I straighten your pillows?" Max stood up, and while making the necessary adjustments, half-whispered, "Why doesn't Simon come to visit?" As she pulled away, she noticed tears welling up in Annie's eyes. She stepped back and gave Annie a moment to compose herself, and then repeated the question. Max repositioned herself back in the chair and waited for a response.

Much to Max's surprise she heard Annie assert, "I'm old, alone and dying! Then she spoke more forcefully, "What good does it serve now?"

Max was not sure what she was referring to, but she remained silent and let her continue.

"Do you have time for a story, dear? I've only told two other people. One is dead, the other is alive."

"Please take whatever time you need." Max realized she was still wearing her coat and sensed she would be there for the long haul. She pulled her coat off her shoulders, retrieved her arms from the sleeves, and let the fabric fall onto the back of the chair. Once again, settled back into the seat, she prepared for what this elderly woman was about to convey.

In a voice even more resilient, Annie began to tell her story. "Before Simon came into this world, I was an investigative journalist for Emit Magazine. I'd been given a bunch of fluff pieces to probe, but there was one story on the horizon that I fought for bitterly and won," she boasted with pride and smiled for the first time. "In 1966,

I was given an assignment to travel to Saudi Arabia and interview a woman who was making inroads in the television industry." Annie continued methodically to lay out the facts as they unfolded. "A few years earlier in 1964, King Faisal had come into power and attempted to modernize and reform the country, and not necessarily within the strict construction of Islamic tenets."

Max knew it was still a society that forbade women to venture into many aspects of the *Islamic* man's world. She wondered if that was the basis for her story.

Annie continued. "But things started to change. In 1965, Saudi conducted its first nationwide televised broadcast. What grabbed my attention was a young woman who spoke on Saudi Radio. In 1966, she became the first Saudi woman to appear on Saudi TV. I traveled to Riyadh to interview her. But it was an opportunity short-lived." Then Annie started to speak as though she were struggling to reconstruct the events in her mind as she remembered them. She described the day she was scheduled to meet for the interview at the newly established television station—only to be met by a mob protest. She explained that a religious fanatical group opposed the modernization, protesting it was in defiance of Koranic law for women to appear on television. It was considered an act of insolence.

Annie again picked up the pace. "As I entered the building, gunshots rang out. A security guard had killed the leader of the mob. I saw the shooting. At the time, I had no way of knowing that the victim was one of King Faisal's own nephews."

Max vaguely recalled reading an article by Nick Ludington, a writer for the Associated Press, who reported on the assassination of King Faisal in March of 1975. Prince Faisal Ibn Musaed, the nephew, admitted killing his uncle in retaliation for killing his brother who was the leader of the television station mob. Max stayed focused on the conversation.

"I didn't understand the political significance, I'm still not sure there was any. But for whatever reason, I was immediately ushered back to my hotel and ordered to leave the country straightaway." Without warning, Annie stopped speaking. She displayed yet another mood swing. This time she became withdrawn. Moments before, Annie's animated speech sounded as if she were reading a bedtime thriller. Now she appeared to be at a loss for words.

Max was reluctant to proceed with her questions, but as the seconds ticked by, she found it necessary to urge Annie to continue. First she asked, "Would you like me to get you a glass of water?"

"No dear, I just need a moment."

The awkward silence remained briefly. After Annie exhaled a deep breath she continued, "I refused to be thrown out of the country. I had a story to report!" she stressed, "It was my big break! So I climbed into my abaya and replaced the hijab, my headscarf."

Annie explained to Max that the long black robe they call an abaya was required to be worn by non-Muslim women, but not the hijab. "But I preferred to wear the headscarf to cover my blond hair. I felt less conspicuous and more able to blend in with the crowd." Then she announced, "I left the hotel prepared to challenge my exile." All of a sudden, as before, her speech trailed off and became almost soundless.

Max was anxious for her to finish, but remained silent out of respect. As she shifted in her chair Annie reemerged, but with less gusto.

"As I ventured out of the hotel and began to wend my way to the local police station a block away, I noticed a black sedan parked across the street. I sensed they were watching me but I kept on walking."

Max studied Annie and noticed her biting her lip as she took long deep breaths through her nostrils. She sensed Annie was on the verge of revealing a significant experience. On impulse, she reached for Annie's hand in an offer of support, but Annie resisted and waved her off.

"I need to finish my story dear. I picked up my pace, wanting to reach my destination. As I approached an alley, right before my turn into the police station, a hand reached out from the darkness and jerked my arm pulling me into the passageway. I was thrown to the ground. Before I realized what was happening, two boys had me pinned by my shoulders, preventing me from moving."

Annie began to tremble, swallowing several times in an obvious attempt to stave off the tears. Then in the strongest voice she could muster, she shouted, "The other boy raped me! They covered my face with my hijab—I couldn't see who or how many had their way with me."

She began to sob uncontrollably.

Max tried to recollect the last time she felt so helpless. She did not know how to respond. The only thing she thought to do was to reach over and hold Annie in her arms. A few moments later, Annie's sobs began to recede. Max felt the weight of her body press into her embrace as Annie began to relax.

"I'm okay dear," she murmured, as she lightly pushed Max away. "It has been many years and it's a relief to be able to tell someone—but there's more."

"Are you sure you want to continue?"

"If you're willing to listen." Annie offered, followed by a gentle smile. "The next morning I left the country never to look back."

"Excuse me, but why didn't you report them to the police?"

"My dear, in those days in Middle Eastern countries, if a woman were to report being raped she'd be accused of having illicit sex. The man would have never been charged for committing the crime."

"Didn't you say they were boys?"

"It sickens me to think that someone so young can be so evil. They must have been twelve or thirteen-years-old. Worse yet, I don't think it was random. I'm positive it had something to do with what I witnessed at the television station. But that was a long time ago."

"You said only two other people knew what had happened."

"Yes, and in a way they became victims too. After returning home, I crawled into a shell and became quiet and reserved. I was twenty-five-years-old and a newlywed with my whole life ahead of me, but I couldn't bear to have my husband touch me. He acknowledged something had happened while I was away on assignment, but he assumed I would tell him when I was ready. He was a very patient and gentle man."

"You were very fortunate."

"For the time being," Annie allowed. "But within a few short weeks, I learned I was pregnant." She continued, but each word dripped with grief. "I'm a devout catholic so abortion was out of the question. That night I had intercourse with my husband and began my deception. With my eyes closed the entire time, I tried to wipe away the past. My skin hurt with every touch and there was nothing I could do to overcome the anguish. I remained in our marriage bed and deceived the man I loved more than life. I know it was illogical and proved to be destructive. Over the next eight months, I prayed for a blond, blue-eyed, premature, healthy baby to arrive." Annie spoke with unfettered self-incrimination. She closed her eyes in an attempt to wrestle with reality.

Max gave Annie time to compose herself and then asked, "What was the outcome?"

Staring out into the room, she sighed, "My baby boy had olive-toned skin with dark hair and large beautiful brown eyes." She turned slightly to face Max and divulged, "Understandably, my husband felt betrayed. Yet, he never broached the subject until we returned home with our new baby boy named Simon. That is when I broke out in tears and told him the entire story, precisely as I relayed to you. He was an amazing man. He didn't blame me for what happened in Riyadh and he promised to rear our son as his own. I promised to end my career as a journalist. But he never forgave me for the deceit—for not believing in him enough to tell him the truth from the beginning. That was my cross to bear and bear it I have. Unfortunately, it gets heavier as the years go by."

"May I ask in what way?" Annie had been forthcoming, but Max suspected the story did not end there.

"As the years passed, I believed my husband had forgiven me, until one day when we had a bitter argument. A month earlier, he had lost his job. Bills and frustration mounted. He reached his limit and in a rare and unusual outburst, my husband shouted that he could no longer pay the college tuition for my bastard son. The quarrel deteriorated at a rapid pace. We rehashed the entire incident. Having returned home from college for a surprise visit, we were not aware that Simon was in the house. He must have overheard our conversation because after the shouting subsided we heard the kitchen door slam shut. Simon had stormed out."

"What happened when Simon returned home?"

"He never mentioned it, nor did we. Conceivably, that was a grave mistake. Simon must have suspected long before that day. He didn't resemble either of us, except for his smile that mirrored mine. A smile he perfected through emulation and used when necessary to charm his way out of trouble. As a youngster, he shied away from malicious behavior, but tended to be mischievous in nature. Simon always tried to pull off the impossible. I apologize dear, I'm getting off-track. A year after the revelation of his birth, he dropped out of college and disappeared for a few years. After that, he would pop in and out of our lives, but never for a prolonged period. He never brought up what he had overheard. It did create some tension at times." Annie lamented. "It's a sad tale my dear, and you've been very patient. Does any of this help?"

"To be honest, I'm not sure. It may explain his actions over the years, once we figure out what he is involved in. I don't mean to be vague. I wish I had more information to share. Do you mind if I ask you a few more questions?"

Annie cocked her head. "You want to know more about Simon?"

"You haven't mentioned anything about his adolescence."

Annie answered with candor, "I'm ashamed to say, both Simon's father and I were less than ideal parents. For the first few years, I would look at his precious face with those dark eyes peering back at me. I'd then begin to relive that awful day and then recoil at the thought. It probably wasn't until he was four or five that I began to look at my son through a mother's eyes."

"What about his father?"

"I said he was a gentle man. He kept his word and was kind to Simon. He played with him, as a father would with a son, but was not overtly affectionate. Although over time, I started to believe that our family had come together. But that was before his genius began to emerge." Annie's face appeared contorted, as she elaborated with obvious regret.

Max, entranced by her mix of emotions, allowed her to continue uninterrupted.

"Simon's school principal recognized his extraordinary intelligence, as well, and asked us for permission to have him tested. We agreed. He scored one hundred and ninety. Only one other child in the world at the time had a higher IQ. I remember his name was Kim Ung-Yong, born in 1962 in Korea, with reportedly an IQ of over two hundred and ten. At the time, I was researching child geniuses hoping to learn how to live with one."

Max was dumbfounded. *Simon was highly intelligent, but I had no idea to what extent,* she thought with some trepidation, as she reflected on the havoc Simon had committed thus far. The concerns heightened not knowing what he was planning next.

Annie caught sight of the expression on Max's face but continued to describe Simon's childhood. She saw no point in holding back.

Max listened with great interest.

"He started to live in his own bubble." Annie attributed it to the lack of affection Simon had received as a child and as he grew older, he became more detached. "When I asked why he wouldn't play with the other kids, he'd reply, 'Eagles never flock.' So he spent hours alone in his room playing his music turned up loud trying to shut out the world and me."

Max sensed Annie was about to retreat into self-blame and interjected, "He must have had some interests other than his music"

"Other than his obsession with Bach, he learned to rely on himself for emotional stimulation and gratification. He spent much of his adolescence attacking challenges he'd create for himself. His perpetual challenge was to exceed his expectations." Annie paused, and with an odd sense of maternal pride, she added, "It appeared to be a creed by which he lived." Soon she reverted to sadness once again, and bemoaned, "It also forced his father out of his life."

Suddenly, Max had a flashback of the scorched CD recovered from Simon's getaway car. "You mentioned Bach, an odd choice for a young boy."

"Bach's *Art of Fugue* was one of my favorites and the last of Bach's great monothematic cycles. I would play it often when Simon was a baby. Then one day the album disappeared until I heard it playing repeatedly from his room."

"Outside of music, did Simon have other interests?"

"My son truly was a genius. At eight-years-old, he built his own computer. At the age of ten, he had designed his own programming language. I didn't understand a lot about technology at the time, but he said he wrote a language similar to c-o something or other."

Max interjected, "You mean COBOL?"

"Yes, that was it. In fact, I remember him saying that Bach's genius inspired his code. I had no idea what he meant. But he explained that his code was a permutation of this COBOL you mentioned. That's about all I know. He's been out of our lives for years. It was all techie gibberish to me. Does any of this make sense?"

At the mention of Simon developing his own code, Max glommed onto a possible twist in their theory. She promptly answered, "You've given me a clearer picture of Simon's life, which may prove to be helpful." Max concluded there was no additional information to glean. She needed to get back to Washington. She needed Noble's expertise to sort out all she had uncovered. "Annie, I've taken enough of your time and I thank you for sharing your very intimate story. It will be handled in confidence and with the utmost discretion."

"Oh, I thank you dear," she offered with great sincerity. "You've helped me to lift an enormous burden from my shoulders, one I've been carrying all these years—ashamed and afraid to tell anyone and my time is running out. You struck me immediately as a sincere person of intelligence. You know dear, as a former journalist, I refined my instinct for trusting people," she boasted with a tender smile.

Max leaned over and kissed Annie on the forehead, surprised by her own display of affection. She readjusted her pillows once again and smoothed out her bedcover. For reasons Max could not fathom, she empathized with the lovely but lonely woman lying in the bed. "Here's my number. Please call me if there's anything you need."

Before accepting the business card and with tears again welling up in her eyes, she asked in a quivering voice, "I have but one request. If Simon is guilty of these horrible crimes and you're able to capture him, please spare my son's life."

Annie took Max's card with her trembling hand.

Max could feel that both of their hands were shaky.

Slowly, Annie's gentle smile returned and she said, "You're very kind, my dear."

Max forced herself to return the smile and then left for the airport to return to Washington.

22
KNOCK KNOCK

South Sacramento is thirty miles southwest of Folsom, and a place reportedly housing large-scale counterfeiting operations, especially in the production of documents for illegals. While the major operations had been shut down, a cottage industry of ex-cons selling their talent continued to thrive. For the most part the local police left them alone, hoping to use them to land bigger fish. FBI agents had swept the seedier neighborhoods weeding out the list of counterfeiters supplied to them by the local authorities. Agent Burke took the short list; he arrived at the last address.

"Who's there?" asked the voice from the other side of the intercom.

"A customer," Burke replied.

From the peephole, the shop owner detected Burke was no ordinary customer. The precision-style haircut was a giveaway. He opened the creaky door. "What can I do for you Agent?"

Burke flashed a photo of Simon and the composite drawing derived from the used car dealer's description. "Have you seen this man?"

"He doesn't look familiar."

Burke edged his way passed the door. "You know, you're starting to look very familiar."

"Come on man, I'm just trying to earn a living." He pointed to the sign over the counter that read, *Passport and ID Photos.* "This is a legitimate business."

"Look at them again." Burke held the photo and drawing under the light fixture hanging from above to provide a better view, not that he conceived the lighting was the problem.

"Oh, yeah. He came in for a passport photo."

"No, he came in for photos for passports and driver's licenses. Does that jog your memory?"

"Okay, okay." The forger described the various documents he prepared for Simon and each of the different disguises. "But he never looked like that guy in the photo you're holding."

"What else did he ask you to do?"

"Nothing—just to prepare the documents."

Burke was an expert at reading body language. He persisted with his questioning. The forger was lying, but his expression changed ever so slightly. *Finally, a breakthrough,* he thought. He could feel it coming.

"On second thought, he might have asked for information," the forger admitted as he rubbed his fingers together looking for payment.

Burke did not relent.

"As I recall, he wanted to know where he could get his car detailed. It was worth a C-note to him. It's got to be worth something to you."

"Hey genius, my payment will be my faulty memory when I meet up with your parole officer." Burke handed him the pad of paper and pen that was lying on the counter. "Write down the address."

The forger reluctantly obliged.

"If this doesn't pan out, get ready for a homecoming back in your cell block."

Burke opened the creaky door and left.

23
DATE AND TIME

Noble heard a rap on the door. "What?"

"And a good morning to you."

"Sorry Doris, you startled me," he said without turning to greet his intruder. Noble had been staring intently at the five grids on the large screen display. They were copies of the same grids discovered in the underground encampment. He felt as though they had transfixed him for hours.

"What time did you arrive?"

"Yesterday morning."

"Noble, you have to stop pulling these all-nighters. This case is going to drive you to your grave."

He turned and smiled. "No truer words spoken. I managed a few winks on the sofa."

"I'll get you a fresh pot of coffee and order you a hot breakfast from the dining room." As she turned to head out the door, she could hear Noble say, "Thanks, you're a doll."

"Start off with what you know," he said aloud, addressing himself.

He played out the entire scenario logically in his mind. The first security breach was at the control center in Birmingham on November 4. The second was in Taylor on January 6 and the third was in Folsom on March 7. The other centers likely to be breached are in St. Paul on May 9, Carmel on May 13, and the last one on July 5 in Mississauga, Canada.

"The last three dates could change if Simon chooses to escalate his timetable."

"Did you say something?" Doris asked, as she walked over to the conference table and placed the food tray down beside him.

"Just talking to myself. I didn't hear you come in."

"Eat this, it will help your think more clearly," she ordered in a motherly tone.

"I wasn't hungry until I smelled the bacon. Thanks. And Doris, please hold my calls, except the short list." Noble glanced at his watch. "Also, I'm expecting Major Stanton to arrive at eleven o'clock, please send him in."

"Eat." Doris left the room.

Noble moved his papers aside and slid the tray in front of him. As he downed his eggs and bacon and took several swigs of coffee, he maintained eye contact with the large screen display. Suddenly, something caught his attention. He focused on the numbers scribbled on each of the upper right-hand corners of the electrical grids. Using the virtual keyboard, he typed in each of the numbers with the corresponding dates of the past and expected breaches. Once again, he focused on the monitor.

Birmingham	11/4/2016	309
Taylor	1/6/2017	6
Folsom	3/7/2017	66
St. Paul	5/9/2017	129
Carmel	5/13/2017	133
Mississauga	7/5/2017	186

"Odd, the first number is the largest and the others are sequential from low to high." In his own world, he continued to speak aloud as he stared at the monitor. "They're multiples of three, even odder." He continued to concentrate on the numbers. "Of course!"

Unexpectedly, the buzzer aroused him. "Yes, Doris."

"Agent Burke is on the line."

"Burke."

"We found the forger. He had no clue what Simon looked like, but he took photos of him in three different disguises. Simon walked away with forged driver's licenses and passports."

"Did you confiscate his camera?"

"No. Simon took the memory card. But I sent in the sketch artist and I think we have three pretty good likenesses. Also, get this. Simon asked if our forger could recommend the name of a good car detailer. I tracked him down and he reported that a man fitting one of the descriptions brought in a white Ford Bronco and asked to have it painted navy blue. I've updated the APB—Director, he's one clever son-of-a-bitch."

"Trust me, he hasn't used half of the tricks in his bag." Noble harked back to Maryann's mention of contact lenses found in the toiletry kit in Simon's duffle bag. However, Simon did not need to wear contacts, so he was either changing the color of his eyes or the retina scan. He enlightened Burke to the fact. "Good work. Are the helicopters in the sky?"

"Yes, but no sightings as of yet. He could be taking the back roads or traveling at night as I had suggested. But we'll keep on his tail."

"Keep me posted."

"Will do, Director."

Noble made a mental note to give a heads-up to Enzo about the additional disguises. Burke was right; Simon was smart, tremendously smart, somewhere off the charts. And while every bone in Noble's body ached to nail Simon, his first priority was to break the code and save the electric grids from shutting down. He was antsy to get his hands on the wristwatch and to hear Stanton's briefing, hoping other clues would emerge.

∽

It was 9:50 a.m. Noble continued to stare at the grids with glazed eyes a skosh longer and then removed them from the monitor. He left the conference room to return his breakfast tray to Doris, and he was pleased to see that the major had arrived early.

"Major, thank you for making the trip." He shook Stanton's hand and escorted him back to the conference room. He glanced back toward Doris.

"I know. Hold your calls."

"Director, I take it you've been waiting for this?" Stanton handed Noble the watch.

Noble excitedly turned the watchband over and slid open the panel. "Amazing."

"According to our mole, the QR code contains the backdoor code for the Folsom facility only. Simon cleverly changed the code slightly for each facility."

"The backdoor code doesn't concern me except that it may help me to identify the failsafe code that I need to crack."

"Of course, you'd have legitimate access to the facilities operating system without needing the backdoor." Stanton observed.

"What have you derived from the interrogations?"

"May I?" Stanton gestured toward the virtual keyboard.

"Be my guest."

The major tapped away furiously at the keyboard until he accessed his cloud and then downloaded a document to display on the monitor.

Noble studied the screen as the major spoke.

"Out of one hundred and nine detainees, we were able to ascertain that ten were recruited to provide technical support for the command center. Our mole was the leader of this group. Their job was to build an impregnable communications center for the underground encampment, one that could withstand a bunker buster bomb. We showed several photos of the other detainees to the techies and they identified five that played the role of recruiter."

"How were the detainees recruited?"

"Aside from our mole who was recruited directly by Simon, the others were bombarded with Facebook postings and emails. They were identified through various networking sources; many were disaffected loners. Simon must have targeted countless potentials and selected few. They contacted the recruiter and the recruiter arranged a meeting. Once on board the recruiter presented the required identification; a photo badge from the Department of Homeland Security."

"Obviously, Simon's handiwork," Noble interjected.

"They were led to believe they were enlisting in a top secret classified mission sanctioned by the president." Stanton explained that after they signed on and the training began, they were further misled to believe the mission was to prepare for an impending attack. He continued at length, describing the different forms of training they received and each of the roles they would play. Their testimonies varied, but one point was constant. "They insisted their mission was to protect America."

"Do you think it was a ploy? Covering up for some other cause?"

"I'm not sure, Director."

"What about the training materials from the encampment? All the evidence led us to the 'jihadi cool' indoctrination and to al-Qaeda."

"Director, I teach my men that the way to defeat the enemy is to understand the ideology by which they want to destroy you. You need to get into their heads. They may have been convinced that al-Qaeda was the enemy as a pretense to lure them into the fold. It might explain that damn mantra."

Noble kept the questioning going, but he was confident the recruits were part of Baari's original plan as president, but not important to Simon's plot, which was taking a different tack. He had deciphered that although Baari and Simon had moved in the same direction, their motives were unrelated. It was purely a confluence of events that complemented his strategy. A significant point, one the major did not need to know at the time.

"Anything else, Major?"

"No sir, other than what do we do with them?"

"Continue to detain them. Do you have facilities to allow them some open space?"

"Yes, we have a few empty dormitories that aren't in use."

"The detainees who committed the murders in the Dead Zone

should continue to be treated as prisoners. I want all other detainees out of confinement and free to speak with one another. Give them some benefits, recreation time, TV's, you decide. Express regret for having to detain them. Tell them it won't be much longer."

"May I ask what you have in mind, sir?"

"I still have my doubts, but if they believed their stated mission was to protect the country, then we'll have to release them. Give them some rope, but have your team keep their ears open. I need confirmation."

"What about the mole?"

"He is another matter. He's mine for the present. I'll get back to you."

"By the way, the president is pleased that you've accepted his offer. However, he's agreed that you should continue in your present position until we capture Simon or foil his plot. I still need you out in the field."

"Yes sir, I understand. I'm in this to win."

"I don't want to keep you Major, I'm sure you're anxious to get back to Dugway."

"Actually, I'm spending the night in Washington. I fly out tomorrow."

"Have a pleasant evening." Noble smiled as he offered a handshake.

"Thank you, sir." The major departed.

Noble glanced at the time. He had one call he to make before refocusing on the dates.

24
A WORLD AWAY

Ciao *amico mio*," Enzo groaned. "What a pleasant surprise to hear your voice, even at six o'clock in the morning."

"Sorry my friend, I didn't realize the time. Worse yet, I'm not calling with good news."

"*Qual è il problema*, what's the problem?"

"There's a possibility Simon may be heading your way," Noble informed.

Then he proceeded to fill Enzo in on the details concerning the hunt for Simon, but held back on the specifics as they related to the actual plot. Although Enzo was the director of the police services for Interpol, the impending crisis was out of his bailiwick.

"If we don't apprehend him before he crosses our border into Canada, he most probably will head for Europe. He will be traveling with a United Nations Laissez-Passer passport, under the name Aadam Ar-Rashid. Simon's master disguise for Aadam is short curly hair, salt and pepper in color. He will also sport a full beard and wear thick black-framed glasses. I'll send you a composite drawing."

Enzo chuckled. "*Mama mia*, where did he come up with that name?" He always found Simon's array of aliases interesting, especially his selection for al-Fadl, meaning the *redeemer*.

"This time around he is the *righteous teacher*. Please update your database and I'll keep you posted as we move in on his location."

"I'll call it in to headquarters right away."

"You're not in Lyon?"

"No, I'm in San Marino on business."

"San Marino! Don't tell me Interpol has an office there?"

"*Si*," Enzo announced proudly. "We have a National Central Bureau that works in conjunction with the other three police entities on investigative activities, along with any affair involving public order and national security."

Noble remembered from one of Enzo's impromptu history lessons, while working on the European terrorist events in Lyon, that the Republic of San Marino is the oldest independent city-state in the world. Its first governing body dates back to 1243, although the city's first historical documents date back as far as 885. "Nice boondoggle, Enzo."

"There may only be roughly thirty-thousand inhabitants, but our role is vital in promoting cooperation between San Marino and other member countries. You must come and visit next time you travel to Italy amico mio."

"But Enzo, San Marino is not in Italy," Noble teased.

They both knew that geographically, San Marino is located in the country of Italy, but technically wedged in between two Italian regions, Emilia Romagna to the northeast and Montefeltro in the Marche to the southwest, and is totally independent.

"Bravo, you were paying attention. Seriously, San Marino *che bellezza*. She is a beautiful, charming medieval treasure resting on the top of Mount Titano, with a three-hundred-and-sixty degree view. You can even spot the Adriatic Coast, about a forty-minute drive away."

"I would love to Enzo. You may have your wish sooner rather than later, if I don't stop Simon from leaving the country."

"We'll be on alert, but you'll capture him this time. And when you do, I have the perfect place where you can buy that dinner you owe me."

Noble remembered the outstanding debt, very well. It was offered when Enzo agreed secretly to lend him the use of Interpol's WAASP, the top-secret prototype for an aerial surveillance system. It had the capacity to detect underground structures at great depths through solid objects, including mountains. The WAASP was crucial in determining the exact location of the underground encampment that led to the capture of Simon, the second time around.

"Let me guess—dinner in San Marino?"

"When you put Simon away, you'll be doing the world a great favor. Dinner will be my treat. Besides, you must meet my dear friend Giovanni Righi. He owns Ristorante Righi in the Piazza Libertà next to the Public Palace. The food *e fantastico* and Giovanni is a prince of a man. It's the perfect place for a *buongustaio*, a connoisseur like you."

"You're the food lover Enzo. I've never had a disappointing meal in your company."

"Then it's a deal! Wrap up your case and then let's spend some time together. I miss our conversations and the stories we share about Hamilton." At the mention of Hamilton, Noble realized how he too enjoyed his time with Enzo. It was a way of keeping his dear mentor's memory alive. "It's a deal. I'll keep you up to date on Simon's case. Until later my friend."

"Ciao amico mio."

"Ciao."

25

D-DAY DISCOVERED

It had been over two hours since Stanton left. Noble was frustrated. He shifted his focus from the dates to the backdoor code. It did not resemble Simon's past code. He was apprehensive as he remembered Simon's programming code that unlocked the security code for almost any system he encountered. He called the program NOBLE, a mocking honorarium, meaning No Operands Between Logical Expressions.

"How clever Simon. But you've stumped me this time," he digressed, knowing his mumblings were out of earshot from Doris. As he continued to focus on the code displayed on the large screen, he found himself fumbling with the watch. "Damn!" He tossed the watch onto the table and stood up. "I need some air." He hastily passed Doris and grabbed his suit jacket from his office. He made another pass and headed out the door as he announced, "Be back in a while."

As he strolled down Pennsylvania Avenue, his head began to clear and his stomach began to rumble, reminding him that time had slipped away since his last meal. He took a few more zigzags, until he found himself standing in front of Starbucks. He did not procrastinate. He headed straight to the counter. "A double espresso and a turkey rustico, please." Noble was not sure why, but his decisive choices instantly brought back memories of Florence with Hamilton. The time he spent with his mentor before he died was bittersweet. Then he recalled Hamilton's failed attempt to capture Simon in the Vasari Corridor of the Uffizi Gallery. *Simon, it always comes back to you. There will be no peace of mind until you are in my grasp*—a thought that haunted him repeatedly.

"Sir, excuse me sir. That will be ten dollars and eighty cents."

"Sorry." Noble handed the cashier a twenty. He grabbed his change and his goodies and headed for a table in the corner. After a few sips of espresso he felt much more alert, and the sandwich calmed his stomach. As he looked around the room, he could not remember the last time he had ventured out of his office with no destination in mind. It felt good, until he thought, *playtime over.* Having disposed of his empty cup and wrappers, he headed back to the White House ready to tackle the code once again.

"Max called while you were out," Doris announced.

"Why didn't she call me on my xPhad?"

"She did." Doris raised her right hand and waved his phone in the air. "It took me a while to follow the ring."

"I can't remember the last time I left without my phone." He shook his head thinking, *this day is not going well.* "What did she want?"

"She said something about how the code was a permutation."

"What?"

"Max said you'd know more about that stuff. She was running to catch her flight and she'd see you in few hours."

"Great." Noble looked at his watch; it was 4:15. He anticipated another late night once Max arrived. "Doris, I'm going to head home for a quick nap, a shower, and some clean clothes. I'll be back at six o'clock. Go ahead and lock up, but leave a note for Max."

"Noble."

"What?"

"Your phone."

"Thanks, Doris."

Invigorated after a shower and a clean set of clothes, Noble was ready to tackle the code. As he entered his reception area, he was happy to see the light on in the conference room. Max had returned.

"Hey, Boss. You won't believe the story I have to tell."

"Hold on, I know the date that will trigger the national blackout."

"We already know it's July fifth."

"No it's not. Look." Noble pointed to the large screen display. "What do you see?"

Birmingham	11/4/2016	309
Taylor	1/6/2017	6
Folsom	3/7/2017	66
St. Paul	5/9/2017	129
Carmel	5/13/2017	133
Mississauga	7/5/2017	186

"It's a list of the control centers and the dates that were or will be breached. But what are the numbers on the end?"

"Remember the numbers scribbled in the upper right-hand corner of the electric grids you found in the encampment?"

She studied the numbers for a moment and then exclaimed, "Yes! Seeing them in that format—they are Julian dates! The actual number of days elapsed in a given year. For example, the Taylor breach was on January sixth, the sixth day of the year. 3-0-9 is the largest number because it was toward the end of the prior year." With that, she took a deep bow.

"Well done, except technically they are ordinal dates. A Julian date is calculated within a Julian Period in chronological intervals of seven-thousand-nine-hundred and eighty years beginning in the year 4713 BC. Granted, outside of a historical or astronomical context, the date is referred to as the Julian date in today's pop culture."

"Thank you professor, but that just proves the blackout is set for July fifth, the day after our Independence Day?"

"You're forgetting there was another number, also scribbled in the upper right-hand corner of an organization chart, the one with the director of FEMA circled in red. The number was 2-1-4. It was not a reference number as we first thought. Notice the other numbers are multiples of three. I think Simon randomly selected the dates. But 2-1-4 is a positive composite number. The pattern must have been broken for a specific reason."

While Noble was explaining his logic, Max was tapping away on her xPhad. She looked up from the screen. "Give me a moment—I don't believe it—the two hundred and fourteenth day of the year is August second. It is the anniversary of the actual day of the signing of the Declaration of Independence. What does it have to do with FEMA?— unless of course—it was the day they were to be prepared for a national emergency to occur. That would mean someone else is part of Simon's plan." Her expression turned quizzical.

"Max—hold on—according to my history books, on the same day in nineteen thirty-four—Hitler took over as Führer of Germany."

"You're giving me the creeps, Noble. If I have it right, you think Baari's reasoning for wanting to create a national emergency was to induce the public to demand a third term. Then he could rise up out of the ashes like a Phoenix—and when reelected he would have become the commander-in-chief of a new America." She still was not totally convinced that was a reality, but acknowledged, "You have to admire the irony."

Noble raised his hands. "And now it's conveniently timed to occur under President Post's watch." His frustration was evident. "Talk to me about Simon. What did you find out from his mother?"

Max filled him in on the details of Annie's tragic ordeal in 1966 in Riyadh…"Then one horrible day she was embroiled in a shouting match with Simon's father. They were discussing the origin of Simon's birth. Evidently, he heard them arguing and discovered he was a child of rape."

"His illegitimacy and affectionless childhood may be the genesis and explain, in part, how Simon's motives were formed. As he climbed further into his shell, it appears he rapidly became a lone wolf and even more withdrawn," Noble surmised.

"It might also help to explain his vulnerability and infatuation with the Jihadi movement. When I asked more about Simon's childhood, she began to speak of the complications of his genius. That conversation also revealed his extraordinary computer skills."

"The message you left with Doris mentioned the code was a permutation, which is a reordering of the prime form. There are many permutations: retrograde, inversion, et cetera. I'm not sure I understand."

"I'm not sure I understand. Annie, Simon's mother, alluded to the fact that his programming language was inspired by Bach." Max shrugged her shoulders. "I've have no clue what that meant," she admitted.

Noble had a puzzled expression. "Oh, she means combinatorial permutation."

"What?"

"Never mind, it's complicated. But remember the CD found in Simon's car was Bach's *Art of Fugue*."

"That was the same music Annie mentioned that Simon played repeatedly while holed up in his room," Max stated with an element of surprise.

"When Burke sent me the CD, I was curious as to what fugue meant. Sounding a tad Italian, I called Paolo. Get this, he told me it comes from the sixteenth century Italian word *fugare* which means to chase or to flee."

"How can it mean two opposing words?"

"Sixteen century Latin closely mirrored the ancient Greek philosopher, Pythagoras' *Table of Opposites*, comparing right and left, or odd and even. You mentioned the word permutation. That could be backwards or inverse—Bach was famous for his use of the Pythagorean philosophical principles in his compositions, especially in the *Art of Fugue*."

Max chuckled. "I'm thoroughly impressed. I never knew you were a classical music aficionado."

"You can thank Paolo for his five minute dissertation."

"Do you think Bach is the clue?"

Noble was curiously excited. "I'm not sure, I have an inkling, but I need to check it out further. The programming code Simon utilized in the past for his backdoors was straight COBOL, antiquated as it was. He used the same code in the encampment's command center. Why didn't he use his own proprietary language then?"

"Perhaps he was playing you at the time and he wanted you to understand the code. Now he's using code he doesn't want you to decipher," Max theorized.

"Great! It looks like I have my work cut out for me. I not only have to get into his twisted mind to crack his code, I then have to wade through the code, looking for something that reveals the target date. Aargh! Let's move on." Noble flailed his hands in midair. "Did you think to ask how he pays for the nursing home?"

"Of course," she blustered, and then grinned. "The business office said they receive a cashier's check on a monthly basis. It is always from a different bank and from a different state. I don't think we'll be following the money this time around."

"Most significant is the clue to decipher the code."

"Agreed, but I wouldn't overlook the Saudi incident." Max furrowed her brow, appearing to be in deep thought.

"What's the matter Max?"

"I was just thinking about Ann Hall and the three boys who raped her." Max explained. "Then all of the sudden the number three rang out at me."

"What are you talking about?"

"Remember Simon's Julian—excuse me—ordinal dates, are multiples of three. I found a copy of the Koran in the encampment and discovered within the text the words *The Trio* were circled. In Christianity it would refer to the Holy Trinity, but I was curious as to the significance in Islam."

"Learn anything revealing?"

"Just that Islamists perform certain tasks in odd numbers, such as washing each of their hands, feet, and face three time before prayer. According to the prophet Muhammad, there are three holy cities of Islam: Mecca, Medina, and Jerusalem. The number three also has something to do with Allah. He represents the number one, an odd number, and therefore reportedly loves all things odd. Thus, in Arabic the first plural number is the number three. And according to Sharia law, all dealings with large amounts must be broken down into an odd number that denotes a multitude of three."

"Interesting. One thing's for certain—Simon is no garden-variety, homegrown terrorist."

"Why do you keep looking at your watch?" Max questioned. "Do you have to be somewhere?"

Noble realized they had been working for the past three hours and he was exhausted. It was time to call it quits. "Let's wrap up where we are. We now know the date Simon plans to trigger a national disaster. Burke is focused on St. Paul and still on the hunt for Simon. He will need to capture him before he reaches Canada, where they will not extradite him for a capital crime. And Stanton has his assignment. You need to find a connection between the Superstation and Agenda 21. Meanwhile, I need to crack Simon's code. I'll see you tomorrow."

Without hesitation, Max collected her papers and headed for the door. "Night boss."

"Give my regards to the major." Noble grinned.

Max departed without a retort.

26
NIGHT ESCAPE

S orry I'm late. I had to brief Noble."
"Let's grab a booth over there." Stanton left a couple of bucks on the bar to cover his beer tab and then escorted Max to the booth in the corner.

"By the way, Noble sends his regards." Max smiled.

"You told him." Stanton looked surprised.

"Of course not. Remember what he does for a living?"

"You sure it won't be a problem?"

"No. Technically, you and I don't work together."

"I think we work very well together." He pulled her close for a passionate embrace before they sat opposite each other.

Stanton ordered a bottle of wine and asked for the menus. They quickly ordered and then sat back and waited for their food. While sipping on their wine they reminisced about the first time they had met.

It was during Operation NOMIS. Until Noble arrived on the scene, Max was in charge of the operation, tasked with entering an underground encampment. During that time, she was badly bruised in an explosion that killed two soldiers. She met Major Stanton the next day.

"I remember you were a sight for sore eyes, bandages, and all."

"You must have been blind. I looked like a gorgon."

"Blinded by your beauty."

"Can we change the subject please?" Max loved the affection, but was uncomfortable with verbal foreplay. Fortunately, their meal had arrived.

They spent the rest of their dinner conversation talking about his impending move to Washington. He asked for recommendations on places to live and any insight into his new assignment that she could offer. They spoke a bit about President Post and the changes within the new administration following the Baari fiasco.

Max enjoyed the political exchanges and discovered with each conversation that there were more facets to the major. He was quite intelligent and knew his subject matter. Moreover, he was fiercely patriotic and spoke from the heart. She found that as he talked she would focus on his every word. She also noticed for the first time how his appearance softened when dressed in his civvies, out of his usual military garb. *What am I getting myself into? Am I ready for this?* She wondered.

"Hello Max. Anyone home?"

"Of course, I'm hanging on your every word."

He knew her well enough to detect she was lost in thought. "How about we finish up and get out of here?"

By the look on his face, she knew where they would be heading.

"Amanda." He could detect her breathing on the other end of the line, but there was no response. "Amanda."

"Yes," said the groggy voice.

"Are you okay?"

"Oh, Noble, yes, I was sleeping."

"I didn't mean to awaken you. I assumed you'd still be up at this hour. Go back to sleep darling. I'll call you in the morning."

"No, talk to me. I just had a rough day and thought I'd hit the sack early."

"I wanted to hear your voice before I crash."

"Did you put in another late night?"

"Yes."

"Simon."

"Yes."

"This will be over soon, right? And don't say yes, unless you mean it."

"How about—you start to plan the wedding."

Amanda could not believe what she was hearing. She bolted up in her bed to make sure she was not dreaming. "Can we set a date?"

"Give me a little more time before setting a date. But I assume there are preliminary steps to this sort of thing."

"I love you, sweetheart."

"I love you too. Now go back to sleep."

Noble hung up the phone, but remained seated on his sofa and spouted out to the air, "I need normalcy in my life. This cannot go on much longer. Damn you Simon!" Feeling marginally better after his outburst, he stood up and walked into the bedroom. Then he prayed for a goodnight's sleep.

"No!—Stop!—Stop!—No!" He continued to thrash about until finally he awakened himself. He felt the bed sheet soaked in perspiration underneath him. Abruptly, Noble sat up and clasped his knees to his chest, as he worked to slow his breathing. "This has got to stop!" He breathed in and out several times. "Freud, you've got it all wrong." He continued to castigate himself with no one in hearing range, grateful Amanda had not witnessed his reaction to the nightmare a second time. Finally, in a calmer state he looked at the clock. It was 5:58 a.m. He maintained his crouched position and continued to stare at the clock briefly. Then the annoying buzzer sounded off.

27

DAY FORTY-FIVE

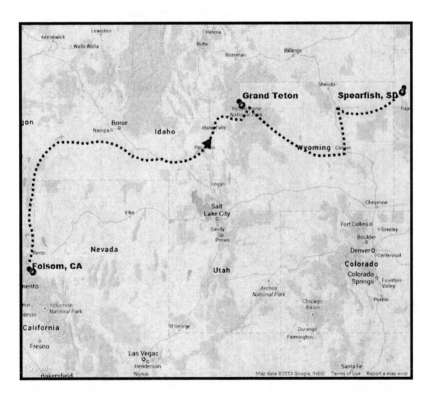

The ray from the morning sunlight pierced the window. It was aimed directly at his face, nudging him awake. He pulled the comforter over his head and resumed his sleep for several minutes more before grudgingly rising out from under the bedcovers. He had had the best night's sleep in weeks. He drove for five days before he reached the Signal Mountain Lodge, instead of the fourteen hours it would normally take to drive from Folsom to the Grand Teton National Forest. It was a straight shot on I-80, but he could not risk it. He took the back roads through backwater towns, into the backwoods and through national parks. Now, with a bit of time on his hands, he basked in a rare luxury. Although months away from the trigger date, he still needed to put the finishing touches on his next planned breach. He also bore in mind that as soon as he accomplished his mission, he needed to flee the country. He rolled over and grabbed the room service menu. He was suddenly famished.

"Yes, I'd like eggs benedict, hash browns—No mimosa. I will have a bottle of champagne. You can keep the orange juice—Also, I want a copy of the local newspaper, and the New York Times—Yes. That's all."

While he waited for breakfast, he sat up in bed and tossed another pillow behind his back. Then he opened his xPhad and began to tap away. Checking the map, he calculated the distance ahead of him, assuming he stayed off the major interstates. He estimated that in five days, he would arrive in St. Paul and breach that facility in accordance to plan. It had to be timed perfectly. He knew that three days after the breach the National Cyber Security Division would send in a member of their geek squad to investigate the source of the hacking. Without his trusted mole, he would now have to reenter the system and piggyback on their time. First, he would have to remove the hacking code and then install his creation—his backdoor code. All had to be done without having his activities traced by security at the installation. He also anticipated the techie on site would take at least four hours of probing, before announcing it was a blip in the system to the director of the control center.

His strategy was in place.

He had arranged for a late checkout, so when it was time to depart he would leave appearing in the same disguise as when he arrived.

Now safely inside his car, he exchanged the cropped gray-haired wig and beard for the dark brown, shoulder-length hair, which he tied into a ponytail, and then attached a Van Dyke beard. After he switched the pair of silver-rimmed glasses with the pair of dark rounded frames, he swapped driver's licenses in his wallet. He made one final inspection in the mirror, and then ventured out under a dark sky toward the back roads of Nevada heading east. In nine hours, he would arrive in Spearfish, South Dakota.

28

THE ODD INTERCONNECTIONS

Max dashed past Doris and swung Noble's office door open. She attempted to announce, "It's not a..."

"Hold on! Before you get started, you might find it interesting to know that I cracked the code." Noble beamed and then noted, "By the way, you look like hell!"

Max waved her arms, blowing off his observation. She had worked late the night before and then spent the rest of the night with Stanton. *My life is out of control*, she thought. After a momentary distraction, she refocused and blurted out, "You have to hear this first! I believe I found the connection between Agenda 21 and the Superstation."

"Okay, you've got my undivided attention—what is it?"

"It's not a what, it's a *who*—it's the Godfather."

"What!"

"The link is Stronghold Management. The Godfather is the Chairman for the International Advisory Board for the Stronghold Management companies." Max was not about to back down this time. With a curious grin, she questioned again, "Now do you think he is one and the same?"

"We have no way of knowing for sure. Baari's so-called Godfather worked behind the scenes. In fact, Paolo and the other members of Baari's Administration admitted never having met the Godfather, so it's conjecture. However, Paolo, using his deductive talents, believes he not only knows the identity of the Godfather, but also that of Baari's bagman, the Financier, as well."

Max shook her head. "When I said earlier that this was starting to look like a *Three Stooges* movie—well now it appears to be a theatre of the absurd. I had to work through a labyrinth of information to make the connection to the Godfather. It was swimming upstream all the way." She explained that when she first looked through the roster of directors and investors for the Superstation, there was no reference to the Godfather. Then she checked the Stronghold Management's Website and again there was nothing.

"Then I remembered that the Godfather hung out in Beijing and Stronghold Management had an office there, so I checked their roster and there was still no mention of the Godfather."

"Now you have me really confused. How can you say he was on the Advisory Board? That would have been our link."

"Here's the attention-getter. I started searching the Internet for any business connections between the Godfather and Stronghold Management, and the only thing that popped up from the various sites was a quote from the president of Stronghold Greater China in 2005. He was referring to China being the economic engine of the world and the role the Godfather played in helping the Chinese government to move forward. It was the same year the Godfather first moved to Beijing. This guy also had a short stint as the Senior Vice President of Sustainable Development in Stronghold's Denver office between 2005 and 2006."

"Wasn't that the same period of time when Stronghold Management was being heavily fined for radiological contamination of workers?" Noble questioned.

"I was wondering if you picked up on that detail." Max paused and then took a deep breath. "Get this. In 1992 he was the Chief of Staff to the Secretary General of the U.N. Conference on Environment and

Development..."

Noble interrupted abruptly and finished Max's statement. "And in 1992 the Godfather was the Secretary General and his boss. But this only implies that they know each other intimately. How can you prove the Godfather has a direct influence over Stronghold Management? I don't see it."

"I asked myself the same question and continued to hunt for confirmation. Unable to get anything from the Stronghold Management sources, I began to scour renewable energy companies in Asia and I came across Euro Asia Energy Limited, or EAE. They are primarily gas and oil traders, although they did expand into investments for renewable energy. Their website lists the nine partners, along with their bios, that make up the team at EAE. One of the partners is the Godfather and his bio clearly states that he is the Chairman of the International Advisory Board for..."

"The Stronghold Management companies," Noble droned.

"Exactly! So your source who gave you the napkin appears to be implying that the Godfather has influence over Stronghold and, therefore, the Superstation."

"It would appear that way, but the Godfather is still an enigma," Noble alleged.

Max agreed. "All this stuff has been in the news, albeit scarce and short-lived. Only the conspiracy theorists highlight his antics. The mainstream press ignores the facts. Moreover, while some investigative reporters connected the dots, for some unknown reason the news coverage disappeared. Since 2012, there has been absolute silence. It's bizarre."

Noble grasped her point, but elaborated. "What's bizarre is that a group of investors pushing for renewable energy would engage a company with a record of failures and questionable behaviors. Certainly their conduct is questionable as it relates to the removal of nuclear waste."

"Considering Stronghold funneled ten million dollars to the failed solar manufacturing plant, do you think it's possible a portion of the two billion dollar stimulus fund was redirected to the Superstation?" Max questioned.

"Let's be careful not to disparage all the good that Stronghold Management does for companies around the world. To be fair, they were rated one of the world's most ethical companies by Ethispere.com one year, but it does raise suspicions in the realm of renewable energy and waste disposal. It's a distraction for now and we can't afford the time to go off on a tangent."

Max noted the concern on Noble's face, but there was more that he needed to hear.

"I discovered a few other tidbits about our man of mystery. He also established the Tianjin Climate Exchange in China that mirrors the bankrupt Chicago Climate Exchange bought out by the Intercontinental Exchange. You recall the Godfather was also the architect of the Kyoto Agreement that granted profitable concessions to developing nations such as China, courtesy of the U.N."

"So he is now involved in China's carbon trading?"

Max shook her head affirmatively. "I also remembered that you said the president spoke about the IUCN Covenant in your meeting with him and mentioned that the Godfather was a patron."

It was evident Noble was becoming weary of the name. "Yes, along with the Prince of Monaco, Queen Noor of Jordan, and a long list of rich and powerful supporters."

"I guess it is one of the places where the rich continue to scratch each other's back," Max quipped. "Seriously, Noble, the final draft of the Covenant is constructed with seventy-nine articles. There are only seven articles in the U.S. Constitution, which is the framework for how our government is to function. It has survived for over two centuries. To date, it has been amended only twenty-seven times. Can you imagine if the Covenant is adopted as a global constitution? For openers, it would turn our Bill of Rights into confetti."

"I can't argue that if we were to follow the Covenant it would trample the tenth amendment and states' rights. Not to overlook the restrictions that would be placed on our second amendment right to bear arms, our fourth against unreasonable searches, and our fifth amendment right to private property."

"In essence, our Constitution would cease to exist."

Max mirrored Noble's frustration.

"As dire as this all seems, it still doesn't tie Simon to the Godfather."

"Remember the Godfather's quote: 'We may get to the point where the only way of saving the world will be for industrial civilization to collapse.'"

"So you are suggesting that the Stronghold Management connection to the Godfather could explain why Baari needed a plan to push the Superstation into operation. And if our assumptions are correct, Simon picked up where Baari left off for motives seemingly unrelated to Baari's original plan to trigger a blackout. But it quite possibly conforms to the Godfather's goal for global governance."

"That was a mouthful Max, but it seems to be a plausible explanation for Simon's actions. We will never really know for sure until we have captured him. I dare ask, is there anything else?"

"One last thing—and it has nothing to do with assumptions, presumptions, or suppositions. When I conducted the research to find a connection, I switched over to the Google search engine. Every single time I'd searched for *the Godfather, Covenant, Stronghold Management,* et cetera, a bizarre message appeared at the end of each search string." Max demonstrated an example on her tablet. "Check the ending; notice the last word."

https://www.google.com/search?source=ig&hl=en&rlz=&q=the+covenant
&btnG=Google+Search&aq=9&aqi=g10&aql=&oq=birthers

"I guess you've been tagged." Noble smirked. "Even the SIA is in the NSA's radar."

Max added, "When it comes to surveillance, it's not comforting to know that the executive chairman of Google spearheaded the former president's team to develop their personal data mining project that paved the way for his election."

"I agree. He also invested millions of dollars in a company called Civis Analytics, which continues to be the fountainhead for liberal campaign data. Civis Analytics' staff is comprised exclusively of the former president's supporters."

Max stepped back. "Let's move on, this is starting to freak me out. You said Paolo mentioned his opinion as to the identity of the

Financier."

"When I met with Paolo he referred to Hank's comment about Baari's handlers being the Godfather and the Financier. We know who he presumes is the Godfather, but when I asked him who he thought the Financier was, all he said was to follow the open society."

"Hold on! If Paolo was referring to the Open Society Institute then he was clearly referring to its founder," Max opined.

"I suspected as much when Hank referred to the rapid increase of 501(c) (4) groups that sprouted up during Baari's first presidential campaign. So I checked into the founder's background more thoroughly. His network of non-profit activist groups—which some have called a *shadow party*—gives him enormous political clout. What is surprising is that his influence extends to numerous interest groups that include foreign affairs."

"So he was not just your typical *financier*, but a person with an agenda beyond the money." Max was curious. She understood that the well-known philanthropist believes in capitalism as a means of generating funds to support his liberal causes." Max read from her tablet. "Right here in his book, *Open Society: Reforming Global Capitalism*, he describes that his mission is to promote freedom, democracy, human rights, rule of law, social justice, and social responsibility as a universal idea. It's also common knowledge that *he* was influenced by his professor Karl Popper at the London School of Economics where he advocated for an open society that combined socialism with liberty."

"Evidently, the concept of an open society was the primary motivation for who we now suspect is Baari's Financier to reignite the progressive movement. That provided him a mechanism to promote a larger government to manage the affairs of the American people," Noble surmised.

"It would help to explain why he blurs the line between his social agenda and his political endeavors. He is on record for pouring millions of dollars into his activist groups to destroy the conservative agenda and its supporters, considered to be a roadblock to his open society."

Noble added, "the Financier also openly stated, speaking in economic terms…"

A lot of positive things are happening. I see Africa together with the Arab Spring as areas of progress. The Arab Spring was a revolutionary development.

"What is most confusing is his rabid support of the Arab world and the Muslim Brotherhood with their self-professed mission to 'destroy Western Civilization from within.'"

"Where did that come from? I didn't think that was part of his game plan."

Noble explained how he did some probing of his own. "My research shows that some elements of the Western media had promoted the Arab uprisings repeatedly as a positive development for the U.S., while claiming citizens from oppressed countries were fighting for freedom and democracy. But there was very little reporting about the opportunities that were being created for the Muslim Brotherhood, as they waited in the wings to take advantage of the events."

Noble tapped on his tablet and shared his additional eye-opening findings. He described Chris Matthew's interview with Brian Katulis on his MSNBC *Hardball* segment. "Katulis is a senior fellow for the Center for American Progress, funded by the Financier. In the interview he stated..."

The Muslim Brotherhood today wants to enter politics...let them be part of the Egyptian politics.

He scrolled down and cited another collaborator. "Marwan Muasher is the former prime minister of Jordan and currently the Vice President of Studies at another enterprise underwritten by the Financier, the Carnegie Endowment of International Peace. In an opinion piece for the Guardian, Muasher stated..."

Governments use the fear of Islam to justify closed political systems that clamp down on all forms of discontent.

"Muasher was also interviewed by ABC's correspondent Christiane Amanpour. In that interview he stated..."

*The Muslim Brotherhood has been used for a long time as a
scare tactic. This is not to say that they don't have designs, but
I think that in closed systems, protest votes will only go to the
Brotherhood.*

"What is curious is that Amanpour let the statement go unchallenged
and didn't even ask what he meant by the word *designs*. These are
examples of the media glossing over the issue."

Max, with an index finger to her temple, pondered, "Each person
you cited gives the impression of downplaying the impact of the
Muslim Brotherhood. But by all accounts, the Brotherhood has stated
emphatically that their goal is to move in and replace the disposed
leaders in the Middle East to create a Sharia caliphate."

"Their plans for the U.S. are even more devastating according
to Frank Gaffney, Founder and President of the Center for Security
Policy. He cited from an internal document crafted by the Muslim
Brotherhood where they refer to the Ikhwan, meaning brotherhood or
an Islamic religious militia. One paragraph states…"

*The Ikhwan must understand that their work in America is a
kind of grand Jihad in eliminating and destroying the Western
civilization from within and 'sabotaging' its miserable house
by their hands and the hands of the believers so that it is
eliminated and God's religion is made victorious over all other
religions.*

Max was stunned. "Are you linking the Financier to the Muslim
Brotherhood?"

"Only stating the facts ma'am." Noble remained solemn. He further
described the *International Crisis Group*, and stated, "They claim
to be 'an independent, non-profit, non-governmental organization
committed to preventing and resolving deadly conflict.' The Financier
who is on their executive committee heavily funds the group. He uses
his investments to push for globalization. Mohamed ElBaradei is also
a board member along with Kofi Annan and other luminaries."

"ElBaradei!" Max knew Mohamed ElBaradei was the former Director General of the International Atomic Energy Agency, the IAEA, and a U.N. organization. She also was aware he played a significant role in ousting Egypt's President Hosni Mubarak and his successor, Mohamed Morsi. However, she was not making the connection.

"Remember in 2013, ElBaradei was sworn in as the Vice President of Egypt. Then one month later, he resigned after a violent crackdown of Morsi supporters that left five hundred and twenty-five people dead in its wake. He cited his reasons in his resignation letter saying within the text something about, '...I always saw peaceful alternatives for resolving this societal wrangling...'"

Max pondered a moment and then asked, "What does he have to do with this web you are spinning?"

Noble chimed in. "Conversely, prior to his short stint as vice president he entertained running for the presidency, but retracted after the Islamic Nour Party opposed his candidacy. However, before renouncing his candidacy ElBaradei stated, 'If Israel attacked Gaza we would declare war against the Zionist regime.' Rather contradictory in nature, I would say."

Max was agape.

Noble continued. "What is more shocking is that the Egyptian Muslim Brotherhood nominated the liberal, secular opposition leader Mohamed ElBaradei as their spokesperson." Noble put his fingers to work again and tapped on his tablet to retrieve a newspaper clipping. "Here it is—an opinion piece in *The Washington Post* written by the Financier. He stated..."

The best-organized political opposition that managed to survive in that country's repressive environment is the Muslim Brotherhood. In free elections, the Brotherhood is bound to emerge as a major political force, though it is far from assured of a majority... The Muslim Brotherhood's cooperation with Mohamed ElBaradei, the Nobel laureate who is seeking to run for president, is a hopeful sign that it intends to play a constructive role in a democratic political system.

"However, the Financier neglected to mention his long-standing, personal association with ElBaradei."

Noble raised an eyebrow. "And there's more." He tapped a few more times on his tablet to retrieve his notes. "In 2008 the International Crisis Group, at which both the Financier, ElBaradei and Annan have a seat, released a report titled, *Egypt's Muslim Brothers: Confrontation or Integration?* It stated in the opening summary…"

The Society of Muslim Brothers also has altered its approach. It is using its sizeable parliamentary presence to confront the government and present itself as a major force for political reform…One of the first recommendations made to the Egyptian government was, 'to set guidelines for the establishment of a political party with religious reference.'

"This is all so unbelievable. How is it possible for the Muslim Brotherhood to coexist in a democratic process such as in the West, when they do not support the separation of church and state?" Noble questioned.

"It doesn't equate. Also remember the Godfather said something about, 'the purpose of economic life is to meet the social needs of people.' From that perspective it certainly appears both the Godfather and the Financier are joined at their ideological hips; remember the Chery Automobile debacle? Now when you throw Kofi Annan and Mohamed ElBaradei into the mix—the interconnections are frightening and never-ending. But they are loose connections at best," Max cautioned.

"Perhaps not." Noble believed there was one commonality. "While many of their endeavors are seemingly altruistic, the actions of these self-appointed interlocutors for a *global society* are at odds with their words and may prove to be destructive, especially to the U.S. Whether or not we know the true identities of Baari's handlers, it gives the impression the Godfather was molding the social policies for Baari's administration, while the Financier was working in the foreign policy arena to cement his supporters."

Max agreed. "That would help to explain why Baari helped set off the spark that propelled the Arab Spring starting with the protest in Tunisia and leading to the ousting of Qaddafi in Libya. The consequences have been deadly, as evidenced in Baari's homeland with the subsequent brutal deaths of a U.S. ambassador and three other American citizens in Benghazi."

"Then the ousting of Mubarak set off another firestorm in Egypt that continued to burn throughout the Mideast and led to the horrific gassing of the Syrian people by one or both of the combatants in the civil war," Noble interjected.

Max took a moment to ponder the facts and then alleged, "It's inconsistent that the instigators are pushing for a global society, which is the antithesis of the Muslim Brotherhood's mission to create a closed society shrouded in Sharia law. As I see it, global governance does not embrace the restrictive precepts of their religious beliefs. Evidently the Brotherhood was smart enough to use the turmoil to solidify their position."

"In any event, these warring factions would be natural partners for Simon to carry out his mission," Noble ventured.

They both sat in their seats for a moment of contemplation. Then having had enough frightening thoughts for one session, Max switched the focus, "Okay, *Code-breaker*, talk to me."

Noble smiled at her obvious attempt to change the subject. "I can see we are both exhausted by the realities and their implications. Go grab us a couple cups of coffee and I'll meet you in the conference room in a few minutes. I have a quick call to make first."

Noble punched in the number.

"Hello," Adam responded.

"Adam, Amanda told me you were quitting the lobbying firm. I just have one question."

"Not now, Noble."

"Then when—it's important—Adam, can you hear me?"

"Give me a minute—I'm thinking. Tonight I'll be at the Kennedy

Center. The performance ends at ten-thirty. Meet me in the parking garage; it should be empty by eleven. I'll be on the lower level in the reserved parking area."

"What about Nancy? I assume she'll be with you."

"I'll send her home in a taxi."

"Thanks Adam. I'll see you this evening."

29
BUSTED

"Watch the coffee, it's hot."

"Thanks Max." Noble took the cup and then reached over and hit a button on the virtual keyboard.

"What's with the music?"

"It's the clue to Simon's code."

"What? It sounds like something from a horror movie." Max sipped her coffee as she thought, *Noble really needs some down time.*

"Actually, you've probably heard it in a number of music scores from movies like *Aviator, Schindler's List, Quartet,* and *Fantasia,* to name a few."

"So this is how you've been spending your time."

"You're listening to Bach's *Toccata and Fugue in D minor B-W-V 5-6-5.*"

"Dadada daa! The same music Simon listened to as a child and the same composer on the scorched CD."

"By the way, you just mimicked Beethoven. But yes, it was the same composer. Although the music on the CD was a more obscure masterpiece by Bach known as the *Art of Fugue B-W-V 1-0-8-0.*"

"What's with the B-W-V?"

"It is Bach's numbering system for his compositions. BWV is the German acronym for Bach-Werke-Verzeichnis. The English translation is Bach Works Catalogue."

"Impressive, Noble."

Noble smiled and then hit another button on the keyboard and the renowned Glen Gould appeared on the screen playing the opening theme to Bach's most enigmatic work that continues to fascinate musicologists for its genius.

Max watched as the maestro played. "Now I remember, The Art of Fugue!"

"Bach's music is the clue to Simon's programming language."

"Okay Boss, elaborate on your brilliance. Though try to make it a light conversation. No more—Pythagorean philosophical principles—please."

Noble continued to sip his coffee as he listened to Max egg him on. Then he turned off the music. "Bach's music is preferred among geniuses, primarily because Bach was obsessed with numbers and puzzles which he incorporated in his music. Simon emulated Bach in many of the games he has played with us. Interestingly, Bach fixated over two particular numbers; three and five."

Max was astounded. "The ordinal dates for the breaches are multiples of three and three is the first plural number in the Arabic numbering system. Simon is attacking five grids."

"Pythagoras…"

"Noble, please, Simon's code!"

"I'm getting to it, but first you may find it interesting that Pythagoras considered the number three the *noblest* of all digits for a number of reasons I won't bore you with, but it held the secret to Simon's code." Noble noticed Max was not partaking in his humor and moved the conversation along. "Bach encrypted many different hidden enigmas in his music and especially in his fugues. An example of one of his motifs was using his family name. He substituted B for B-flat and H for B-natural in German musical nomenclature, resulting in B-flat–A–C–B-natural. Then he often permutated this motif in various ways such as in inversion or in retrograde where he reversed the notes to play B-natural–C–A–B-flat. While reflecting on Bach's permutations of his fugue it hit me—Simon used Bach's retrograde or reverse code for his backdoor code."

"So he reversed the naming conventions in the failsafe code as well."

"Not exactly—at first, the code in the wristwatch was confusing. It did not resemble the code he has used in the past. It was a clash between a Rubik's cube and Sudoku. However, when you told me what Simon's mother said about Bach being his inspiration, it all came together. The code actually was the same as the backdoor code that he used to break into the various banking systems."

"You just said it wasn't the same."

"It was the same code, but instead of reversing the wording, like Bach, Simon reversed the commands. The code would appear to be valid but would execute the opposite instruction. The only way it would be discovered is if a programmer followed the logic through thousands of lines of code."

"I'm confused. My head is still spinning from our earlier conversation so this is making no sense."

"Max, hang in there."

Noble explained that in Simon's version, he changed the command for example, *EndCount* to mean *CharCount* and *CharCount* to mean *EndCount*. However, he had to distinguish his commands from the actual commands, so he added an additional letter. Therefore, when he wrote *Move 1 to EnddCount* he instructed the program to *Move 1 to CharCount* or *Move 1 to CharrCount* instructed the program to *Move 1 to EndCount*.

"In essence he created his own source code and designed his own undetectable failsafe code."

"Do I really need to know this?"

Noble grinned and spared Max the programming lesson. "Fortunately, FERC convinced the directors at the control centers to grant me temporary access to each of their operating systems, along with providing the actual program name where the failsafe code is stored. The program name is different at each facility for security purposes."

"So how did Simon actually modify the main operating system's program to execute his failsafe program? Please, just a rough outline."

"The only changes Simon made were to add a few lines of code to the main program. He inserted a statement that said if the date was equal to 0-8-0-2-2-0-1-7, for the month, day, and year, and the time was 0-9-0-0-0-0, for the hour, minutes, and seconds, adjusted for various time zones, then the command would go to the next line of code. That line of code would execute his failsafe program; otherwise the main program would continue to function as normal."

"Can I assume his failsafe program modified the original instructions from reallocating power from the other grids to shutting down the entire grid?"

"Precisely, otherwise everything would continue to function normally until August second at nine o'clock a.m., at which time the main system would execute Simon's failsafe program—all five grids would shut down simultaneously."

Max was still somewhat mystified. "If Simon created his own code, inserted his own naming convention, and edited the source code, wouldn't he have to recompile the program?"

Noble was impressed with the little knowledge Max had for programming. "It would be virtually impossible for Simon to recompile the code. It would have to be recompiled by a programmer actually on the premises."

"You mean there are more moles in each of the facilities?" Max was surprised.

"No, I suspect Simon knew the regular maintenance schedule for each facility. He entered the backdoor shortly before the system was brought down, inserted his few lines of code, and installed his failsafe program. After the programmers made their routine changes to the operating system, they would recompile all the programs before bringing the system back online. They would have no inkling that the new code had been incorporated."

"That's absolutely brilliant."

"I agree. The simplicity itself is ingenious. That's our Simon."

"So there is no way he can now bring down the grids?" Max asked, looking for solid confirmation.

"Thus far, I've removed his lines of code, his failsafe program, and his backdoor code at the Birmingham, Taylor, and Folsom facilities. If we don't catch him first, we'll let him go ahead and do his fancy work at the St. Paul control center and then move on to the one in Carmel. I can easily go in behind him and restore the system. He'll be none the wiser. For the present, the threat is over, but now we have to intercept him before he escapes to Canada. He could still trigger the Mississauga blackout, which would be a repeat of the massive blackout that incapacitated much of the U.S. in 2003."

"Why do you think Simon set up a rigid time schedule?"

"He knew he had to execute his plan before the Superstation goes operational or he'd be automatically locked out of the system. He also needed time between facilities to create his own failsafe program. I suspect August was as far out as he could push his plan. In his usual cunning way he chose the signing date of our Declaration of Independence."

"It's ironic that Baari's strategy was to expedite the process for firing up the Superstation and conversely for Simon it was an impediment to have the Superstation in operation."

Noble snickered; he appreciated the satire.

Max joined in and then asked, "Have you heard from Burke?"

"I spoke with him earlier. He's setting up roadblocks on the major roads heading in to St. Paul. I also informed him that Simon would likely do his damage shortly before the operating system is brought down for repairs. He's aware of their maintenance schedule. So let's keep our fingers crossed."

"What are your plans if they capture him?"

"I have the company jet standing by. Within an hour, I can be at any one of the locations. I'm not going to miss the moment. I'll need you to manage things here."

"Not a problem. But let's hope it ends there."

30
THE SOURCE UNLOADS

Noble walked toward the shadowy figure leaning against the column between two parking spaces. "Adam," he whispered.

Adam stepped out into the dimly lit parking garage and responded in a deep throat, "What's so important?"

"Is this the reason you're leaving the firm? Noble handed him a cocktail napkin. A line was scratched through the words Agenda 21 and scribbled below was a name. "Why is he a threat?"

"It's not him; it's all the defenders of the Covenant, the jazzed-up version of Agenda 21."

"I'm not sure I understand."

Adam kept his voice quiet and low as he explained, "The Kyoto Protocol and the climate exchanges have been cap-and-trade impediments to my clients. The government's policies continue to kill coal and natural gas production that make up close to seventy percent of our energy resources. So I started to delve into the issue in an effort to save the fossil fuel industry by questioning global warming."

Noble interrupted and asked for clarification. "Pardon me; you believe those policies only made our country more dependent on foreign energy resources?"

"Yes, they are killing our industry. The cynic I am, I almost believe the turmoil in the Middle East was calculated to drive up the cost of oil. The crux of the problem is that the urgency for *renewable energy* lacks a viable infrastructure. I'm all for renewable energy, but it can't happen overnight, yet those pushing for green energy want it yesterday. It has to evolve slowly over time."

"So your contention is that the environmentalists are purposely pushing global warming as a means to justify the presumed urgent need for renewable energy?"

"Yes! Even my former boss at the DOE stated, 'I'm not interested in debating what is not debatable,' stopping the conversation on global warming in its tracks." Adam took a moment to collect his thoughts before furthering his argument. "To my point, Germany tried the same approach shutting down their nuclear power reactors and dismantling coal-fired plants to encourage renewable energy. As a result, Germany has coined a new term, *energy poverty*. In 2013, it was reported that their energy costs had spiked over thirty percent in a five-year period, having risen during their rapid transition. Renewable energy sources lack the technology for long-term energy storage—when the winds don't blow—and the sun doesn't shine."

"Are you suggesting energy poverty can be expected in our future?"

"Unless we slow down and take a more methodical approach— yes." Adam carried on, but parsed his words carefully. "Aside from increasing our energy dependency and increasing our energy costs, it will decrease jobs. The Secretary of the Environmental Protection Agency said she did not want to talk about jobs anymore as she wrote new job killing regulations."

"Excuse me, but won't the jobs be simply replaced with green energy jobs?"

"Renewable energy projects are basically capital projects requiring large amounts of capital and labor up front. Once the facility is up and running, however, it will require less labor to manage. There will be no light bulbs to replace," Adam jibed. "On the other side of the spectrum, the oil and natural gas alone supports over nine million jobs, contributing to more than one trillion dollars to the United States' G-D-P per year, as pointed out by Senator Tim Scott from South Carolina. Renewable energy won't be able to make up the difference."

"I was under the impression that there was an energy boom in 2012?"

"Granted, according to CERA, the Cambridge Energy Research Associates, the oil and natural gas production contributed two-hundred-and-eighty-three billion dollars to the G-D-P. This was all due to the revolutionary technology resulting from hydraulic fracturing, referred to as fracking. Nevertheless, the administration continues to place bans on fracking and stricter environmental regulation to block other avenues of new sources of oil and gas production. The Keystone pipeline was a glaring example. Jobs became less important and the push for renewable energy became the driving force. Appallingly, the key players pushing the renewable energy agenda profit from their investments in green energy at every turn."

Noble, somewhat dubious, invoked, "Investors are in the game to make money."

Adam hesitated and then opined, "But they profit from keeping the global warming argument robust, when there are considerable amounts of scientific evidence to the contrary. So I ask you, which dishonesty is worse? Pushing a false premise or profiting?"

Noble displayed a feeble grin and assumed Adam was not looking for an answer, but he certainly had a question. "I understand the issues you tackled for your clients, but I'm unclear as to why you fear the opposing forces enough to bow out of the game and leave your firm."

"As I said before, when I started to delve into the global warming issue, I found myself digging deeper and deeper. That is when I exposed what I believe to be *the global warming camouflage for global governance*." Adam stressed.

"Are you suggesting that is the crux of the matter?"

"I hold that it is the primary impetus for the redistribution of global resources for the sake of what is described as sustainability." Adam took a breather and then said, "Deep down in the inferno—I also discovered a host of powerful people pushing the Covenant—a clan of mumpsimus souls. That's when I realized I had lost the battle."

"How can you walk away? It appears you've made tremendous headway."

"My clients have picked up the cause to protect their own interests. I am through tussling with the government. However, the DOE thinks I am fueling the fire, so the threats have continued even though I have backed away. I've clearly been targeted. It isn't worth it anymore."

"Where do you go from here?"

"First, I'm going to take a time-out, maybe take my wife on an extended vacation. In time I'll decide, but I won't go anywhere near the energy industry or the U.S. Government."

"I know Amanda is saddened by your imminent departure. She's enjoyed working with you."

Adam offered his first comforting smile. "She was one of the best confidantes I've worked with; I'll miss her. I hope we can continue to socialize, but let us keep a distance for a while. We must avoid the threat of guilt by association."

"Adam, I understand and I respect your decision and I thank you for your candor. I've kept you long enough my friend." Noble offered him his hand.

Adam shook Noble's hand and offered a smile of gratitude. Then he turned and disappeared into the darkness.

31
DAY FIFTY-ONE

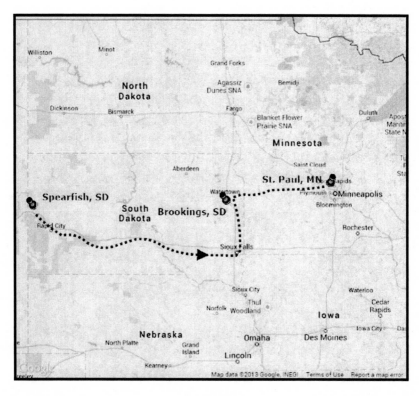

The last several days, he remained holed up in the *All Stars Travelers Inn* in Spearfish, South Dakota, where he endured the solitary confinement and planned the next step of his plot with precision. He ventured out of the hotel only to scrounge up his meals. His unwholesome choices were between the Pizza Hut and Arby's, located across the street. Eager to move to the next target, he had to force himself to proceed with caution. Days had passed; the time had arrived. He downed the last slice of pizza, grabbed his duffle bag, and left his room.

When he first checked in, he prepaid for four nights. On checking out, he stopped at the reception desk to pay for the two extra nights after having to delay his stay. He shuffled through his wallet, pulled out a crisp one hundred dollar bill, and handed it to the night clerk.

"Please call me a taxi."

"Yes sir, one moment." The night clerk placed the call to his Johnny-on-the-spot brother-in-law. "Your taxi will arrive momentarily. Have a safe trip."

He offered a brief smile and headed out the door. Outside the sun had set; it would be dark within the hour.

He handed the driver a slip of paper. "Take me to this address."

It took twenty minutes to reach his destination, but upon arrival he spotted his vehicle straightaway. It was parked in the last row in the deserted parking lot. He paid the driver and then waited until he sped away out of sight. Left alone, he used the spare key to unlock the car and quickly hopped inside. Within minutes, he was back behind the wheel of his freshly painted red Ford Bronco driving away from Spearfish thinking it was worth the extra days. He was still on schedule. In seven hours, he would arrive in Brookings, South Dakota shortly before sunrise, where he would spend one night. The following night, under the cover of dark, he would ease into St. Paul, Minnesota.

32
SKIP A BREACH

Burke was confident that Simon was heading in his direction and had taken all precautions. Roadblocks had been set up at all access roads leading into St. Paul, Minnesota. Anyone crossing the junction onto either State Road 280, Route 35, or I-94 would be stopped for visual identification. All hotels had been alerted in the area surrounding the Mideast ISO control center. The local authorities maintained around-the-clock stakeouts.

Nothing more could be done—other than to wait.

Burke understood that Simon would likely hack surreptitiously into the facility's network directly and it would be untraceable. However, he would have to be within range of the source. Burke set up surveillance along the perimeter of the control center at Energy Park Drive and North Lexington Parkway. He also arranged for the parking lot at the apartment complex adjacent to the center to be patrolled.

It had been a frustrating week. The situation had remained stagnant and Burke's confidence had eroded. The time had come to report in to the director.

"Burke, what's the status?"

"Nothing has surfaced. There have been no sightings of Simon and no unusual activity at the center."

"Do you still have the roadblocks set up?

"Yes, but he must have eluded us in some way. In fact, only one Ford Bronco was stopped." Burke explained that the particular vehicle was red and that the plates did not match. The two occupants were males with proper I.D., but the driver was a nineteen-year-old college student heading to the University of Minnesota. The passenger was an older man with short blond hair and dark blue eyes with his right arm in a sling. "That's the closest we've come."

"BURKE!" Noble shouted. "Get their descriptions out to the local hotels. See if anyone resembling the pair checked in or out within the past few days. Call me right back." Noble slammed the receiver back into its cradle.

Noble tapped feverishly at the keyboard to access the St. Paul computer system. Within minutes, he located Simon's telltale code. Simon had left his imprint. They were too late—at least to capture him. It took Noble another thirty minutes, to remove the trigger date along with Simon's permutations and delete his failsafe program, leaving the original program intact. On a hunch, he entered the computer system for the Carmel control center and located Simon's failsafe program—he had already penetrated that system as well. Noble quickly performed the same procedure and restored the original code.

Then after moments of contemplation, he deciphered that Simon had changed the failsafe codes at both installations from within the St. Paul's control center. At that point, he sat back and stared at the screen. *Simon, what are you planning next?* "Shit, he never intended to go to Carmel," he blurted aloud. He hurriedly pulled up a map of the country on his computer and zoomed in to The Great Lakes region. After studying the map further, he concluded there were several options for crossing over the border into Canada.

"Doris, please get Agent Burke on the line."

Noble stood up and paced his office reevaluating his conclusion, while he waited to speak with Burke.

"He is on line one."

"Thank you." Noble took a calming breath and hit the button. "Burke, did anyone see our duo?"

"Your instinct was correct," Burke sighed. "The person fitting the description of the passenger checked out of the Best Western at Bandana Square two nights ago around eleven o'clock."

"You mean Simon."

"I'm afraid so. The location of the hotel would make sense. It is a seven-minute walk to the Midwest ISO building. Moreover, there is an apartment complex located between the hotel and the facility. The resident's parking lot can be accessed without difficulty and is situated essentially outside the control center's door."

Burke continued to inform Noble of another possible lead he had received moments before from one of the other agents. "Yesterday night, the local authorities conducted a raid at a local chop shop in Dubuque, Iowa, suspected of conducting illegal activities other than the obvious. The owner is a two-time felon on parole."

"Agent, please cut to the chase." Noble's eagerness was evident.

"Director, the felon didn't ask for his legal mouthpiece but asked to speak with the feds. He wanted a deal. Our blond-haired, blue-eyed passenger traded his red Ford Bronco for a souped-up silver 2010 Dodge Challenger. I just sent out an updated APB and I'm in the process of setting up roadblocks heading into Carmel." Burke hoped it was the lead Noble wanted.

"Forget it Burke, he's not heading to Carmel. He is heading to the Canadian border."

"Sir, with all due respect, how can you be sure?" Burke held his breath and waited for the reproach. He was pleasantly surprised when Noble explained his logic with composure.

"Simon already infiltrated the Carmel facility using the St. Paul network. Therefore, he is on his way to the Canadian border and to the final facility in Mississauga—but which way, we do not know. He could either head north toward Sarnia, Ontario or to Fort Erie, Ontario via Buffalo, New York."

"Director, how can we be sure that he won't charter a plane or a boat to transport him across the border?"

"He'll take the route we don't expect, purposely to tie up our resources. Simon needs to be in control and the fewer people he has to interact with the better. I still contend he will drive to the border." Noble feared his reasoning may prove to be irrational, but it was worth the risk.

"That would make sense, Director. He would not switch cars on the way into town, but would on his way out of the country. Dubuque is eight hours to Sarnia and eleven to Buffalo. I suspect he'd take the shortest route."

"Again we can only speculate. Simon has gotten this far without a trace."

"We still have some time in our favor if he heads toward Buffalo. Let's focus on Sarnia first. I'll send up a helicopter to see if they can spot him, but if he continues to travel at night it will be near impossible."

"I'm afraid Burke, our best bet will be to capture him at the border. But which border?"

"Director, I'll arrange for the traffic to be rerouted to prevent border crossings, and coordinate with the local feds and the Mounties to move in at a moment's notice."

"Get to work. Alert me the second you know anything. And Burke, sorry about losing my temper. Simon has the tendency to get under my skin."

"No worries Director. He's getting to all of us. In fact, I think he's living under my skin."

"Call me back after you have everything in place."

"Will do."

Noble tried to make sense of all of the events that had occurred, but knew there was a missing part to the conundrum. He asked himself, "Simon, what do you and the other players in this drama have in common?"

33

ALLUSION OR CONCLUSION

Noble looked up from his desk and noticed Max heading out of her office. He called out to her and waved her into his office. "I just received a call from Burke."

"Please tell me he has captured Simon."

"No such luck. He's still on the run but we know for sure he's heading to the Canadian border." Noble filled her in on the details as relayed to him by Burke.

"Conning a college kid to drive him to St. Paul was a nice ploy." Max was amazed Simon had eluded detection for so long. However, there was something else she needed to discuss. "Can you spare a little time? There is something that's been gnawing at me."

"Sure, what's up?"

Max sat in the chair across from Noble's desk as she carefully phrased her words. "We've thwarted Simon's plan thus far—and he's only days from being in our grasp—so understanding his motives at this point may be of less importance."

"True, but where are you going with this?" Noble was curious as to her hesitancy.

"Here it is. Throughout this investigation we have uncovered a number or remarkable facts, inferences, and a host of fascinating characters."

Noble eased back into his chair and said, "It's interesting that you'd bring this up now. I've been toying around with the same thought, trying to make the connection between them and Simon." Then he offered a hint of smile and pointed to the white board behind where Max was sitting.

Max turned and looked at the scrawling on the board that appeared to be a mathematical formula, it read:

$$\frac{\text{Godfather \& Financier} + \text{Agenda 21} + \text{Covenant} + \text{Resolution 16/18} + \text{OIC}}{\text{Sustainable Development}} = \text{Global Governance}$$

"Exactly! And they all seem to have one common denominator—the United Nations."

"But I still can't make the connection to Simon," Noble admitted.

At that point, Max was confident she would garner Noble's support and announced, "I have a theory."

"I'm all ears!" He was always interested in Max's theorizing no matter how outlandish, even when she was brusque and challenging.

Feeling back in her groove, Max returned to her animated self. "I drilled deeper, going beyond the facts we had uncovered—mostly for my own edification. I figured we were so far into the weeds, what's the harm?"

"Go on," he said with a hint of trepidation mixed with excitement. He had learned that when Max was excited, he should be ready for anything.

"First, we know that the Godfather of the Environmental Movement had a well-publicized career in the U.N. and continued his intimate relationship for years afterwards. From his own words he believes wealthy nations should help pay for poor nations by redistributing the wealth, which could only happen through some form of global governance."

"Let's not forget his thrust was couched in the name of sustainability and we've deduced that global warming was his catalyst," Noble reminded.

"Certainly with the help of Al Gore and company, they were able to perpetuate what now appears to be a questionable argument, at best. Even the I-P-C-C, the highly regarded Intergovernmental Panel on Climate Change, continues to dial down the hysteria with each successive report. In fact, as far back as 2013 Matt Ridley, a British scientist, framed the global warming debate. He said that climate change is either the most urgent crisis facing mankind requiring almost unlimited spending—or it is a hoax dreamt up to justify socialism. Ridley takes the middle of the road approach and states his 'lukewarm third way—that climate change is real but slow, partly man-made but also susceptible to natural factors, and might be more dangerous but more likely will not be.' Both sides attack his argument."

"Didn't the Environmental Minister Patterson from the U.K. state that more deaths are attributed to cold winters than hot summers, also pointing out that longer growing seasons for crops could extend farther north in some of the colder areas due to global warming?" Noble questioned.

"That debate continues to *ping pong* as to the number of deaths and the real causes. The reverse argument, of course, is that more people have central heating to protect them against the cold, but fewer have air-conditioning in the event of extreme high temperatures. In terms of agriculture, the extension of growing seasons is less debatable."

Max halted a moment, and then pointed out the consequences of the offshoot of policy decisions. "Ignoring the naysayers on both sides, savvy investors continued to make millions of dollars in green energy and carbon trading products. As a direct result the U.S. in particular has lost jobs and the ability to become energy independent has not met expectations."

"We can't be sure there's a direct correlation, but evidence does suggest that the green energy craze may have had a negative effect on jobs," Noble challenged.

"In either case," she countered, "it is an effective argument the advocates of global warming have launched. By keeping the discussion alive, some believe it gave credence to the Covenant—taking us back to global governance and to the United Nations, as you laid out in your formula."

"Don't get carried away. I still don't see a link to Simon," Noble replied with a puzzled look.

"It's coming, but first the players."

Max took a deep breath.

"We know that the Godfather and the Financier have worked together hand-in-glove. Moreover, four years earlier in 2013, the Financier's Open Society Foundation collaborated with Harvard University to offer an internship program on Rights and Governance Global. It started with a ten-day seminar in Budapest, followed up with a six-week intensive internship at a non-governmental organization. It seems they were sowing the seeds everywhere for a one world supranational-government."

"You know one of the things I found most puzzling is the Financier's involvement in foreign affairs. I've always connected him with reigniting the so-called progressive movement in the U.S.—not in the U.N.," Noble admitted.

"I was getting to that point."

"Come on Max, you're not trying to make a connection between Simon and the United Nations?"

"It may merely be a coincidence, but Baari's handlers and Simon appear to be attempting to polarize America to support their varied causes. The ElBaradei connection piqued my curiosity at first, and then I remembered your conversation with the president about the OIC. I checked them out more closely."

"What did you find other than that they are a powerful voice representing the Muslim world?"

"That's an over-simplification, and only scratches the surface. Historically, the Arabic/Islamic states have voted over seventy percent of the time against the United States in the U.N. General Assembly." Max grinned as she sarcastically pronounced, "You can bet the ranch on that fact; it was reported by Snopes.com."

They were both aware that it was frequently reported—though unsubstantiated—that the Financier funded the Snopes' fact-checking website heavily. Some have even posited that it has political leanings that are similar to those of the Financier.

Noble caught her verbal jab, but he was disturbed by the data. "The revelations are more extensive than I had realized."

"Please bear with me. I'm going to load up on quotes to support my premise. So this requires your full attention." Max caught Noble's eye. "And your patience." She then glanced at her tablet and read from her notes. "The OIC was established in 1969 with a charter 'to safeguard and protect the interests of the Muslim world in the spirit of promoting international peace and harmony.' Their charter was extensive, but here are two of their goals..."

> ...*to the principles of the United Nations Charter, the present Charter and International Law...to preserve and promote the lofty Islamic values of peace, compassion, tolerance, equality, justice and human dignity to [endeavour] to work for revitalizing Islam's pioneering role in the world while* <u>*ensuring sustainable development, progress and prosperity for the peoples of Member States.*</u>

"That was a mouthful," Noble stated, "although it sounds very positive. You have my attention; this is becoming more intriguing by the minute."

"You will be pleased to know that the United States, along with over twenty nations, agree with you that it is positive. And that gives the OIC an exceedingly powerful voice as the largest but unofficial voting bloc in the U.N., including on the Human Rights Council."

"Even the Human Rights Council?" he asked with great interest, recalling OIC's request particularly for a seat on the Security Council.

"OIC's *current* charter is to fight fearlessly against *Islamophobia*, an emotionally charged euphemism for 'defamation of Islam.'"

"That makes perfect sense. Since 9/11 it has been difficult for the Muslim community to fight discrimination, especially within the U.S." Noble was openly sympathetic.

"I agree that feelings have been aroused since that tragic day, but then I became confused by a statement I discovered. It was made by the Secretary-General of the OIC at a press conference at the General

Secretariat Headquarters in January 2012. Ekmeleddin Ihsanoglu stated…"

> *The OIC's actions and objectives are governed by a new*
> *Charter which embraces modernity and the new universal*
> *values that <u>do not contradict with the teachings of the **noble**</u>*
> <u>*Islamic Sharia law. The latter has brought lofty principles*</u>
> <u>*and **noble** values that are equal or superior to those of other*</u>
> <u>*modern day positive laws.*</u>

"Quite *noble*, if you pardon the reference. Wouldn't you say?"

"I'm not sure it adds luster to my name." Noble raised an eyebrow. "That's an about-face! He's now endorsing Sharia Law; therefore his statement embracing modernity is a contradiction in itself. It certainly is in conflict with western values, and clearly erases the OIC's earlier charter to commit to the principles of the United Nations Charter and International Law. *Not to contradict,* converts to conformance with Sharia Law according to my interpretation."

Max caught Noble's facial expression. "My research became more confusing as one fact led me to another. It was like stepping on a hornet's nest. Are you acquainted with the Istanbul Process?"

"Only vague rumblings about a U.N. resolution where Istanbul was mentioned." Noble shifted in his chair and listened intently as Max laid out the details.

"The official name is the Istanbul Ministerial Process. The topics ranged anywhere from economic cooperation to counterterrorism within the Mideast countries. The major focus shifted to rewriting the language in the U.N. Human Rights Council Resolution 16/18."

"Do I have it right? I recall it was a resolution to combat defamation of religions worldwide. Ostensibly, it covered all religions and has been in existence and debated since the late 90s. Again, it provided a positive approach to embrace the Muslim community and an obvious attempt to stem off a feared tide of terrorism."

"You're correct, but what is not common knowledge is that in 2011 the U.S. State Department asked the OIC to help draft language to protect free speech and still address the problems of Islamophobia.

The then-Secretary of State Hillary Clinton participated in several meetings with the OIC at the Istanbul Process."

"What was her involvement?"

"She worked directly with the OIC to change the language in the Resolution 16/18 to criminalize speech insulting religions." Max averred.

"To criminalize? Where's the free speech?" Noble exclaimed.

"Specifically, points five and six of the resolution explained its full intent. It reads…"

Speaking out against intolerance, including advocacy of religious hatred that constitutes incitement to discrimination, hostility, or violence…adopting measures to criminalize incitement to imminent violence based on religion or belief.

"How would it be possible to observe and/or to enforce?" he asked warily.

"The Secretary-General of the OIC stated at an Istanbul Process meeting in London…"

We need an Observatory at the international level with the broad mandate to monitor and document all instances of discrimination and intolerance on religious grounds. It must have global coverage.

"This is shocking! Call it what you will, but it's akin to a form of global governance."

"Wait, in Geneva at an Istanbul Process meeting, the Secretary-General acknowledged the important element of Resolution 16/18. He stated…"

It is most significantly characterized by divergence of views on the adoption of measures to criminalize incitement to violence based on religion or belief…

"Secretary of State Clinton was involved in helping to draft the language. What was she thinking?"

"Noble, this can only place further limitations on freedom of speech. And how does one decide what is incitement—and what is imminent?"

"You have to admit that the video by Nakoula Basseley Nakoula, the California-based filmmaker who criticized the Prophet Muhammad, was clearly meant to incite, even if it didn't apply directly to Benghazi. But he was prosecuted within the context of the U.S. legal system."

"Let's take it one step further. One should ask—if Resolution 16/18 is adopted with that language then who would determine the fine line between free speech and hate crimes—a sovereign nation or the world court?" Max posed. "Any process that would convict an American citizen outside of the U.S. court system is a scary concept."

"If the United Nations ends up controlling the criminalization of hate speech, it presents a slippery slope pitched away from our first amendment and places the U.S. on the precipice of global governance." Noble shook his head at the worrisome thought.

"Perhaps that is their intent—putting us on the edge of that cliff."

Max then cited Abigail Esman, a contributor to *Forbes Magazine*, who pointed out that criticism of Islam, such as criticizing the Prophet Muhammad, is punishable by death in particular OIC countries. "In essence she highlights, 'Your free speech allows you to insult my prophet; my freedom of religion compels me to kill you for it.' It is her belief that the OIC is playing a high stakes game of *Gotcha*."

Max paused and made direct eye contact with Noble. "Esman makes a finer point, no less important. She suggested that… 'by agreeing to curb speech that could lead to *imminent violence*, we in essence accept the blame for any terrorist acts against America (and the West). We agreed not to provoke, after all.'"

Noble was aghast. "Max, your conspiratorial mind is working overtime. You're not suggesting that our government outwardly and tacitly approved the riots in Benghazi over the video—as a gesture to show solidarity with the OIC and the Istanbul Process?"

"*What difference at this point does it make?*" Max asked mockingly, recalling the former secretary of state's response when questioned at the Senate Foreign Relations Committee hearing on Benghazi.

Max noticed Noble's *not nice look*, fashioned to thwart any overreach on her part. She dutifully waited a moment for him to consider the possibility before continuing to make her argument. "We've become apologists and it could at least explain the Administration's rush to judgment by citing the tape as the cause."

Max clued Noble in on the report from *Al Jazeera's* Imran Khan, exposing a $70,000 expenditure by the U.S. for a commercial designed to convince the public that the government did not have a hand in the so-called Benghazi video. After appearing on seven Pakistani television networks, it was deemed a failure, much to the disappointment of the former U.S. president and secretary of state who appeared in the commercial.

"Max, be careful. You're skating on thin ice," Noble cautioned.

"At least there is sixty percent more Arctic ice to skate on," she quipped, harking back to Brian Sussman's report. Then she quickly added, "Their sound bite didn't discredit the rioters. It was actually engineered to discredit the video itself to pacify the Islamist," replacing her sarcasm with a tad of ire.

"Seriously, I don't see how this explains any logic for falsely identifying the video as the cause of the riots in Benghazi."

Max pushed back. "According to an opinion piece in *The Daily Caller*, the writer referred to the commercial as a political tack. He stated it was either for the purpose, '…to deflect the blame for the Benghazi killings or…they were using the Alinsky tactics to implement the Istanbul Process and U.N. Resolution 16/18…'"

"Isn't that a bit farfetched, even for you? And it still doesn't make a connection to Simon?"

"Hear me out! The writer also cited many Alinskyisms from his book, *Rules for Radicals*. You may find them quite interesting." Max read from her tablet:

The organizer's first job is to create the issues or problems…
An organizer must stir up dissatisfaction and discontent…The
organizer must first rub raw the resentments of the people of
the community…Fan the latent hostilities of many of the people
to the point of overt expression.

"The last one was my personal favorite," She jabbed. "Interestingly, the former Secretary of State Clinton's senior thesis at Wellesley College widely reported was titled, *There Is Only the Fight . . .: An Analysis of the Alinsky Model.*"

"Hank and Baari would be so proud!" Noble enjoyed the irony, but was still confounded. "How does that square with Resolution 16/18?"

"It doesn't. That's what's puzzling. First go back to the point that Esman made when she said, 'we agreed not to provoke.' Then consider the purpose of Alinsky's rules; they are designed to incite people to take action. Our former secretary appears to have attempted to straddle both proxies."

"Let's not get off track," Noble cautioned. "I can see where Simon's interest might align with Alinsky philosophies. But I don't necessarily see how it supports the full-blown terrorist attack that we suspect Simon plans to launch."

"Remember during your interrogation, Simon told you of his conversation with Osama bin-Laden when he claimed to have presented a better strategy to destroy western values. And I couldn't help but remember what Muammar al-Qaddafi once said..."

We don't need terrorists and we don't need homicide bombers.
The fifty-plus million Muslims in Europe will turn it into a
Muslim continent within a few decades.

"By all accounts, the population is projected to be over sixty million by the year 2030 in Europe alone. The Pew Research Center forecasts the Muslim population of the world will reach two-point-two billion and comprise twenty-six-point-four percent of the projected world population within the same time frame."

"Isn't that precisely why they would need representation within the United Nations?"

"Representation yes, but they are governed by a religious ideology that dictates their own set of laws. They are not a nation, as in the *United Nations.*"

Noble picked up on Max's point. "Perchance Simon and Baari had more in common than anyone suspected. I can't forget Baari's Libyan roots go back to his childhood and to the influence of Qaddafi in his life."

Max nodded in agreement as she continued to read from her tablet. She stated, "Quoting the writer from the *Daily Caller* once more..."

> *In the vein of* **Fast and Furious,** *if there could, just by chance, be a spontaneous riot incited that could be blamed on someone insulting Islam, then it would be used as the justification for a rush for Americans to give up a part of their free speech rights.*

"I suspect if it were to occur it would be subtle and would go unrealized by most of the public. But are you suggesting that the decision in Benghazi on the part of the State Department tacitly endorsed the OIC's language to criminalize speech that allegedly defiled Islam?"

"Perhaps, it was the better alternative than to blame the riots on Islamic extremists."

"If I understand you correctly, you submit that if Simon were successful in creating a national blackout to foment what is accepted as a catastrophic terrorist event, it would incite anti-Muslim sentiment. It could then force the U.S. government to go into overdrive to defend the Islamic community as a whole, to live up to its commitment to the OIC." Noble paused, and then with some skepticism acknowledged, "Interesting theory—maybe even plausible."

Max, sensing she was making headway, furthered her point that the effect that the Istanbul Process and Resolution 16/18 had on the U.S. government was based on the State Department's action as cited in Deborah Weiss's blog, *ACT! For America.* "Weiss first postulated, 'This is not necessarily a direct result of the resolution, but of the implementation of the concept of combating defamation of Islam.' In the course of her investigation, Weiss uncovered that the Department of Homeland Security, Department of Justice, National Counterterrorism Center, and the Federal Bureau of Investigation have 'purged any mention of Islamic terrorism in virtually all of their national security and counterterrorism training.' In addition, the DHS is focusing on *terrorist behavior* and conveniently disregarding the motivating religious ideology behind the behavior. She stated that the criminal framework had displaced the war framework in prosecuting terrorists."

"It appears that the more we capitulate to the Islamic community, the more power they gain on the world stage." Max frowned a bit as she began to question her own theories.

"Are you okay?"

"I was pondering—could it all be that simple?"

Noble began to wonder. "Assuming the Arab Spring was meant to strengthen and inspire the Islamic Council—think about this—Baari's machinations and a misguided foreign policy partially contributed to protests in Tunisia, the ousting of Mubarak in Egypt, the Day of Rage in Libya, and the uprisings in twelve other countries in the Mideast. Assume again that Simon was the quarterback and Hank was the executioner of the strategy, to strengthen the Islamic cause by giving more power to the OIC. Hank had to have known what was going on but he never told all, only enough to keep himself out of trouble," he countered.

"Noble, another disconcerting aspect is that the OIC has been linked on many occasions to being in cahoots with the Muslim Brotherhood. We saw it in Libya, Egypt, and Syria, among other countries. Back in 2011, during the Egyptian revolution the liberal party organized the Free Egyptian Party. In 2013, their spokesperson Ahmed Said sent a letter to the former U.S. president. Hold on and let me grab my tablet— here it is. It stated..."

> *Let us first inform you about who the Muslim brothers are:*
> *They're an unlawful organization operating outside the realm*
> *of Egyptian law, receiving foreign funding and laundering*
> *money in a flagrant breach of international law. Their aim is*
> *to rule the world through a so-called Islamic Caliphate, as they*
> *believe is their absolute supremacy.*

"Where does that leave the Human Rights Commission?"

"Boxed in a corner. For example, when it comes to denouncing Islamic countries that continue to force young girls to marry against their wills, they can't criticize the Islamic practice or they would be defaming Islam. It has the effect of muzzling free speech."

"It would appear the Human Rights Commission is not the only one boxed in the corner. How can the U.S. defend Israel against the OIC countries that declare 'Death to Israel,' when our actions as a nation give the appearance of strongly supporting the OIC? It defies logic."

"Point well taken. With Israel feeling alone and isolated on the world stage it may give them no choice but to take action unilaterally, as Netanyahu stated in a speech to the U.N. It's also likely Israel's enemies will attempt to provoke them into action," Max intoned.

"So Baari and Simon, with different motives, each planned to muck up the Middle East intentionally? An ironic oddity that they chose the same battleground." Noble shook his head in disbelief.

"Let's look at Baari's record: he reduced the amount of privately-held land, reduced the ability for Americans to bear arms, created redistribution of wealth through taxing, and whittled away our rights of privacy with the increased actions of the NSA. These actions combined to push our country closer to the Covenant."

"So in the end Baari was the true puppet. He literally spent his time in office as Kipling's *Man Who Would Be King*." Noble eased up and displayed a slight smile.

"Without a doubt, Baari energized warring factions on the issue of economic disparity, pitting the haves against the have-nots, and seemingly joined forces with his puppet masters to help build an oligarchy."

"He followed Alinsky's Rule number thirteen to the tee: 'Pick the target, freeze it, personalize it, and polarize it.' Once he had the citizens motivated to support his goals, they would cede him the power he sought. Incredible."

"Evidently, it was a rule Simon and Baari adhered to," Max added blandly.

"So coming from different perspectives, they sided with Islam. But what do Baari's socialist handlers have in common with Islamic extremists?"

"I suspect it has to do with Islamic Socialism, but it's conjecture."

"Is there such a thing?" Noble was surprised, since he heard the term used infrequently in the past.

"I looked it up. In 1975, Qaddafi published a short book setting up his philosophy called *The Green Book*. It described what he called 'Islamic Socialism.' Muslims use the term to describe a spiritual form of socialism. And many passages in the Koran dictate economic and social equality."

"Of course Baari would have been familiar with the concept, having grown up in a Muslim country where its leader coined the term."

"It's amazing that Baari's handlers sat at the table poker-faced without revealing their ultimate goal, yet at the same time they unknowingly played into Simon's hand."

"Nice metaphor Max, but Simon played upon the aspirations of both of Baari's handlers, to carry out his single goal—to spread Islam and create the caliphate sought out by the radicals. Although, we can't be certain until we capture him."

"And when that happens let me sit in on the interrogation. After all my involvement I deserve to hear the answers to these questions first hand," she said forcefully.

Noble sat back and remained silent for a moment.

At that point Max did not interrupt. She had made the sale and decided to close the book.

"You're right! You've earned it Max," was all he said.

She smiled in relief. Then her joyful expression waned as she said, "My speculations may simply be grand allusions."

Noble, maintaining his composure, said, "Sometimes allusions can lead to conclusions."

34
DAY SIXTY-ONE

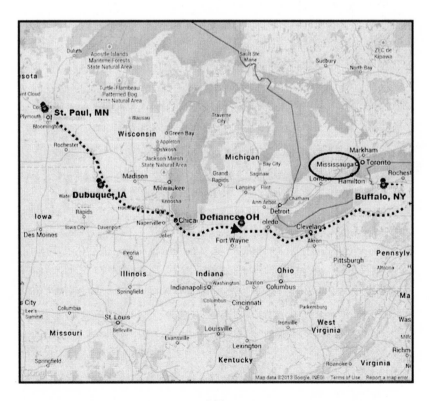

The night sky was blacker than black, except for the crescent moon and a single star. The streets were desolate and the only sound was the hum of his engine. He had been driving for over four hours; he had five and a half to go. He decided to drive for one more hour and then take a quick pit stop. By his estimate, he would be across the border by ten-thirty a.m. He counted on the Monday morning traffic to work in his favor. One more facility and he would be finished—mission accomplished.

✑

Noble rolled over at the sound, robbing him of his first good night of sleep. The clock read 3:00 A.M. He grabbed his xPhad and grumbled, "This better be good."

"We have a Simon sighting!" Burke exclaimed.

Noble bolted upright, "What have you got?"

"Evidently, Simon checked out of a Super 8 Motel around midnight. Get this—he was looking like his old self, obviously feeling confident. But the night clerk remembered seeing his photo posted in a local establishment and called the sheriff; he called us."

"Burke, where?"

"Defiance, Ohio!" he bellowed. "Can you believe it, Defiance?"

Noble heard Burke chuckle from the other end of the line.

"Simon's having fun with us. He's close to the end of his mission, so he is just playing a little cat and mouse game. It's obvious he wants us to believe he is heading toward Buffalo." Burke sounded as though he was talking from an echo chamber. "Where are you?" Noble asked.

"Hovering over *holy* Toledo!"

"Now who's trying be funny?"

"Seriously, I'm in the helicopter. We'd been searching the roads up toward Sarnia when I got the call."

Noble wiped the sleep from his eyes, while at the same time formulating a plan.

"Director, can you hear me?"

"Hold on—meet me in Cleveland in two hours. Have the helicopter standby and be ready to take off at five a.m."

"Director, the quickest way over the border is across the Peace Bridge in Buffalo."

"Agreed; if we don't catch him before he reaches the onramp, the bridge is our best option to seize him in the U.S. Have everyone ready to move into place."

They were both aware that the Peace Bridge is an international bridge between the United States and Canada. It is located at the east end of Lake Erie, the source of the Niagara River, and about 12.4 miles upriver from Niagara Falls.

"See you in a few hours." Noble hung up and called Max.

"Who is it?" Noble heard a voice say in the background. It was not Max's.

"Noble, it is three fifteen in the morning."

"My apologies, but I need you to get to the office and set up a command post." He filled her in on the events, the call from the sheriff, and his plan to meet up with Burke in Cleveland. "Max, determine the various routes Simon might take to get from Defiance to the Peace Bridge. Consider all highways, byways, toll roads, and back roads. Calculate the shortest distance and get back to me as soon as you can."

"Why did he choose that border crossing? It will take him several hours longer to reach his destination."

"Because he assumed that we'd think he'd take the fastest route and head to Sarnia."

"Noble, I think we should also check all seaplane operations heading into Canada and have the coast guard on alert. Remember Lackawanna?"

Max knew Noble would recall how security had tightened around the Buffalo area after an al-Qaeda cell was arrested in Lackawanna, a neighbor of Buffalo, in September of 2002. The members of the cell were naturalized American citizens of Yemini descent.

"Good call; gotta go!"

Noble hurriedly dressed and headed for the door.

cℐo

Noble stepped out of the company jet and spotted Burke standing outside the helicopter. He quickly rushed toward the agent. "Has everyone been alerted?" he asked in a loud voice, compensating for the blades that rotated precariously over his head.

"Director, I arranged for the Buffalo police to begin rerouting traffic away from the Peace Bridge. The border patrol is on alert and the Mounties and the feds are standing by awaiting orders."

"Good work. Let's go!" he shouted.

Burke and Noble hopped into the helicopter and headed east. During the first hour, the roadways were only sprinkled lightly with vehicles.

"Simon, where are you?" Noble mouthed, but no one took note, distracted by the whirling sounds overhead.

"All we've seen are truckers!" Burke yelled, forgetting it was no longer necessary inside the copter.

They continued to study the road for any signs of Simon's car.

Noble's xPhad vibrated. He tapped the *Answer* key. "Max, we've been up here for an hour and nothing but semi-trucks and trailers have been traversing below. Give me something to go on."

"Noble, I'm sure he will continue to avoid toll roads, especially if he discovers you are following him in a helicopter. He'll likely choose a route that will make it more difficult for you to land. My best guess is that from Defiance he will take US-20 that cuts in and out of back roads. Once he hits Pennsylvania, keep your eye on PA-5 until he reaches the New York Stateline. Simon will avoid the Interstate until the last possible moment. Follow US-62 North through Lackawanna. I emailed you the directions, along with other options. Go get him, boss."

"Good work, Max. Standby, I'll get back to you." He hit the *End* button. "Where are we?" Noble asked the pilot.

"Director, we're approaching Mentor. That's US-20 below us."

"Do you have enough fuel to go the distance?" Burke asked.

"Yes sir. The whole trip is less than two hundred miles. This baby is good for over three hundred. No sweat."

Noble discussed Max's options with Burke. "Her instincts are generally on the mark."

"I agree." Burke instructed the pilot to take US-20 to PA-5 and then cut over to US-62 heading north."

"Okay everybody, we're looking for a silver Dodge Challenger," Noble reminded them.

It was 6 o'clock in the morning and they had spotted only a few cars among the trucks, none of which fit the description. Noble and Burke were becoming antsy. Simon could be across the Peace Bridge and in Canada before lunch. They had four hours to capture him. It would be their last shot at keeping him out of Canada's welcoming arms where he would be able to avoid extradition.

Excitedly, Noble shouted. "There!" He spotted what resembled Simon's car. "Can you get a little lower? But don't spook him."

Burke directed the pilot to fly close enough to force the driver to look out at them, and then he immediately turned on the surveillance camera.

The pilot swooped down.

"Got it," Burke said.

"Pull back. I don't want a chase scene," Noble ordered.

Burke was successful in snapping a photo of the driver using the 2100-mega pixel camera, and then zoomed in on the suspect on the display screen. "I love this technology. It feels as though we are standing next to the guy. Evidently, he hasn't shaved."

"That's him. That's Simon," Noble confirmed.

"If it is him, he's in a disguise we don't on have on record. Are you sure Director?"

"There is only one person I know with that unmistakable signature grin." Noble continued to focus on the face on the screen. "Where are we now?"

"We are passing through Ashtabula on US-20. Shortly, we'll be crossing into Pennsylvania and approaching PA-5."

Noble and Burke discussed the possibility of landing the helicopter and cornering Simon, but the options were rapidly becoming limited. The traffic was starting to build up as the day edged into the hour of the Monday morning commute. They feared Simon was armed and considered the possibility that he rigged his car to explode. Simon had nothing to lose—he was desperate.

"We'll take him on the bridge," Noble announced.

Burke got on his phone and began to issue orders. In the meantime, everyone kept their eyes on Simon's car. The pilot followed instructions and veered off occasionally, and then returned for a flyby so as not to lose sight of him.

"Director, we are approaching Lackawanna. He is less than a half hour from the bridge."

Noble and Burke were tense, each taking turns from glancing at their watches to eying Simon's car in the distance.

The pilot was completely at ease and seemed to be enjoying the chase. "There he goes. He's picked up speed. Look! He's veering onto I-90."

Simon had arrived at the ramp entering the bridge. "Get everybody in place," Noble ordered. "He'll be trapped with no way out. This time I'm taking no chances."

Burke got on his phone at once. He called out, "Move in!"

35
A BRIDGE TO NOWHERE

Simon had spotted the sign for Exit 9 seconds before the GPS railed out the next set of instructions in military style, *Peace Bridge Fort Erie Canada*. Following the electronic voice, he quickly veered onto the northbound off-ramp. He heard the helicopter again hovering about, but he had no choice—he had already entered the ramp. Within minutes, he was on the bridge speeding past the tollbooths, positioned to process the passengers entering New York. As he glanced to his left, he noticed the absence of other vehicles. No one was waiting in line for the mandatory customs inspection—and there were no other cars ahead of him either. His ears pricked as his sensors warned him something was seriously wrong. He soon approached what appeared to be the center of the empty bridge.

He slammed on the brakes, stopping short.

Then with reluctance, he forced himself to look in his rear-view mirror. Stretched across the three-lane highway was a threatening cordon of federal agents. Checking the opposite end of the bridge, he clearly viewed an identical line of Mounties at an equal distance, blocking his only access to the Canadian border. He felt as though he was standing near the fifty-yard line, with no place to punt. "Shit," he snapped. He stood in the midst of contemplating his rapidly disappearing options, while his fate hung in the balance.

Without warning, a familiar voice resonated from a hovering helicopter.

"All parties stand back and hold your fire—I repeat—hold your fire. This is SIA Director Bishop. Do not approach the suspect. That is an order."

Simon was so stunned from the sound blasting from the bullhorn he almost ignored the whirling sound of the blades. The helicopter had touched down in front of the row of federal agents standing ready, adding to his apprehension. Now, men prepared to shoot on order, blocked his only escape routes at both ends of the bridge. Simon's options had come to an abrupt halt. He quickly glanced to the passenger side of the vehicle and then through the rear window. He caught a glimpse of Noble as he stepped out of the helicopter and walked toward him. Desperation took over as he reached for the door handle and stepped out of the car.

Noble immediately issued orders once again, for everyone to stand back. Then he stopped within thirty feet of his longtime nemesis. He locked eyes with Simon. He had an eerie premonition it would be the ultimate faceoff. Slowly, Noble removed his jacket and handed it to the agent standing close by. Then he carefully raised his arms, brandishing no weapons, and walked closer and closer. "See, I'm not packing," he shouted.

Simon remained frozen in his stance, staring back while reassessing his options. His patent Cheshire grin was absent; only an odd expression shrouded Simon's face.

"It's over Simon. Please come with me and no one will be hurt. It's not worth it." Noble spoke calmly as though he were talking a friend off a ledge. *After all these years, it is finally over*, he thought, simultaneously feeling a pang of sympathy.

Suddenly pandemonium erupted.

Simon yelled, "This is it!" He quickly peered toward the passenger's seat for the last time and pulled his hand out of his right pants pocket.

In a resounding crescendo, one shot rang out unexpectedly and then in an instant another shot pierced the air.

"Hold your fire," Noble screamed.

Everyone obeyed orders and stood down—there were no follow-up shots.

All eyes watched seemingly in slow motion as Simon, obviously wounded, staggered toward the bridge railing. When he reached the side of the bridge, he placed one leg up onto railing and rolled over his body without a sound. A trail of ruby red droplets marked his path.

Noble was temporarily in a state of suspended animation. Simon had deprived him of the long sought-after capture he envisioned. *This is not a befitting end to Simon's life,* he mused, as he tried to grapple with what had occurred. Confirming all doubts, he dashed toward that point of the bridge. He looked down over the railing. All he could see was a black hole, reliving his recurring nightmare—but there was no face staring back. Noble forced himself out of his momentary lapse and refocused on the source of the shots. It was difficult to decipher who pulled the trigger—but the sight of Simon taking his grand leap was undeniable.

On impulse Agent Burke, who had been standing by the helicopter, ran to Simon's car. He quickly ordered his agents to seal off the area around the crime scene and instructed them to encompass a wide area. He immediately alerted the U.S. Coast Guard stationed a few miles south of the bridge to embark on a search for the body without delay. As the crime scene was cordoned off completely with the familiar yellow tape, Burke eyed Noble hightailing in his direction. Briskly, he raised his hand and halted his approach. He then walked toward Noble and prepared the director for another shock.

"Director, there's something else you must see." He motioned with his hand as he walked back toward the car.

Noble followed in an uneasy lockstep, curious as to the agent's resolve.

The other federal agents awaited further orders.

The Mounties stood back as well, having agreed not to interfere with a crime scene that had occurred on the U.S. side of the bridge. Burke had already been in touch with the senior officials who agreed to allow the feds to determine the next steps.

Noble used caution as he leaned over to peek into the car. Slumped over in the passenger's seat lay a body with the face pressed into the knees and a single bullet hole in the left temple.

"There's no pulse," Burke informed. "I suspect he was killed instantly by a ricocheting bullet."

Noble stood upright and shouted, "Everyone stand back!" Then he looked head-on at Burke standing to his side and ordered, "Keep everyone outside the tape. Agent Burke, please stand away as well." Noble held out his right hand to receive the pair of latex gloves Burke handed him and then turned toward the car.

Burke, without haste, followed Noble's directions and cleared all personnel from the scene.

As Noble pulled the gloves on, he leaned into the car once again and stared at the corpse. Even with a full head of white hair and a long beard, there was something unnerving about the body. Noble's heart pounded. He proceeded to walk around to the other side of the car as he heaved several shallow breaths to ease the tension. Then he opened the door on the passenger's side, reached in to lift the corpse's head, and peered into the dead eyes. Once again, the tension returned. He too checked the victim's pulse to confirm the unthinkable. Then without hesitation, he grabbed his xPhad and hit the speed dial.

"Max, I want you and Stanton at the Peace Bridge in Buffalo straightaway. The company jet is headed back to Washington. Call the pilot, have him refuel and head this way."

"What's happening, Noble?"

"Just get to the Buffalo Niagara Airport A-S-A-P. I'll send a helicopter to pick you up. And tell Stanton to bring his forensic bag of tricks—and a body bag."

"Simon?"

"No—he decided to take a hundred foot plunge off the bridge. His body should be floating over the Niagara Falls by now and down the Niagara Gorge. If the fall didn't kill him, the Falls will. I'll explain everything to you when you get here. There's no time now."

"If it's not Simon, then who's the dead one?"

"Max, I want the body and the evidence collected and back in Washington this evening. No one is to know what you've uncovered."

She persisted, "Noble—who's the corpse?"

There was complete silence except for Max's bated breath as she anxiously waited for the I.D. She sensed it was bad.

Noble eyed Burke standing guard. He then moved away from the car and walked over to the railing for privacy. "Max—it's the former president—Abner Baari."

"Abner Baari! What the hell was he doing there?"

"I'll clue you in when you arrive. Hurry!"

"Burke—Max and Stanton will manage the crime scene with your help. Please send the helicopter to pick them up at the Buffalo Niagara Airport; they should arrive within the hour. I want you to keep other law enforcement officials informed, but do not reveal anything about the corpse. Also, identify the trigger-happy agents who fired the shots. Use your charm when it comes to the Mounties."

"Yes sir, but what about the body, Director?"

"No one is to go near it—no one!" Noble glared until it was clear the agent understood his orders.

"Yes, sir. Will you be leaving on the helicopter?"

"Not now, I'll wait for Max and Stanton to arrive."

Noble walked away and stood off to the side against the railing, far from the corpse, but within eyeshot of the crime scene. From time to time, he would peer over the side at the fast moving waters a hundred feet below, half-expecting to see Simon's face sneering back. Still in disbelief, but with an odd sense of relief, he placed a call to Enzo and filled him in on the demise of Simon Hall. He ended the call by stating, "It's finally over, my friend."

When Noble tapped the *End* key, he noticed a new email had arrived. He had forgotten that his xPhad vibrated just as he stepped out of the helicopter. Now, away from the scene, he casually retrieved the message. "What the…?" he was thunderstruck by what he read; **I CONFESSℭ**. There was an attachment.

36
THE CONFESSION

Noble waited a moment, wondering if he was ready to read Simon's exposé from the grave. He anticipated he would need time and concentration to dissect the words of his onetime nemesis. Just then, he spotted an agent coming his way.

"Director, Agent Burke said you'd be here for a while..."

Noble cut him off. "Any word on who fired the shots?"

"Sir, Agent Burke is still interviewing some of the other officers. I'll let him know you're awaiting the report. By the way, I'm going to take off to see if I can scrounge up some food for all of us. Is there anything we can get for you?"

"A large black coffee and a sandwich would be great. I'll be in the car over there." Noble pointed to the black sedan nearest the crime scene. *I will need to sit down for this one, I'm sure,* he thought.

The agent departed.

Noble settled into the not-so-comfortable back seat of the car and took time to reflect on the morning's events. Finally composed, he clicked on the attachment and unfolded his xPhad. On his tablet appeared a lengthy confession. He stared at the first word for a moment, causing a flashback to his Harvard's days when Simon tagged him with the nickname.

Lordy,

It took Noble several more minutes, before he finally ventured on with what appeared to be more of a personal message addressed to him.

Here is the confession you tried to nudge out of me at Draper, where I admit the repartee was delicious. I also confess a lingering admiration for you and I did not want to leave this world without giving you the answers to your questions. You might consider this my farewell thesis. So sit back my brother, and let me enlighten you.

First, I want to you know one of my greatest disappointments was your refusal to join us in La Fratellanza. I always play to win and I needed the best team. However, if you are reading this, then my disappointment has been eclipsed by my sudden, unfortunate demise brought on by you, my friend. Please believe me when I say I hold no resentment.

Simon, why do you feel the need to confess? Noble pondered. *Perhaps in his own egotistical way, he needs to remind the world of its great loss. I suspect, Simon, you simply wanted to prove you are smarter than I am. More devious, yes, smarter, no.* "Simon, you lost the game," he mumbled. Noble let out a sigh of satisfaction and then continued to read as he scrolled down the page.

As an eighteen-year-old college sophomore, I set out on a journey to the Mideast to satisfy my intense interest in the Islamic culture and to find my father. You may be surprised to know that I never knew my biological father.

It was 1984 when I flew to Karachi. That is when I took the name Mohammed al-Fadl. Within days, I was in the midst of helping funnel arms into Afghanistan to fight against the Soviets.

Things began to move at a rapid pace. The fight continued
and there were rumblings of a new group emerging, calling
themselves al-Qaeda. That is when I had the good fortune of
meeting Osama bin-Laden. From our first encounter, I became
enthralled. I lost sight of my original mission and with total
commitment joined the cause. I spent two years developing a
wire-transfer system for Osama's organization to move funds
undetected between Hawalas in the U.S. Over time, I started to
question the wisdom of al-Qaeda's mission.

Noble laid the tablet on his lap as he remembered the story Max told
him about the horrific ordeal Simon's mother suffered and that Simon
was a child of rape. In a way, both he and Simon shared mutual internal
strife. It invoked memories of the horrible car accident that took both
lives of Noble's parents while he was attending Harvard. He recalled
the kindness Simon showed him during that time. He even loaned
him the money for his tuition for the last semester, without which he
would not have graduated. On occasion, he pondered as to whether
Simon had any culpability in the accident. Years later, he dismissed the
possibility—over the past sever al months, the possibility of Simon's
blameworthiness had resurfaced.

From the corner of his eye, he noticed a welcome sight, as an agent
approached with a bag and a large cup. Noble had not been able to
sleep on the plane and upon landing before he was swooped up by
the helicopter. So much had happened in the course of the morning,
none of which included rest or caffeine. He checked the page number
of Simon's confession and expected there were more revelations. He
needed to be alert and decided to take a short break.

"Sir, the best I could do was McDonald's."

He thanked the agent and then without giving it much thought,
devoured the burger and fries, and downed the steaming hot black
coffee. Finally sated and marginally energized, he picked up the tablet
and reread the last statement.

I started to question the wisdom of al-Qaeda's mission.

He ruminated for a moment as he looked over toward the crime scene. Then he took a deep breath and began where he had left off.

I returned to my studies in the States. Meanwhile, the bombings in Nairobi and Tanzania had occurred, compliments of al-Qaeda, which was gaining strength and stature throughout the Mideast. Through my experience with Osama and the influence he exerted, coupled with my coursework on the teachings of Saul Alinsky, I fixated on one particular quote. At the time, Alinsky was quoting Dostoevsky:

> *Taking a new step is what people fear most...*
> *They must feel so frustrated, so defeated, so lost,*
> *so futureless in the prevailing system that they are*
> *willing to let go of the past and chance the future.*
> *This acceptance is the reformation essential to any*
> *revolution.*

On the other side of the spectrum, when I studied Sharia law I became acquainted with the writings of Sayyid Qutb. He became the genesis of the jihadi movement, spurring al-Qaeda to accept that without Sharia law the Muslim world would not exist. After traveling throughout the U.S., Qutb described the American culture as obsessed with materialism and fraught with injustices. He returned to Egypt, and formed the Society of Muslim Brothers, referred to today as the Muslim Brotherhood. Excerpts of the opening of his book *Milestones* contain the following view:

> *The period of the Western system has come to an end*
> *primarily because it is deprived of those life-giving*
> *values which enabled it to be the leader of mankind...*
> *Islam is the only System which possesses these values*
> *and this way of life.*

For the first time, I began to see the marriage of these two dynamic philosophies that were to have a profound influence on my future. Then on the streets of Florence, I heard Hussein Tarishi speak. In a revelation, I discovered how I could realize a great undertaking: to achieve al-Qaeda's mission without violence. I returned to the states and spent the next two years constructing my plan and selecting the members to help carry out my plot with meticulous care.

Lordy, you think you understand the rest, but read on my friend.

Noble smiled at the fact that it no longer annoyed him when Simon referred to him as Lordy. He was not sure if it was because he considered it an endearing gesture from a friend, or because he would never hear it spoken again by his nemesis. Noble readjusted in his seat and continued.

When I called my La Fratellanza brothers together in Chicago in 2000, they voted unanimously to turn our thesis game into reality. Then after al-Qaeda destroyed the World Trade Center and steered a plane into the Pentagon, I returned to Pakistan, again as Mohammed al-Fadl. I arrived in Kursu and met several of Osama's followers who remembered me. Once again, I was sitting across from Osama and his two perpetual bodyguards, his inseparable friends since boyhood. I pleaded with him to give up the strategy of blowing up the buildings one at a time. Instead, I lobbied for a strategy to bring America to her knees by destroying the very foundation on which she has built—her government. Attack from "within" as Alinsky espoused. I also stressed that destroying buildings and killing innocent civilians would only cement the resolve of the American people.

My plan fell on deaf ears. They called me an infidel, saying I was doomed to failure. Osama then called for one of the lieutenants to escort me unceremoniously down the mountain.

A pity bin-Laden died a few months later on December 14, and was not able to see what I had accomplished. The 2011

melodrama of the raid on bin-Laden's compound was staged
by the Baari Administration and the public was content even
without a body. I am digressing.

"Get on with it Simon!"

Burke suddenly appeared and knocked on the window. Noble
realized he must have heard him yell aloud.

"Everything okay, Director?"

Noble opened the door, unable to roll down the automatic window
and assured, "Everything is as well as can be expected, Burke. What's
up?"

"I just finished interviewing our agents. Only one admits to firing
his gun. He said he fired only one shot toward the suspect when he
heard a shot come from the car." Burke noticed Noble's expression.
"What are you thinking Director?"

"Let's wait for the forensic evidence to be processed."

Burke then informed Noble that the Mounties had retreated, many
of the federal agents had dispersed, and the traffic continued to be
rerouted. "Is there anything else you want me to take care of for now?"

"Just stand by and wait for Max and Stanton."

"Yes, sir." Burke left and walked back toward the yellow tape to
speak with some of the other agents milling about.

Noble gave pause to the agent's update and then continued to read
from the tablet.

By 2009, I, with the help of La Fratellanza, had
accomplished the impossible. Hussein Tarishi, an illegal
immigrant, morphed into Abner Baari and was elected to
the presidency. I was ready to take it to the next level. Then
you chose to round up La Fratellanza and interrogate them,
discovering Baari's true identity. Now you understand the story
did not end there.

Baari was always willing to be manipulated as long as
he would acquire the ultimate power. He took direction
from Hank without question, as he laid out his own policies,
utilized his executive orders freely, and eroded the capitalistic

society of the U.S. Then during his second term, he became
unmanageable. His ego became elephantine. After years of not
caring who pulled the strings, he demanded that Hank give
him the names of his anonymous backers. Hank offered up
only me. I agreed to meet. That is when Baari laid out his plan.
Yes—his plan. I am loath to admit it was brilliant. So together,
we began our plan to transform America from within.

Now here is where it gets interesting.

Baari was behind this—all along! Noble told himself with skepticism.

Right now Lordy, you are rather skeptical.

Simon was always able to predict my reactions. Noble shuddered at the
unsettling thought.

Baari described to me the efforts of two of his major
benefactors; he referred to them as the Godfather and the
Financier. I could not believe my luck. I am sure your mind is
racing, but read on.

I hate it when he does that, Noble thought.

Remember after the death of bin-Laden, al-Qaeda
became more fanatical and indiscriminate in the violence
they undertook. As part of Baari's strategy, he dismissed their
importance and succeeded in changing the American psyche.
He was also successful in weaving in his social agenda as he
increased the size of government to control many aspects of
daily life. He also recognized his days were numbered and
that one day, you would be standing on his doorstep calling
for his resignation. Which you did! But not before Baari
and his benefactors abandoned a public seemingly ripe for
revolution, surmising they would be so absorbed with the
national calamity generated by Baari, they were incapable
of making rational choices. With Baari having already set the

stage, I willingly hopped on the bandwagon to take advantage
of the situation. For me, it was the perfect solution.

Baari had prepared for the inevitable, but he had one more
self-serving trick in his bag. He wanted to create a national
catastrophe by bringing down the power grids in major areas
across the country. He was aware that the Tres Amigas Project
was about to go online and he planned to use the Superstation
to restore the power, confecting the image that he had saved a
grateful nation from a disastrous crisis.

My role was to reprogram the control center's operating
systems and then await his instructions to flip the switch.
FEMA and the military would have then stepped in to restore
order according to plan. Capitalizing on the public's fears,
Baari would label the event a homegrown terrorist act.
He held to his maniacal notion that the American people
would be ready to support a revision to the Twenty-second
Amendment to allow him to serve a third term to resolve the
national crisis. The militia I was training was a backup force to
protect him in case of backlash.

"Fortunately, that plan backfired." Noble glanced out the car window
and noticed the agents standing nearby. Although he was out of hearing
range, he suspected they noticed him periodically speaking to himself.
He smiled at the thought and then continued to read.

I concede at times, I questioned the purpose of Baari's
militia, thinking it was to support him in the staging of a coup,
something akin to a banana republic mentality. Baari had
reduced the U.S. to behaving much like a third world nation,
so it held an ounce of plausibility. I had studied enough Sharia
law to recognize that when people are at their most vulnerable
they can be led with little resistance. When Dostoevsky said,
"They must feel so frustrated, so defeated…," that struck
a chord. Baari's plan to turn out the lights appeared more
than plausible. I laid the groundwork for an unprecedented
national emergency, which you have now zeroed in on.

Even you, Lordy, would have to admit it was brilliant! You should be aware that Baari ripped the blueprint out of the President's Book of Secrets. You can let Hank off the hook. The underground encampment, identified by the blueprint, is where I also constructed the plan to create the national energy disaster he sought. The location was ideal. He also devoted his efforts to confiscate the surrounding land, to prevent any intrusion by drilling and mining interests.

Then when Baari resigned and left the U.S., he became embroiled in the Libyan turmoil and adopted their anti-U.S. strategy. He later realized that his original narcissistic plan could still provide value—this time to weaken American resolve. To my surprise, he risked reentering the U.S. and joined me in the encampment. In fact, he left only days before you sent in the troops.

I owed you for revealing at Draper the planted evidence in your interrogation that implicated me in the European bombings. It compelled me to return the favor with this confession. Actually, the bombings were instigated by Baari camouflaging them to look like attempted assassinations—all as a distraction. The deaths were unintended consequences. I always expected Baari would try to set me up, although he did plan my self-serving escape from prison. I am sure you also discovered that my darling Maryann was an accomplice in my escape, but cut the senator some slack.

Anyhow, I decided to let it play out. I knew eventually, I would find the right time to exact my revenge.

Simon's last statement struck a nerve. Noble remembered the exact words Agent Burke said, *He must have died from a ricocheting bullet.* After discovering the body, Noble instinctively checked the glove compartment—there was no gun as Maryann had reported. Suddenly, he had a flashback of the moment just before the first shot rang out. *Simon pulled his hand out of his pocket.* "Son-of-a-bitch. Simon fired the first shot."

Noble laid the tablet on the seat cushion and took the opportunity to rub his eyes. He was tired and operating on fumes. The Baari revelations were appalling and the events kept spinning in his head. He rubbed his eyes once again as though he could somehow erase the events from history. Then he picked up the tablet and began slowly to scroll past Simon's words.

As I said before, Baari and his handlers deserve the credit for setting the stage. The American citizens are complacent and desensitized to terrorists' threats, abetted by an administration that repeatedly dismissed those threats. The American public had capitulated emotionally and believed the government was in complete control and mother government would tend to their needs.

So when I flipped the switch, it would have been blamed on an unforeseen terrorist attack, immediately weakening the U.S. economy. According to plan, anti-Muslim sentiment would erupt and the U.S. government would be embroiled in a battle with the OIC. They would be forced to abdicate action to the U.N. where the Islamic community would have the greatest sway.

The final blow in this whole ordeal is that unbeknown to Baari, I discovered the identities of the Godfather and the Financier and their personal quests. You cannot imagine how astonished I was to find out that all three of us were setting out to achieve similar goals, but for different motives. They each wanted to transform America by obliterating her western values and diminishing her influence on the world stage, and to advance the cause of global governance. By hitchhiking on their efforts, I was able to pursue my goal to strengthen the power of the Islamic world, which paradoxically is not their agenda.

It is almost satirical that I began to help one man to destroy America from within, albeit his reasoning was skewed— but then with the unwitting help of his handlers, I would accomplish my goal with one flip of the switch. It was a win-win for me all the way around.

"In part Simon, in part." He fingered the tablet, scrolling to the next page—there was more.

> Your one lingering question must be—what was the driving force behind my actions? This answer will put it to rest.
> The pivotal moment happened on a mountaintop in Kursu. I stared into the eyes of three men as they mocked my plan and called me an infidel. They said I was doomed to failure. From that very moment, I discerned from whence my seed had come. The eyes do not lie. When the trio rejected my proposal—it was as if my father rejected me as his son.

Noble rested the tablet on his lap. Stunned, he recited the words, "My father rejected me as his son!"

Slightly shaken, he glanced once again at Simon's confession, or rather his last declaration.

> My ultimate revenge would have been to achieve a goal Osama himself had not been able to achieve—to give the Islamic Coalition at the United Nations a powerful seat at the table. My friend, if you are reading this confession then the ultimate revenge will be yours to enjoy! But be careful, Baari and I were only bit players in this drama—Act Three has yet to begin—watch out.
> Stay safe Lordy.
> Simon

Noble slouched back in his seat dumbfounded by the entire affair, finding it difficult to comprehend. It had finally ended.

Without warning, the rap on the window startled him. His deep penetrating thoughts kept him from hearing the whirling sound of the helicopter that landed less than fifty feet away.

It was Max.

Noble stepped out of the car still holding the tablet.

As anticipated, Max bombarded him with her first question. "What the hell is going on?" Then she quickly noticed the look on his face and calmly asked, "What's happening, boss? You look like you just saw a ghost."

He flashed the tablet. "Simon's confession. Evidently, he had composed it sometime in the past, but based on the date and time on the email, he sent it minutes before we cornered him."

Max was stunned. "Did you find anything revealing?"

"We'll discuss it when we're back in Washington. Where's Stanton?"

"He's working the forensics on the car. The body is in the bag."

"Max, are you okay?"

"No, Noble. I am hiding what some consider a national icon. And I am sure there's a crime in there somewhere."

"Just bring all the evidence back to Washington as quickly as possible. I need to get back to inform the president."

"What about Senator Townsend? Baari was her husband."

"I'll handle it."

"I guess I had the senator figured wrong. Maybe she was telling the truth about Baari threatening her and forcing her to help Simon."

"Max, you have your orders," Noble stated sternly.

"Understood." Max let up. It was obvious that everyone was frazzled. She backed off and changed the subject. "We'll take care of things on this end and then meet you back in Washington in a few hours. I have the pilot standing by at the airport to take you back."

"Thanks, to both you and Stanton." Noble replied, modifying his prior sternness. Then he turned and headed to the helicopter.

Once airborne, Noble took one last look at the crime scene below encircled with the yellow tape. It was a strange view as he also saw the spray from the Falls in the background.

The pilot noted the distraught look on Noble's face and interjected, "Sorry Director Bishop that he got away. It's common knowledge among us agents that al-Fadl was a personal quest of yours—perhaps you'll have another chance to nab him in the future."

"Excuse me, you and I witnessed the same scene." Noble responded with annoyance.

The pilot stole a quick glance, making eye contact. "I guess you're not aware that in June of 2011, a woman in her thirties jumped off the Peace Bridge—and survived."

Noble stared straight-ahead attempting to push the slightest possibility out of his mind.

POSTSCRIPT

Today's society's preference is to absorb knowledge via some form of entertainment. Fiction is one medium that has satisfied readers' tastes since time immemorial. My goal is to increase the awareness of readers to current events by embedding factual knowledge in an entertaining fictional format. The plots in my books are pure unadulterated fiction conjured up in my imagination, but generously sprinkled with unassailable facts. Any facts conveyed are supported by intensive research, in fairness to my readers.

To quote Francis Bacon: "Truth is so hard to tell, it sometimes needs fiction to make it plausible." So what if it could happen? What if it did happen? What if it is happening? One should not avoid asking these incisive questions. To ponder these questions sheds the needed light on critical events.

The most severe problem facing our nation is not the issue of global warming; it is the dilution of our basic values. Our complacency, our detachment, our inability to give up our "stuff" for the greater good, and our unabated willingness to compromise our individual freedoms preciously fought for by others—sow the seeds for the downfall of the greatest nation in history. We see the erosion of our values in our daily lives. Rugged individualism has been sacrificed on the altar of government dependency. Personal accountability is disappearing rapidly.

Years ago, I learned from a wise professor about the *Five Threads* that shape and bind our society. She taught me that the political, social, cultural, geographic, and economic effects—or threads—touch every aspect of our lives. The threads that weave the fabric of our society should be compatible and progress in unison. If one thread is seriously out of balance and dominates, it leaves the others in knots. Today, the political thread has created chaos in all parts of our society. It is time to recapture our basic values and bring balance to our social order.

The tapestry created by the five threads is becoming worn and tattered as we stray further from the values that shaped this great nation. The possibilities exposed in "The Simon Trilogy" will become reality played out in our streets and inside our government, if we stand back idly as the threads unravel. If, after reading *The Ultimate Revenge*, you ask yourself the all-encompassing question "What if?" I urge you to read *Agenda 21* by Glenn Beck and Harriet Parke for a futuristic tale of the potential aftermath of our failings, if we do not act.

—Sally Fernandez

ACKNOWLEDGEMENTS

I offer my deep appreciation and gratitude to my publisher, David Dunham, for his continued confidence in me as a novelist, and for giving of his own time to see my projects to fruition. I am eternally grateful to my dear friend Susie Coelho, who opened up this opportunity by bringing David and me together, sparking this whole adventure.

My profound thanks go to my special inner-circle of talented readers whose suggestions and insights helped enrich all three books in "The Simon Trilogy"—Ann Howells, Donna Post, and Alfredo Vedro.

Lastly, there is no way to thank all of my friends and family who continue to support my efforts and forgive my frequent absences.

ABOUT THE AUTHOR

 Sally Fernandez' career background includes project management, business planning, and technology, with additional experience in technical and business writing. Her books of fiction are based on knowledge garnered from careers in banking, computer technology, and business consulting, while living in New York City, San Francisco, and Hong Kong.

Fernandez' foray into writing fiction began in 2007 when the 2008 presidential election cycle was in full swing. The overwhelming political spin by the media compelled her to question the frightening possibilities the political scene could generate. A confirmed political junkie, she took to the keyboard armed with unwinding events and discovered a new and exciting career.

The Ultimate Revenge is the conclusion to "The Simon Trilogy." Her earlier books in the trilogy, *Brotherhood Beyond the Yard* and *Noble's Quest*, provide an exhilarating platform for the launch of this final chapter of a gripping narrative that challenges the reader to put the book down. The ever-elusive Simon's daring escape from a high security prison allows him to add unheard of dimensions to the classic cat and mouse game he has played with Noble, the SIA Director.

A world traveler, Ms. Fernandez and her husband split time between their homes in the United States and Italy.

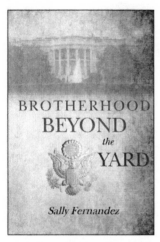

In 1990, an extraordinarily talented young man was discovered on the streets of Florence, Italy. His gifts are readily apparent, his ability to lead unmatched, and the possibilities for his future endless. Several years later, a group of scholars at Harvard known as La Fratellanza devise a brilliant thesis in the form of an intellectual game. When the game morphs into a real-life experience with the election of President Abner Baari, no one could have foreseen the consequences—or ramifications.

Director Hamilton Scott of the States Intelligence Agency is dispatched to Florence to coordinate a sting operation with Interpol to trap a terrorist, but as he digs deeper, he finds himself in a complicated mystery that has the fate of the United States, even that of the president himself, on his shoulders. As Hamilton drives the investigation forward with clear-headed integrity, Brotherhood Beyond the Yard provides an array of disturbing possibilities while delivering a rush of thrills.

Sally Fernandez's crackerjack international thriller expertly weaves seemingly disparate events into a cohesive whole leading to a shocking, shattering climax; a classic blend of character study and well-plotted action sequences keeps the pages turning faster and faster. There are no sacred cows here as Fernandez drives straight to the highest seats of Washington and questions anyone—and everything. A hair-raising page-turner from start to finish, Brotherhood Beyond the Yard examines political ideology, the international banking crisis, the role of Internet technology, and international terrorism with ferocious insight.

www.sallyfernandez.com

NOBLE'S QUEST

Fresh on the heels of her acclaimed first novel, *Brotherhood Beyond the Yard*, Sally Fernandez has penned a sequel that will add more sparkling thrills to the trilogy she is authoring. Major earth-shaking events in Europe and the USA converge to fuel Interpol and the States Intelligence Agency to join forces.

Although seemingly detached, the threats prompt Noble Bishop, Director of the SIA, and Enzo Borgini, Executive Director of Police Services for Interpol, to conduct joint investigations. Leading-edge technology is used to unravel the labyrinth of connections. The events are not coincidental. The enormous risks facing the USA and the world eventually draw the newly-elected president into the picture.

Land grabs, political manipulation, and a terrorist camp—along with sea changes in the American psyche—are skillfully woven to form a tapestry of intrigue. Readers of *Brotherhood Beyond the Yard* will renew their acquaintanceship with some of the characters in the sequel. This time their roles are more expansive and transparent, adding to the lingering intrigue. The widely sought mastermind of the global terrorist threat adds a breathtaking twist that lends even more intrigue to the narrative.

Written in the author's patent style, readers will be beguiled by the artistic marriage of established facts with a storyline that lifts creativity to new heights. Readers are challenged to separate fact from fiction, in the true Fernandez style.

www.sallyfernandez.com

CPSIA information can be obtained at www.ICGtesting.com
Printed in the USA
LVOW11s0747090214

372803LV00003B/6/P